KING'S RANSOM

OIL KINGS - BOOK TWO

MARIE JOHNSTON

LE PUBLISHING

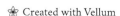 Created with Vellum

It was supposed to be a simple case of revenge: get to know King Tech owner and CEO Beckett King, learn his secrets, and ruin his life like he ruined my brother's. But Beckett King offered me a deal I couldn't refuse.

Not only does he want me to pretend to be engaged to him, he needs to marry me to get his grandmother off his back. And at the end of the year, we can go our separate ways, only I'll be a whole lot richer.

I won't fall for his irresistible good looks, or that *aw, shucks* country-boy charm he still possesses from growing up on a ranch. I am smarter than that. He has a lesson to learn and I am the best one to teach him.

But that's the tricky thing with revenge. It doesn't always go as planned.

CHAPTER 1

va

ADAM WASN'T FIT to care for himself. I sighed and pressed my hand to my forehead. In the kitchen, my brother couldn't see me from his standard spot on the couch. If he stayed there any longer, he was going to grow roots.

The backs of my eyes stung, but tears wouldn't fall. They never did. Crying was a luxury. I had too much to do.

Sighing, I pulled the plug in the sink. I had a day off for once, but I wasn't going to lay idle.

Popping out of the kitchen, I veered to the window and opened the blinds. Light streamed in, chasing away the shadows, but not the ones that lingered in my brother's eyes.

One more time for good measure, I cursed the man who had done this to him, then plastered on a pleasant smile. "I'm going out for a bit."

Adam didn't spare me a glance as he focused on his multiplayer game. "'K."

He'd woken up before ten in the morning and I'd even gotten him to eat breakfast. It was a good day for him.

"Need anything?" He needed food and a job, one from the many applications he'd submitted—if he'd actually uploaded his resume and hit submit. I had my suspicions. We needed so much, but with only one of us working, it was all I could do to keep the internet on. Without it, I feared what the extra empty time would drive Adam to do.

"Nope."

Stepping back into the kitchen, I grabbed one of my to-go bags of cat food. Outside, I locked the door and peered down each side of our apartment.

The setup was like a one-story row house. Each apartment shared its walls with its neighbors and had an outside entrance. No garage, which sucked in the winter, but I took the light-rail as much as possible.

Adam and I had grown up here and it had felt like a home when our parents were alive. I couldn't name many of our neighbors. The guy to our left was my age, and from the number of random guys doing the walk of no-shame in the early morning hours, he was single and loving it.

The couple to our right fought all the time and I certainly knew his name. It was Mike You Motherfucker. Their fights were only verbal so far and they were in the off portion of their on-again, off-again relationship.

The other person in our fourplex was an elderly lady who had seemed ancient when I was five. She didn't want to talk to us any more now than she had twenty years ago.

I stopped before hitting the sidewalk. At the end of the building, a line of shrubs had started losing their leaves for the winter even though it was late August.

"Here, Kitty." If the other tenants knew about Kitty, they didn't care. I'd found her last year as a kitten, but since Adam was allergic, I couldn't take her in. She wouldn't have let me anyway. It'd only been recently, and with a lot of feedings, that she'd let me get this close.

"Hey," I cooed. Squatting, I stretched my arm through a break in the branches to pour the food into the little plastic dish I'd set out—and froze. "Oh, Kitty."

The cat was there, curled up in a pile of leaves. At her belly was a mass of squirming fur. Kittens.

I poured the food into her dish and counted her kittens. One, two, three, four—holy shit—five kittens. She gave me a lazy blink.

"Mama's tired? I would be too." I wanted to pet her, but I hadn't fully earned her trust. The food in the dish looked like a pittance. It wasn't that I didn't want to feed her more, but I had me and Adam to buy food for too.

The feeling swarmed over me. The one full of desperation, where I wondered how in the hell I was going to keep going until eternity claimed me. There was a time I'd wanted more in life. Today, I'd settle for more cat food.

Straightening, I shoved the empty baggie in my pocket. All baggies got reused. Ramming my hands in the pockets of my jeans, I followed the same path I did every day, but instead of heading toward my catering gig or the place I bartended, I was going to the heart of Denver.

I was looking for a man. Why today of all days, I didn't know, only that I was sick of stalking him online. It was time to see him in person. I needed to see him to fuel my anger, to motivate me to work harder to help Adam through his deep depression, to hang around long enough to see my brother prove this motherfucker wrong.

I was looking for the man who'd ruined my brother's life.

CHAPTER 2

eckett

I REGRETFULLY INFORM you that I'm handing in my resignation, effective immediately.

Archiving the email, I tossed the phone on the seat next to me. Another one gone. Being my assistant wasn't that hard, but it wasn't the easy pass to becoming a millionaire so many seemed to expect.

Across from me, Dad sipped his brandy, his eyes pensive as he looked at my phone. We were somewhere above Montana, where I had flown out for his impromptu wedding to Kendall Brinkley. I was still salty about it. She was closer to my age than his. I couldn't imagine how ashamed my mother would be if she were alive.

I'd thought Grams would lose it, but she'd been stoic during the entire ceremony. Mama had been gone a long time, but it couldn't be easy for Grams to watch her former son-in-law marry a woman the same age as his own children.

But at least Dad's wedding had given me a brief reprieve from her meddling. For a woman who hadn't been terribly involved in my childhood, she was certainty invested in one specific aspect of my future now.

"Trouble in paradise?" Dad asked.

"There is no paradise when I need an assistant and Grams sends prospective fiancées my way. How did she even find out Wilma quit?" But then Grams had talked to my former assistant more than me. Wilma was younger than Grams, but only by about fifteen years, and I missed more than her punctual and proficient work ethic.

I didn't have the heart to turn away the women Grams funneled toward my job opening. Only my open position was not the missionary position, or the wheelbarrow, and it definitely wasn't on one knee to propose. Three of her candidates had already passed through my office and left as soon as they'd realized the only payday they'd hit was their paycheck. Which was still a damn good wage—just not my inheritance.

"She got Aiden married off, now she's turning on you. I'll talk to her if you want, Beckett." He was the only one close to me who called me Beckett instead of Beck. "But I'm not her favorite person right now. Still, I can't blame her, though I'd rather you fall in love and get married instead of what your grandmother wants."

"I'm doing fine on my own." My net worth had hit nine digits months ago.

"Your grandparents worked hard for that money."

"They got lucky." Finding that much oil on our land was only the beginning. It had happened during my grandpa's day, when Mama was just a kid. Dad had been her high school sweetheart and had gone on to spearhead the company after they married.

"Your grandparents worked hard on that land and dedicated their lives to the company. You wouldn't be using this private jet to fly back to Denver if it weren't for them." Dad set his drink down and leaned forward. I refrained from mentioning that I could buy my own Gulfstream, but it seemed a waste when I could use my family's plane. "Your grandparents secured the inheritance you're so willing to give away."

"I'm not exactly willing to whore myself—or anyone else—out for it either."

"None of us want you to."

I gave him a pointed look.

"You're right, but Grams wouldn't consider it whoring. She'd call it a business deal." Dad ran a hand through his salt-and-pepper hair. If he chose to cover his gray, he'd look like he was in his mid-thirties instead of pushing fifty. "Like I said, I can't blame her. You can't fall in love if you don't date, and I want to see you happy. I'd like to see you happy with that money. None of us wants to see the other option happen."

I scowled and looked away. Why, Mama? Why? The rules for the trust were clear, and Mama had built in guardrails. Not only did I have to get married, but I had to stay married for a year. So, yeah, I could find a partner in crime, get legally wed, stay that way for a year, then divorce her and we'd each leave with half.

And if I did that, I would be no better than my older brother. Aiden had found a genuinely nice woman to marry and ignore, a woman who'd had no idea she was just a payday.

But if I didn't do the same, then the family responsible for Mama's death would become filthy rich.

"If the Cartwrights get what's ours..." Dad's jaw flexed and his gaze flicked to where his new, young bride dozed in a recliner. "I will respect your decision not to marry by your next birthday if that's what you choose, but *dammit*, they've taken enough."

The pain in Dad's voice startled me. The guy had just said round two of his "I dos" and he sounded as devastated about Mama's death as the year it had happened.

I lowered my voice out of respect for Kendall. I had to admit, she didn't seem like the gold digger I'd first assumed she'd be. Who knows how she felt about Mama, but she'd just said her vows in front of her new husband's four adult kids, so it wasn't like Mama was a secret.

I didn't want to talk about this anymore. My own work was waiting if I wanted to keep my millions, which now included assistant duties until I filled the position. Yet, when I looked at Dad, his face was lined with more stress than a newlywed should have. "Is Grams riding your ass about this too?"

Surprise flickered through his eyes. "It's nothing I can't handle."

I laughed. "It's not like she can threaten your position at the company. You've been there thirty years."

"Right." Dad's chuckle was uneasy.

I'd kept out of the oil business. When I was a little kid, Dad had worked for the family business while still managing the ranch. Then Grams and DB—what we called our dearly departed grandpa, Donald Boyd—had sold a leasehold for a ridiculous amount of money and retired, leaving Dad in charge. DB Industries had become King Oil. Almost half of that money had been gifted to Mama and Dad, the rest separated into a trust for each of us.

Fuck. Grams wielded plenty of power at the company. Was that how she'd gotten Aiden to marry? "I'll think about it, all right?"

It was bad enough dating as one of the Kings from King Oil. Getting into a relationship as a CEO with a demanding job had its own challenges that I was yet unwilling to deal with. But it was much harder dating after Grams had hinted to every single prospective woman in a ten-state radius that marrying me equaled a lot of money for them. Grams's focus wasn't on who should get the money or who would really benefit from it, but on who shouldn't.

Dad leaned back in his chair and picked up his drink. "Look, your mother had a soft spot for the Cartwrights that I'll never understand." He jerked his gaze out the plane window, his jaws flexing. "If Sarah had known how much her mother would interfere with your lives, she wouldn't have set it up like she did. And if Grams had known what she had planned, the check from the leasehold sale would've been in my name." A sigh leaked out of him and for a brief second, he looked his age. "Knowing any of you had arranged a fake marriage just to get the money would kill her."

I understood Mama's nostalgia for the Cartwrights. She had been best friends with one of them and probably would've married our trashy neighbor if she hadn't had a fling with Dad that resulted in Aiden. She'd taken to Danny's daughter Bristol like a second mom every chance she could. Mama's heart had been in the right place, but her mind had taken the day off when she'd set up the trust.

Instead, her good intentions had become a reverse ransom: produce a wife and then get the money. Happiness for either party didn't factor into the equation, but then I guess that was what Grams thought the money was for.

CHAPTER 3

$\mathcal{E}$va

"Well, don't just stand there. Come inside and get to work."

The brusque, cultured voice behind me rumbled through my body. Whoever it was stood close. Was he talking to me?

I didn't know anyone in this part of town, unless I'd served them at some fancy reception. But I'd bet my nonexistent life savings that I was as nameless and faceless to them now as I had been then. The catered events I worked at weren't held for people like me. And people like the ones flowing around me weren't patrons of the bar I worked at either.

Denver pedestrians swirled around me. I'd been hit up for spare change at least three times on my stroll from the light-rail to Beckett King's spot of prime realty. I was used to blending into the background. Today, it didn't take a white shirt and black slacks. I fit in with the panhandlers in my regular, worn clothing.

"I'm impressed," the man continued. "He worked fast. Were you waiting in reserve?"

Arrogance poured off the words. Whoever this man was, I didn't like him. I took my time turning around in case he was talking to me. My lungs froze. Yes, the man was talking to me—and it wasn't just some stranger. It was *him*.

Unfortunately, I'd know him anywhere. Internet stalking had given me plenty of pictures to stare at. One night, I'd even fallen asleep with his photo on my phone. Good thing Adam hadn't seen or he might've gotten the wrong idea.

Dark eyes glared at me, the muscles of his jaw flexing as if looking at me physically hurt. The rich bastard probably thought I was more likely to ask him for a buck or two than enter one of the offices around here.

"Go on," he said. "I can see Grams is trying another route this time." His dismissive gaze swept down my pale-blue fitted knit sweater, past my skinny jeans, and down to my Toms. From the way his lips flattened, he didn't like what he saw. I'm sure my disheveled pixie hair cut didn't fit his opinion of how a proper lady should look.

"Excuse me?" Did he know me? He shouldn't know me. But that tone of his—if he offered me a dollar, I would whip him with it.

He tipped a dark brow and a smug smile curved lips that were hard not to stare at. So I swept my gaze over his body, adopting the same dismissive expression he had. The look was hard to maintain. It was like scowling at a beautiful sculpture.

His traditional black suit was fitted in the trendy slim style that accentuated his wide shoulders and long legs. And the way his maroon tie offset his black vest made me want to rip his suit jacket off to see what he looked like without it.

Dapper was the word that entered my mind. As if I'd been born a hundred years ago instead of twenty-five.

"Like what you see?" His tone was wry. My gaze flipped up to his. Self-confidence butted against smugness in his expression. He looked good and he knew it.

I scrambled for words before *Yes, yes I do like what I see* could slip out. "I'm not a suit girl."

The smug smirk lightened to a real smile. "Is that how you talk to your boss?"

"No?" What was he talking about? Had I been plotting against a madman? If so, that'd suck the wind right out of my sails. It was hard to get revenge on a guy who didn't understand reality. That'd make me the villain in my sad story.

"What's your name?"

"Eva." I didn't have to ask his. Beckett Parshall King. Twenty-eight-year-old tech giant. Born and raised in Montana, and a self-made millionaire, which totally wasn't fair because the man came from loads of oil money.

"Beck King. What'd my grandmother tell you when she hired you?"

"I've never talked to your grandmother, Beck King. I don't know who you think I am—"

"Good try, but I'm onto her games."

"That makes one of us." He thought I was someone else, and my brain was shutting down. What could I say I was doing here when he figured out I wasn't who he thought I was?

"Did she think that feigning ignorance would actually work?"

"I swear I don't know your grandma, but I'll go out on a limb and guess her name is Mrs. King? If so, that's all I know about her."

He scrutinized me. Realization dawned in his eyes, then a predatory smile lit his face. He stepped back to look me over again. The warm flush moving along my body with his gaze had me shifting my stance.

"It would be Mrs. Boyd, actually. Want a job?"

My mouth dropped open. Of course I'd give that a hard pass, but...I had been here looking for a way to worm into his empire. To rot it from the inside out until Beck King was couch-bound and despondent like my brother.

"Why would I need a job?" I had two already, but his offer was intriguing.

He stepped around me to open the door to the office building. I hadn't dared wander inside. Today was just for recon. I'd learned all I could online about Beckett and it was time to gather information on him personally.

"Come inside," he said. "We'll talk."

Was it my lucky day? Should I buy a lottery ticket? The only way it could get even better was if he sat down and told me his deepest, darkest secrets. Everyone had dirt on them and Beckett wasn't any different. I only hoped he had enough dirt to ruin his reputation in the tech world and cost him his fortune.

It was a long shot to say the least, but I had to do something. For my brother.

"After you," Beckett prompted.

I stared at him. He held the door like it was a given I'd enter. "I don't know you."

"You'll want to. Trust me."

Bold statement. I hated that he was right but loved that he was so wrong about why. Whatever he had in mind, it wasn't what I was after.

"We'll see about that." I strode inside, then stalled. Where was his office? I had only gawked at the building from the outside. The inside was a maze of plate-glass-windowed offices. It was hard to tell where one business stopped and the next one started. I wanted to run but I'd end up like a pigeon in a pinball machine, slamming from wall to wall.

He took the lead so naturally. What was it like to go

through life like that? Expecting people to obey his commands. Not worrying about bills. Strutting through this building like he owned the place. He probably did.

Beckett ushered me down a hallway. Like prairie dogs popping out of their holes, the employees of the businesses we passed rubbernecked and stared. I didn't have to look hard to know that several people admired Beckett as he walked by. Hell, I wanted to swoon with them.

He had a swagger I didn't see too often. Probably the result of growing up on a ranch. A wild horse could charge by, and he'd swing up onto it, suit and everything. At a glance, one wouldn't know the man could herd cattle, fix fences, and whatever else ranchers did. They just knew from looking at him that he had authority.

Beckett King in real life almost made me abort my mission. Why did I think that me, little Eva Chase, could destroy this guy?

He unlocked the door to a smaller office. It, too, had glass windows but only a sparse waiting room with earth-toned chairs, wooden coffee tables, and a walnut reception desk the size of a family sedan. Unlike the clean lines and modern appeal of the corridor, his office was sophisticated. Old school.

"Not what I expected." This space suggested money but didn't scream it like the rest of the building.

"It was like this when I bought it. I didn't want to deal with a remodel."

"You mean you don't own the whole building." Maybe he was more accessible than I'd thought.

But his knowing look and that arrogant smirk said he wasn't.

"Seriously? You do?" I sighed. Did I leave now and scold myself for being naïve about me versus Beckett King? Or did I stay and have it proved over and over again?

Who was I to go up against a guy who could buy a freaking office center in downtown Denver? During the week, I worked for a caterer, delivering heavy trays of divine-smelling food I could never afford. I remained invisible in my crisp white shirt and black pants as I served faceless people and cleaned up the mess they left behind. But it paid more than minimum wage. Then on weekends, I bartended at a local sports bar and my boss didn't care how hard I smacked a patron who tried to grab my ass.

But something about me had caught his attention. I had my in and I couldn't blow it. If he found out who I really was, what would he do? I couldn't sink much farther and my brother was already at rock bottom.

"Let's talk in my office." He led me through the waiting area.

The wall behind the reception desk hid his office door, accessible from either side of the divider. He punched in a key code and opened his door. His office was equipped with the tech he was known for. He could probably log into the security app on his phone and see every square inch of this place.

I'd had to drop cable TV after Adam lost his job.

"Have a seat." Beckett gestured to the plush seat across from a minimalist modern desk. No wood in here. It was all sleek lines and open surfaces. Rounding his desk to his chair, he unbuttoned his suit jacket and shrugged it off.

Oh my God, him in that fitted vest… Was this a test of my dedication to destroy him? It was hard to be equally vengeful and lustful toward the same person.

No, it was actually quite easy.

The sight did not disappoint. The flex of his biceps as he hung the garment on a hook behind his desk made my mouth go dry. The flash of a rock-hard ass as he twisted was just unfair. I was at a severe disadvantage—I doubted I affected him in nearly the same way.

"So." He settled into his ergonomic Herman Miller chair and leaned back. "I need an administrative assistant."

I blinked. That was his job offer? "And you're willing to hire me off the street only knowing my name is Eva?"

"For this, yes. It'll be temporary. Four months, but of course, if you work out, I'd be happy to extend the position."

"Sounds amazing," I deadpanned.

A faint smile touched his lips. His bottom lip stuck out just barely past his first, giving him the sexiest permapout. When combined with his smoldering dark eyes, the look made a temporary four-month position as his bitch almost seem desirable.

"There'd be a background check," he said.

"I certainly hope so." I should be worried, but I wasn't. Adam and I didn't share a last name. Adam had his bio dad's last name, Dickerson, and while my dad had adopted him in every way but the legal one, my parents had just never gotten around to the paperwork. And thanks to Adam, there was nothing criminal in my background.

Familiar guilt ate at my insides. No matter how unqualified I was for this job, I had to see it through.

"There's a catch," he said.

"Do tell."

"You see, ever since Grams learned my executive assistant resigned and moved away over a year ago, she's been sending qualified applicants." Beckett gave me a pointed look. "Attractive, presumably single women who see me as a future payday. They're no longer interested in the job when they find out it doesn't lead straight to my bank account."

His honesty was startling but the story was intriguing. Who'd want to marry their grandson off like that? And he called his grandmother Grams?

"Does your grams own part of your business?" My respect for Beckett dipped. So much for a self-made millionaire. His money went way back.

"No, but she knows they can do the job and that I won't kick them out on their asses for her interference. I have a soft spot for Grams."

That almost made Beckett sound like a nice guy.

I can see Grams is trying another route this time. Yeah, I seriously doubted those candidates had looked like me. They'd blend with the rest of the employees in this office building.

Tension filled my muscles. Beckett hadn't been rude, but I didn't want to sit around hearing about how I was the perfect fugly duckling to get his grandma off his back.

I thought back to his comment about his bank account. "Why would they think that?" Anyone who married into the Kings probably got carpal tunnel signing the prenups.

He considered me for a long time. If he couldn't answer simply, it must be a hell of a story. Was it exactly what I was looking for?

"Grams has an ulterior motive and it doesn't include ensuring my meetings and travel itineraries line up." He kicked a leg over one knee. His slick loafers were as black as his suit, same with his socks. He rubbed his lower lip between two fingers and I couldn't look away. "I have a trust."

"Sure." A lot of people did. Not me. I served people who had trusts.

"I can access it on my thirtieth birthday if, and only if, I've been married for at least a year."

Rich-people drama was so much juicier than regular folks' issues. "What happens if you're still single? Or if you get married at twenty-nine and a half?"

There was that faint smile again. "Mama made her terms

clear. Not only would I not receive it, but someone else would."

According to a newspaper article I'd found, his mom had passed away nearly twenty years ago. That was a hell of a trust to set up for a twelve-year-old kid.

He folded his hands in front of him and looked me in the eye. I wanted to squirm under the intensity of his gaze. "The money will go to someone outside my family, someone who doesn't deserve it, a family that—" His jaw clenched and he glanced away. "I find I'm caught between wanting the funds just because my grandparents and parents worked so hard for them, and letting them go because I don't want anyone dictating who and when I marry."

Details started clicking into place. Temporary. Four months. He turned twenty-nine in four months and would need to say "I do" before then to access his trust. He wanted me to hold down his office so he could find a willing bride.

Irritation built. Guys like him thought people like me were disposable. I wasn't going to leave two jobs to pretend to be an executive assistant for four months. Then I'd be on the streets, doing the application game with no money coming in. But I bet he hadn't thought of that.

"Do you need the money?" I asked. I waved around his office. "I mean, you seem like you're doing okay."

He'd offered my brother 3.5 million for his life-hacking app Organize You. Life-changing money dangled like a carrot, then yanked away.

"I am doing well," he agreed. "But Grams has other ideas. The people it'd go to— Well, I can't blame her."

Reality finally sunk in. I wasn't about to be a rook in the games rich people played and I had a feeling the Kings could play as dirty as they needed to. The patriarch hadn't made billions off an oil empire by being nice, and the matriarch hadn't raised four boys with an oil baron because she was a wallflower. And those were just his parents. What was Grams like?

They would destroy me to get their way. It was one thing to come here, looking to inflict my own little damage, but I hadn't planned on taking on the whole family. Nope. Self-preservation won.

I rose out of the surprisingly comfortable chair. "Sorry, a four-month temp position isn't my idea of a stellar job opportunity. Good luck though." At least I'd leave knowing I'd tried, and also knowing that I was too small of a fish to mess with a frenzy of sharks.

"It could be four months and *one year*."

My answer was still no, but curiosity stalled my exit.

"I'd compensate you for the ruse," he continued. "And if you're good at the job, it'd be a bonus and you could stay on as my assistant. After we divorce, of course."

Dumbfounded, I couldn't quit staring at him. He was speaking nonsense. "Divorce?"

"Be my fake fiancée for four months. If we get along, be my fake wife for another year. We split the money in the end. Whaddya say?"

CHAPTER 4

eckett

I TOOK a measured breath while I waited for the pixie's answer. Her hair gleamed almost black where it was thickest, but the tips around her face and ears were brunette. How fitting that this woman I'd found on my doorstep had hair the hues of oil, the substance that had given my family its vast wealth.

Not many ranchers with operations our size ranched for fun. But my family did. It was in our blood and we took it seriously. Mama's parents had been ranchers before they'd found oil, and Dad's family had ranched for generations. But now I was more interested in software than cattle breeds. I enjoyed rounding up promising apps more than a good cattle drive. Marketing new programs until they earned out seven figures gave me more of a high than I'd ever gotten at the sales barn.

Almost every app I'd bought earned out. I didn't need the

money. But my trust *was* family money. I could do a lot of good with it. Old Man Cartwright would just drink half of it away and snatch up land that he'd let go into disrepair with the rest. The drive to save it from him had taken root.

I'd been prepared to lose the money, and swallow the sour pill of a hundred million going to our land-greedy neighbor, but now I could have the best of both worlds.

My suggestion was crazy. Absolutely ridiculous. But it made sense. Based on our short time together already, I liked her.

I'd get the best of both worlds. With Eva as a fiancée, Grams would leave me alone and we could make it look real enough that it wouldn't upset Dad. If she went through with the marriage, the money would stay in the family, and at the end of the year, she'd get half. It looked like she could use it more than me. She was cute, but her clothes were well loved.

Lord knew they loved her right back. She seemed oblivious to the attention her tight little body attracted. Her ass in those jeans was the first thing my gaze had landed on when my driver had dropped me off. The butter-soft denim was snug against her lush curves, and my fingers twitched to caress it.

Veering back to the present before I embarrassed myself, I studied her. She continued to stare at me, her luminous amber eyes filled with disbelief. A good sign.

The other "applicants" Grams had sent had been fully aware of what they were getting into and had tried to play me from the first false smile. Time was running out. Grams had probably been interviewing another woman before I'd even read the latest resignation email.

It was insulting to me and to the women she viewed as nothing more than heifers she could breed me to. Not long ago, I would've expected that behavior from Dad, not Grams. After Mama had died and he'd broken the seal of sleeping with other women, he'd viewed them as nothing more than a pastime—until Kendall had come along. Kendall had only proved that he was a romantic who wouldn't settle for less than love.

But that still left me and my impending twenty-ninth birthday.

When I'd arrived at work and seen Eva wandering around like she was lost, I'd thought Grams had changed tactics. But Eva's attitude had been refreshing—and inspiring. She didn't know me or the King family. The way she regarded me with caution and a healthy dose of suspicion was real.

The fact that she had to think about it only made me more confident that this might work.

She sat back down, hands on her knees, and looked me in the eye. "You want me to be your fake fiancée to get one over on your grandma because how could you be engaged to someone like me? And then if we get along, we'd get married for real so you can collect your money?"

Part of what she said bothered me. "I didn't ask you because you're the opposite of who Grams thinks I'd like." Grams's choices had been very attractive, and intelligent, and under different circumstances, maybe there would've been a spark. Though none of them had intrigued me like this leery woman with expressive eyes.

She arched a brow. "Instead you opted for grabbing some random off the street and proposing? How is that a better idea?"

The frank way she spoke to me was refreshing. Other than my pain-in-the-ass brothers, nobody talked to me like "a random off the street." People in my life wanted something from me, whether it was my money, or…my money.

I stuck with the honesty she seemed so fond of. "So far it's going well. You're actually thinking about it."

"I am not." A delicate blush brushed her cheeks. I liked it

there. I wanted to be the one who always put it there, but I wanted the reason for it to be passion.

An orgasm would have the same effect on the dusting of sprinkles across her nose, creating a pink glow as she called out my name—

I adjusted myself discreetly below the desk. Good God, it was like I hadn't been laid in… How long had it been? Since Grams had been interfering with my love life. I hadn't trusted my dick around anyone for months.

"Okay, maybe a little," she admitted. "But only because it's a completely ridiculous proposal."

"I can give you a fake proposal out of your wildest fantasies." I hadn't meant to infuse my words with so much suggestion. But she blushed again, so it was worth it.

"The whole situation is absurd."

I shrugged. "Yep. Mama wanted to ensure her rowdy boys would settle down and she thought this would do it."

There was more, but Mama was gone and her secrets with her. Dad was quiet on the subject. I was old enough to remember a few comments though, ones I hadn't been meant to hear.

Like Dad asking Mama, *You think you could've changed him, Sarah? There was a reason you were single when we met.*

Mama's wry reply of *I was eighteen, Gentry, not exactly an old maid* always made my heart ache like I'd lost her yesterday.

Or the one time I'd overheard Mama talking to Grams. *I feel guilty spending this money. It shouldn't have all been ours.*

Eva interrupted my thoughts. "You don't even know my last name."

I'd have a complete background check performed before the end of the week. "Tell me whatever you're comfortable sharing."

Her eyes narrowed for a heartbeat but she reclined in the chair and crossed her arms. "Eva Chase."

"Nice to meet you, Eva Chase." It was the highlight of my week. Hell, of my month. "Do you want me to show you around?"

"I haven't said yes yet."

"Where are you working now?"

I didn't think she was going to answer me, but when she did, she rolled her eyes like she couldn't believe she was either. "I'm a server for Silver Eats Catering and I bartend at Nellie's."

Quickly calculating her current monthly wage, even accounting for the generous tips I didn't think she got at a place like Nellie's, I scribbled a counteroffer on a King Tech–embossed notepad.

"Take some time to think about it. The offer is good for twenty-four hours."

"I'd hate for you to withdraw your offer." The vitriol in her voice was startling.

"My terms are always clear." The first thread of indecision wiggled into my conscience. What was I doing, offering to marry a stranger?

She scowled at the sheet, then directed her perplexed gaze at me. "This much for four months?"

"I do have actual assistant duties for you, so no. That would be monthly."

Her eyes widened, color draining from her face. "That's crazy."

"I'm hardly asking you to fill a nine-to-five position. I work around the clock."

"What if I don't know how to use basic computer programs?"

Shit. I hadn't thought of that. "Do you?"

"Some," she said warily.

"But you can learn."

"Sure." Her eyes narrowed as if she was rating my sanity.

This was adding up to the most fascinating encounter I'd ever had with a woman. The fat monthly salary on the paper in her hand hadn't been enough to change her salty attitude toward me, nor was the promise of half of a giant trust fund should she marry me.

She waved the small sheet of paper. "What do you even do again?

"King Tech invests in the present with an eye on the future. Right now, that's apps. My people and I scour the globe for talented developers, then evaluate their programs. If they make the cut—"

"The people or the programs?" Her lips were thinned and her eyes challenging.

At my level, I was used to my methods being questioned, but her reaction seemed more critical, more personal, than others. "Both. I want to know who I'm investing my money with, especially since my employees are scattered all over the world. That gives them more autonomy and control than most other investors would allow, but the risk also allows me to keep a small workspace and allows them more flexibility in their schedule. If I trust them, I can give them tasks and a due date and know they'll get it done."

"But you keep your assistant in an office with one window?"

Part of my pride shriveled a little. She sounded less than impressed with my surroundings. The window she'd mentioned was behind me. Where she'd sit—or my next executive assistant—there was no view but the expansive hallway.

"The other tenants were already here. When I want wide-open spaces, I go to my mountain cabin." Or home, but I wasn't pining for dusty, manure-scented air. "I'm usually just here for board meetings."

Flicking her finger up and down my length, she asked, "What would the dress code be?"

Form-fitting jeans and another sweater just like she was wearing were fine with me. "Business casual."

"Yeah, about that. I only have casual."

"What do you wear to your other jobs?"

"This, or an outfit that would have all your clients asking what organic gluten-free options are available on the menu."

My lips twitched. "How about anything that's not jeans?" She still didn't look convinced, but I pressed. "Is that a yes, then?"

Her shrewd eyes narrowed on me. "If you really want to me to quit both of my jobs to do this, then I need half the first month's wages up front."

"How do I know you won't take the money and run?"

"Would you really notice the loss?"

Of her? Yes. Of the money? It wouldn't make a dent in my wallet. A ping came from my phone. "There's that meeting I mentioned. Wait here." I went to the empty reception desk that would swallow Eva whole—lucky desk—and grabbed a pen and notepad. "Leave your email. I'll send the forms. Get them back by the time the bank closes and you'll have the money."

She scribbled her email in curt, blocky handwriting. Straightforward, like her personality. "This is risky, Mr. King."

Blame it on my ranching background, but I hated formality. "Call me Beck, and yes, it is."

But I didn't take risks. My brothers had called me Gooder for half my life, short for Do-Gooder. My success came from diligent planning and research. I calculated odds at every turn and bailed when numbers were too low, too high, or too in between, depending on the situation. I'd been known to cut and run when unsavory details about those I was negotiating with came to light. That type of behavior didn't make friends, but it had made me rich. Without the oil money.

"All right, *Beck*. I'll be here bright and early in the morning. For administrative duties."

"Looking forward to it." I could fill in the blanks. Discussion of the fake marriage would come later. She didn't realize that she held all the power. I might have to pay out to get her to work for me, but if she left and never returned, I was out a hundred million dollars.

CHAPTER 5

va

"WHERE THE HELL are you going dressed like that?" Adam rubbed his bloodshot eyes like he was afraid he was hallucinating.

He very well could be. What was this, hour twenty-six behind his controller? One day he'd ferment into the sofa.

I jingled my keys to the apartment deadbolt. "Someone has to pay rent."

"Yeah. I'm gonna apply to some places today." His dead tone promised otherwise.

"Maybe get some sleep first." I hoped that the fear of our electricity being cut off would get through to Adam. But I also feared what he'd do left inside his own mind once the batteries in his phone, Nintendo DS, and iPad died.

I left him behind and locked the door. As I breezed outside, cool autumn air tickled my hair. Yesterday, I hadn't

27

styled it, but today it was slicked up to a peak in front and a little off center. My sides were short but not buzzed.

What would Mr. King say? I doubted his other assistants had my style.

Stopping to feed Kitty, I checked on the kittens. She lifted her head and blinked at me.

"It's the good stuff today." It'd be canned food for the next four months. I'd bought two cases and almost herniated myself carrying it all home until I realized I had enough money to order a ride.

Leaving her with a little extra, I walked to catch the light-rail to downtown. My bank account might have enough for another ride, but getting food home was one thing. Wasting it on my everyday commute when the light-rail was so much cheaper was another.

My new knee-high boots creaked with each step. By the end of the day, I might have blisters, but I couldn't help the purchase. Mr. King—Beckett—*Beck*—had come through with the funds so I could wear more to the office than skull-print leggings and a T-shirt with a rainbow marijuana leaf. That shirt had been on clearance, and I hadn't been about to turn down a three-dollar top.

What I was wearing now hadn't been three dollars. The sweater was a pale pink cashmere that made my eyes glint like a wolf. It fell past my ass to midthigh so only a small swath of my chocolate-brown leggings was showing.

This was the nicest outfit I'd ever worn. Even when I'd gone to prom with the crew of delinquents I hung out with at the time, I had worn a powder-blue tux in defiance of *the man*.

Now I was going to work for the man like the proper little executive assistant I was.

Fiancée. I snorted and the guy next to me on the light-rail gave me a *how ya doing* nod. Like my noise had been a pickup line. I ignored him, my thoughts returning to the previous day.

I couldn't quit thinking about him—it. I couldn't quit thinking about the situation. Pretending I was going to marry the guy who had turned my brother into the couch-bound zombie I'd just left behind? Crazy.

Almost as insane as scoping out his workplace with nothing more than ten bucks in my pocket and my phone. This was fate telling me to go get him. Learn his weak points and bring him to his knees.

Figuratively, not literally.

Imagining him on his knees did naughty things to my body. A hot flush was already spreading, and damn my light complexion, I was probably blushing. If we did the most outrageous thing I'd ever heard of and got married, what would he expect?

He said it'd be fake, but in order to pretend to his family, we'd have to spend time together. I assumed that meant more time than me asking him if he was free to schedule a three o'clock meeting next Tuesday—or whatever my assistant duties were.

Stepping off at my destination, I strutted to the Midland Office Tower. The place my new boss and possible future fiancé owned.

And he'd taken the smallest office in the place.

How was that for a start on dirt gathering? *Tech entrepreneur and oil heir buys tower and gives up entire floor for a hole-in-the-wall office.*

Scandalous.

The guy had to have something in his past. Or if he was squeaky clean, maybe in his future?

For once, I blended with the milling of office drones power-walking to their cubicles. Stilettos clicked on the pavement around me. Men in suits, cropped haircuts, neatly trimmed beards, and mirrored shades zipped by me. I hoped none of these people were executive assistants. Otherwise I was severely underdressed.

But Beckett had hired me in Toms, so…

My stomach fluttered as I strode through the main door to the tower. Each step I took confirmed that yesterday hadn't been a doped-up dream. I didn't smoke pot, snort, inject, or inhale anything else, but there'd been no other explanation for this ridiculous scenario.

Marry Beckett King. In name only, for a year, but still. The more I researched him online, the more I thought I'd need every minute spent together to build a case against him. His reputation was spotless. But he'd pissed enough people off in his short career that it wouldn't be hard to find ears to listen to my woes, so I had that going for me.

If only I could do it before Adam forgot to eat breakfast, lunch, and dinner for three days in a row and landed himself in the hospital. Again.

As soon as I stepped foot in the office, Beckett appeared around the corner, carrying a clipboard.

"For a tech guy, you use a lot of paper." Perhaps this was the time to filter my speech. What an impossible task.

His gaze went from my face to my hair, then drifted down my body. "And you said you didn't own business casual."

"I didn't before last night."

His brows lifted in surprise. Had he seriously not believed me? And he'd still seen me as potential fiancée material. Was he trying to piss his family off?

"I like the physical act of writing and checking items off." He shot me an ironic smile. "And that the paper can be shredded."

"Once online, always online."

"Exactly. It's amazing what I can find out about someone

with a few keystrokes." His words made my heart stop. *He knows who I am.*

But he just set the clipboard down on the reception desk. "Go ahead and get settled. We'll go through my typical monthly schedule."

As my heartbeat returned to normal, I took a seat. Beckett wasn't in a suit today, but he was no less compelling. Softer, maybe. He wasn't all done up in trendy pastel fitted slacks. His pants were charcoal and his sweater maroon. The material wasn't cashmere, but it looked just as soft.

The image of me curled against his massive chest filtered through my mind. I cut it off and summoned my last view before leaving home. My brother, unshaved and unbathed, on the couch. Listless and lifeless, thanks to this asshole. I owed Adam. He was my older brother and he'd always taken care of me. It had cost him everything when it shouldn't have.

"Your background check came back."

I crossed one leg over the other and faced him, forcing myself to breathe normally. My lungs wanted to seize until I ran outside for fresh air. "And what did you find out about me with a few keystrokes?"

"Admittedly, not much. You're a Denver native, you didn't finish college, and you've no criminal record."

Thanks to Adam. "That's me. Squeaky clean."

I was turning to check out the computer when he said, "And you? What did you find out about me?"

I couldn't stop my smile as I tore my gaze off a computer system that would make Adam drool. Between the tower and two huge monitors, I bet it cost close to five grand. Because there was no way Beckett didn't have top-of-the-line gaming capabilities in all his equipment. Did he expect his assistant to test out the programs he was interested in? I had more experience with that than coordinating meetings and travel.

No doubt he assumed I had gone home and researched him all night. Little did he know, I'd done that already, and for far more than a single night. Punching the on button, I spoke while waiting for the computer to boot up. "Born and raised a country boy." I slid my gaze to him, then down to the Oxford shoes that were the polar opposite of cowboy boots, then back to the computer. The screen was bigger than my fucking TV, but not Adam's. His was a remnant from the days before Beckett had destroyed him. "Princeton grad. Self-made millionaire, but oddly, nothing about the trust fund." Grams must've had the women she sent sign nondisclosure agreements. There had been one waiting for me in my packet.

"What else?"

"Is there something else?" His dating life was quiet and drama-free, but I had my suspicions. He'd been linked to an heiress from New York, a social media darling turned self-help "expert," and a local TV news anchor who was so gorgeous it had hurt to look at her picture. She'd been a part-time anchor, but dating Beckett had gotten her on the evening news. Was it Beckett's notoriety or her talent that had gotten her up the ladder that quickly while she'd been seeing him? I hoped it was her talent, but unfortunately, the world didn't always work that way around people like Beckett.

"There's always something else." He perched on the counter next to me. If I looked over, I could revert to my juvenile years and check out how much of a tent his manhood made and start guessing widths and lengths. But I didn't plan to get *that* close to him. "Don't be afraid to tell me about the negative stuff you read. I know it's there and I know what they've said. Many have said it to my face."

If he wanted honesty, I'd go for it. "Your competitors think you're a heartless bastard with an eye for the bottom line, not the people behind the product. They think it's because of your age and your lack of attachments. When your supporters argue that you're tight with your family, the haters challenge them to produce recent photos of you with your family. Or of you at home in Montana. They can't, which leads them back to heartless bastard who doesn't care about people."

Beckett's expression went colder with each word. He was going to bust some teeth soon. It wasn't as satisfying as it should have been. I wanted to know more.

"And then there are your exes, but I have a strong feeling that due to NDAs, what they can say is restricted. But that heiress? 'Let's just say, previous relationships have taught me to expect more out of a real man.' She's good at throwing shade. Like expert level."

The corner of his mouth twitched. "She also has exceptional aim with solid objects."

I couldn't see Beckett dodging vases and phones and whatever else was in the luxury condo of a professional party girl. I could see him clenching his jaw, spinning on his expensive heel, and marching out without a word.

"Well, I hope she doesn't visit," I said as I pointed to the login screen. The backdrop of a mountain lake looked like the sort of wallpaper that came preinstalled on computers the world over, but there was something different about this photo. The blue sky came alive above snow-peaked mountains and the lake glittered like it was rippling across the screen.

"Is this photo real? I mean, like one where you grew up?"

Beckett leaned over to open a screen where I was prompted to set my own password—in the highest definition possible. It was going to be hard to get used to real life when I looked at more pixels than God had intended. "Yes. Near our family's place."

His tone lacked inflection, most definitely not the pride I'd expected to hear. The scenery in this picture was crazy beautiful. I might be a Denver native, but I'd rarely left the city's limits. Mom used to take us to public parks, and she and Dad had discussed big plans to camp in Yellowstone "someday." Someday hadn't arrived before the accident.

No more was said about the picture. He led me through setup and customizing my desktop—which I could've done myself, but him leaning next to me wasn't something I wanted to shoo away—then he disappeared into his office. The rest of the morning was spent combing through apps and familiarizing myself with the various companies under the umbrella of King Tech.

There were so many. I didn't recognize three-quarters of the names, but they ranged from tiny one-person operations that Beckett had a use for inside King Tech, to complex programs that millions of people had on their phones and computers. One title I recognized from a billboard for a security firm in front of my apartment complex.

Hours later, he popped back out. "How's it going?"

"It's going to take me more than a day to get all this down," I said, stunned. New respect bloomed for the nameless, faceless suits I'd passed on the way here.

"You've got a week."

When my gaze flew to him, his eyes crinkled in the corners. "Kidding."

Beckett didn't outright smile much. If I'd grown up with stupid-full bank accounts and a ton of well-adjusted siblings, I wouldn't stop smiling.

He hit a few more buttons and handed me a phone. "The password is the same, and the scheduling program is on both."

I swallowed hard at the name of the program he used. It was the one he'd purchased after backing out of the deal he'd offered Adam. My brother bordered on obsessive, and organization was like a drug. Even as a dud on my couch, Adam had his shit arranged. His dirty cup, always on a coaster, sat three inches away from his bag of chips. His games were organized, but not alphabetically. It depended on his moods. Sometimes I found them arranged according to gaming systems or by rating. Once in a while, he switched it up to the level he was on, or the main character's hair color. Role-play, individual or group mode. When Adam was going to college and had to juggle due dates, real dates, and his work schedule with group classwork, he'd designed a program they could all log in to and coordinate together. It wasn't a highly unique program, but Adam made it fun and easy, more like a social media app, and word had spread.

Beckett pulled me out of my memories when he glanced at his watch. "Why don't we break for lunch?"

"What time do you want me back?" I would've packed a lunch, but after splurging on clothing for the first time in my life, I'd had the impulsive idea to eat out for lunch. There were so many eclectic eateries downtown. I'd walked past them for years. Today, I was going to be one of those people who went out for lunch instead of grabbing cooled leftovers from serving trays and peanuts from the bar.

"We'll go together."

Right, the fiancée bit. We hadn't discussed those terms yet, or if I would indeed be hired for that role too. He probably wanted to get to know me before planting a big diamond on my finger.

That meant I had to spend time with him, not just trying to ignore the soothing smell of his aftershave and the way heat rolled off his body every time he leaned over to use the keyboard. I'd fallen into the mindset of office drone learning new tasks. I'd forgotten I was here to possibly marry the guy.

Good thing I'd never been the type of girl to dream about my perfect wedding and my perfect man.

"Where should we go?" he asked.

"You'll have to choose. I've never eaten downtown."

His eyes widened. "And you've lived here your whole life?"

I wasn't ashamed of being raised on a limited budget. "If it didn't have golden arches, we didn't eat there."

Understanding darkened his eyes. He must've put my statement together with the fact that I had worked two jobs up until yesterday and figured out my family's income level growing up.

"What do you like?"

"Broke kids don't grow up to be picky." Not when they were broke adults.

He blinked. "Gotcha. There's a burger place on Sixteenth that's amazing. We'll start there."

The walk to the restaurant was brisk and…interesting. It was hard to study Beckett when he walked next to me, but unlike the clipped strides of all the guys around us, Beckett swaggered. With his rolling gait, he hadn't been raised on concrete like I had been.

Curt greetings breezed past us. "Hey, Mr. King." "How's it going, Mr. King?" Or just a short "King." It was a given that their gazes slid to me and back to him. I was dismissed so easily, it was as if I were in a bubble of invisibility.

Beckett greeted each person by name. I tried to take notes in case that was expected of me in my new "job" but quickly gave up. I hadn't bothered to remember regulars' names at the bar. Once they became permanent fixtures on the barstool, their tips didn't change because I could say, "How's it going, *Bill*?"

We reached the burger place and he held the door open for me. It was an automatic move for him, one no doubt ingrained from childhood. The warm glow blooming in my belly had no business there in the first place.

I wasn't special. I was another business deal for this guy, complete with contracts like the ones I'd filled out yesterday.

Once settled into a booth, I fiddled with the paper band around my silverware. I didn't know this guy and I wasn't used to dining with my bosses. I bullshitted with Frank at Nellie's, but he was probably as old as my dad would be if he were still alive.

Beckett tapped through his phone like I wasn't there and that was just fine with me. These few moments before ordering gave me a chance to study him out of the corner of my eye.

Still as good looking as before, but even better up close. His hair was trimmed close to the scalp and he was clean-shaven, but I could picture him with a little scruff and a cowboy hat pulled down low.

Flutters rippled through my belly. All kinds of men filtered through Denver. Ultra athletes. Yuppies. Even cowboys and ranchers. Somehow Beckett could fit in with any of those, except the men I hung out with.

Not that I dated much anymore. Work consumed most of my time and the rest was spent cleaning the house and making sure Adam didn't shrivel up on the couch.

The server appeared at the booth. I ordered first as Beckett clicked his phone off. His complete attention was on the college-aged waiter. He was direct, polite, and efficient.

How would I have handled serving Beckett? Customers came with all kinds of personalities, but I lumped them into two categories: those who saw me and those who didn't. Some nights, I was relieved to wait on those who didn't see me. They ate, drank, paid their tab, gave me a mediocre tip, and left with no drama.

The ones who noticed me were lumped together. They

pitied my lot in life either because they were super friendly or because they had once waited tables and pitied me. Then there was the subsection of those who wanted to date me, and I'd have to coax and bribe them to pay their damn bill so I wasn't left covering their unpaid tab when I turned them down.

Beckett wasn't giving off a pity vibe, but he'd probably leave a big tip, subconsciously grateful he wasn't in the food service industry. I'm sure my ragged look had influenced his proposal. Give the pauper a hand up, not a handout.

"I have a meeting this afternoon," he announced.

"I'll be fine in the office." I doubted anyone would stop in. What a tomb. In my first hour, I had missed my catering gig and the hustle and bustle that came with it. There, I only watched the clock to make sure we had food placed and presented on time, or tables broken down and loaded by a specific hour. I ran in and out of buildings as we loaded and unloaded platters and prepped food.

Most of the places I catered at least had windows.

His dark gaze pinned me. "You'll need to come with me, take notes, and add dates to the master schedule, and afterward, I usually rely on my assistant's general impression of how the meeting went. And about the people involved. Will that be a problem?"

I could opinion the hell of out his meetings, but I didn't think those were the kinds of observations he was looking for. Another detail bothered me. "If we're going to come out as engaged in the next four months, won't it be weird that I started as your assistant?"

"It'll be stereotypical."

"That happens a lot?"

"In reality? I don't know. In other people's minds? All the time." He shrugged and scanned the restaurant. "It doesn't matter to me."

His phone buzzed and I lost his attention.

If I had been his legitimate assistant and not some chick he'd hired off the street to stick it to his Grams and the legal confines of his trust fund, it would totally matter to me. I took pride in good honest work. There'd been a time when my actions had been less than honest. I'd taken the easy route to earning a living and it had turned into the hardest part of my life, a part I was still dealing with. But I wasn't his legitimate assistant, so it wouldn't matter to me either.

Our food arrived and I carefully cut my burger into smaller slices so I wouldn't be wearing ketchup on my blouse to the meeting. Beckett had no such hesitation and I tried not to be jealous of how everything came easy to him.

After I finished, I pushed my basket to the side. "What's this meeting about?"

Beckett hadn't looked at me once throughout the entire meal. I'd dabbed my mouth until my lips felt dry, quadruple-checked my front for globs dropped on my chest, and fiddled with my hair. Is this what I had to look forward to?

"I'm evaluating a new-to-market app." The muscles of his jaw flexed. "It has limited uses, at least for a guy, but I can see the potential."

Limited uses for a guy? Was Beckett just a tech bro and the app was for lipstick, or clothing, or...whatever he thought women were supposed to be obsessed with?

He cleared his throat and gazed across the restaurant. "That's actually why I want you there. It's a program that tracks the intimacy between couples and makes recommendations. It's loaded with suggestions, challenges, and...stuff of that nature."

Feeling wicked, I shook my head like I didn't understand. "What stuff? And why wouldn't that be useful for a guy?"

The bastard must've smelled the challenge. "Because men are already sitting around thinking about how they can get their girlfriend to give them a hand job in a public place. And whether they can go down on their partner in a dark movie theater without getting noticed. Most of us don't need to be encouraged to fuck our partners more."

Heat wicked up my body and I struggled not to squirm against the seat. Each suggestion he made created a vivid image in my head—and he and I were the stars.

I took a slow sip of water. His pupils dilated and his jaw clenched as he watched my throat work, but he didn't look away. I couldn't let him dominate this conversation or my role in this farce would be fucked. He'd bulldoze me and I'd plant myself beside my brother.

"Mmm. I don't know about that." And I wasn't just being contrary. "My years as a bartender have taught me that men have insecurities and periods in their life when virility isn't pouring out of them. The middle-age spread starts. Little kids keep them up all night. Their wives or girlfriends are tired and depressed and the guys are frustrated and feel powerless because for once, sex won't solve everything. That's on top of all their own career concerns, bouts of depression, and stress over a massive mortgage."

Beckett's expression sharpened with each point. He relaxed into the booth and considered what I said. "So an app like this—would it help?"

I snorted. "Advertise in the bathroom stalls of every bar in Anytown, USA, and it'll get downloaded."

The corners of his mouth twitched. "I want more than a flash in the pan. But she's a marriage counselor, so I think it's worth looking at."

"The app's cheaper than her hourly fee, right?"

Another ghost of a smile. "That's actually close to her tagline."

The server came bearing the bill. I was about to reach for my card when Beckett handed him a hundred. "Keep the change." He slid and stood, the server already forgotten. Beckett wasn't looking at me to see if I was impressed with his generosity toward us poor folk. "Ready?"

Nope. His mind was on work. *Emotionally withdrawn and professionally selfish*. No wonder the guy was still single.

CHAPTER 6

eckett

LUNCH HAD BEEN A TEST. How long had it been since I'd been so sex starved that I couldn't control my body when an attractive woman ate? But her lips. Plump and pink...they'd keep me up at night.

And her cunning amber eyes. They spoke louder than her matter-of-fact statements. She'd been uncomfortable going out to lunch with me, painfully so once the food came and she was worried about spilling on herself. But then I'd mentioned our meeting and she'd had spot-on insight. Thanks to her experience as a bartender, she knew more about the male population than I did. I had my dad and my brothers to go off of. A sex app? A waste of gigabytes.

But to Mr. and Mrs. Joe Blow? It could help them weather the doldrums of their life together, or even save their marriage.

Only now I was going to have to go to a meeting and talk about sex—with Eva sitting next to me.

"My driver will be waiting by the office tower." I almost held out my arm for her, but we weren't there yet. Being with her, thinking about marriage, yet not touching her and teaching her the inner workings of my day, scrambled my brains. I had four months to get to know her. We'd be married in name only.

Although she hadn't asked about that part of the arrangement. I got the sense that she was feeling out the job—and me. If I turned weird, she'd be gone, and that thought fueled my stress levels.

I'd never worried about my real dates' lack of commitment. It wasn't usually a concern. None of my relationships had lasted more than six months. The women wanted more. More talking, more emotions, more access to my life—one had even tried to break into my computer. They asked about my dad, about what happened to my mom, and begged to see the ranch. Until Dad's wedding, I'd been home only once since I left ten years ago, and that had been for my oldest brother Aiden's wedding last year.

He was following in Dad's footsteps, running King Oil, but he'd married a librarian, taken her on a whirlwind honeymoon, and changed her address from Mountain View, Montana, to Houston. He'd married her because he wasn't about to lose the trust money. All of us had known but her, the poor girl. She was a woman in love, swept off her feet by the oil tycoon. As soon as they'd said their vows, I'd left.

Disgusting.

I wasn't going to be that guy. Eva knew the deal. As payment for her time, she'd get half of the trust when we divorced. Thanks to Mama, the trust was immune to any prenup. I was paying Eva enough in the meantime, and pleased that she might actually be a competent assistant. I had a virtual one that had taken over many of Wilma's old duties, but a real person to bounce ideas off of was invaluable.

That it would be Eva was getting better and better.

A black sedan was parked in the loading zone in front of the office tower. I opened the door for Eva. She peeked around the interior as she slid inside and greeted the driver.

I went around to the other side and got in. "Rick, this is my new assistant, Miss Chase."

"Eva, please." She buckled herself in and muttered, "This is weird enough as it is."

"We're meeting Dr. Magdalene Herrera at her clinic in Boise."

Eva had been looking out the window, but she whipped around to look at me. "Idaho?"

"It's a quick flight there and back. The meeting will be no more than an hour." Eva's brow was still scrunched. "She made room in her schedule, but her clients come first." I wasn't often pushed off, but Dr. Herrera thought she had the power. I wasn't the only company interested in purchasing her program.

Unlike the others, I didn't need her program. Though the idea of technology paired with human relationships hit close to home. So far, no human had paired well with my technology.

Eva stared out the window. "When do you expect we'll return?"

"You'll be home no later than eight. Is that a problem?" I respected my employees' personal lives, but was Eva really balking at working late on the first day?

"No. That should be fine." Her tone was brighter, but there was a ring of insincerity to it.

She might as well get used to my schedule now. Rick took us to the airport and she didn't say a word. My brothers and I shared a private plane, thanks to King Oil. Eva shadowed me as I ran through the itinerary with Rick and the pilot. Her acute interest in our surroundings was hard to miss.

Wide eyed, she studied the airport, the car, then the Gulfstream in front of us. I pointed to the stairs leading to the plane's entrance.

"I hope you paid attention. You'll be the one discussing the details with them next time," I told her as we boarded.

She stalled at the landing, gawking left and right. The flight attendant greeted her and ushered her forward to one of the bucket seats in a pod of four facing each other. The other woman ran through buckling and safety pamphlets. A delicate line formed between Eva's brows as she listened intently to each word. I was puzzling over the attendant's sudden interest in catering to Eva when it hit me.

The attendant had recognized a first-time flyer before I had.

I took the chair across from Eva. Usually when I flew with Wilma, she sat in a different pod to give me room to work while she wrapped up last-minute plans. During the flight, she did crosswords or knitted. All my brothers had handmade stocking hats from Wilma. And scarves and socks. Wilma had two grown kids, and before the grandkids started arriving, my family members were the recipients of her projects.

After checking with me, the attendant stepped away.

"You haven't flown before?" I asked.

Eva kicked back in her chair and adopted a haughty expression. "Yes, darling. I went to Paris last weekend." The plane started its taxi and Eva clutched the armrests. She winced at her white knuckles. "Is it that obvious?"

"Not at all."

She smiled at my wry tone. We didn't speak as the plane

took off. I pretended to work on my phone, but I was paying more attention to the wondrous expression on her face.

She leaned over to stare out the window. "Whoa. So, this is your life? A driver? A plane? Do you have a home in Cherry Creek? A cabin in the mountains?"

My lips thinned. Coming from her, my life sounded absurd. When I dated someone like Cara, an NYC heiress with a lavish lifestyle and actual weekend trips to Paris on her private jet, I felt too normal to relate to them. But around someone like Eva, *I* was Cara.

Eva chuckled. "Nailed it, didn't I? Bachelor condo or brick mansion?"

Her question was teasing, but her tone accepting. I answered, "Brick mansion."

"Good choice." Those bright eyes of hers sparked with mirth. "And the cabin? Aspen or Snowmass?

I inhaled a slow breath, hating that she'd pegged me so easily. "Aspen."

She shook her head. "I can't believe it."

"Can't believe what? I work day and night. My life is my career. I earn every penny." She was about to open her mouth, but I held up a hand. "And before you point it out, yes, my family is an advantage. But my father worked every minute of every day to grow the company and we paid for it as a family. I'm personally tired of apologizing to people because their parents didn't provide them with silver spoons."

"Maybe their parents died before they could afford more than thrift-store silverware."

I bit the inside of my cheek. Damn, I'd forgotten that she'd lost her parents to a car accident.

She shook her head and grabbed the tablet I'd given her as her mobile office. "Anyway, there's nothing wrong with admitting that money makes parts of life easier. Whatever my boss orders me to do, be it cleaning up a frat boy's vomit or piss all over the walls, I have to dance for my money. But at least I'm in a position to decide whether it's with my clothes on or off. If I had a few million, I might still have problems, but there are a ton I wouldn't have."

"Eva—"

"No, Beckett. I get it. It's the way it is. Someone who can plumb an entire house still worries about paying the mortgage on their own. Construction crews risk life and limb to fix a few potholes. A cashier can get mugged any day of the week but barely brings home minimum wage. They won't ever get paid as much as the idea guys, the ones who make deals for breakfast and reap the benefits by lunch. Sports stars and actors have paydays in the millions simply because they can entertain us. I get paid in tips of 'Maybe if you smiled more' or my favorite, 'Another refill wouldn't have killed you.' I'm sure my landlord will take a fourth refill on his Diet Coke and a grin for rent next month." She clamped her lips shut, a look of alarm passing over her face.

Her tirade didn't upset me. People had actually said that to her? I wanted to hunt each one down and shake their pockets out until she got what she deserved. But was I any better? I was paying her well, but the money came with expectations. "I'm sorry."

She gave me an appreciative smile. "Don't make me clean your vomit and we'll be cool."

"I'm from Montana, I can hold my drink," I drawled. "And I don't piss on walls. Wilma would've walked before she put up with that."

"Wilma?"

"My previous assistant, the reason I have an opening that's become a revolving door." I pointed to an earth-toned blanket folded neatly over the back of one of the chairs. "She knitted that. There's one on board for each of my brothers, and the crew sets out the correct one, depending on who flies. That one's mine."

"What'd you do to make Wilma leave?" The curve of her mouth told me she was kidding, but her question soured my mood all the same.

"Her husband got a job in Florida and she claimed her old bones were done with winter. She's only fifty-two and a Disney addict, so I didn't believe her for a minute."

Eva giggled, a sound that could quickly become my obsession. Her overall look could be considered…sharp, but with a soft edge if you earned it. She presented a resting bitch face to the casual observer, but I saw deeper. She was always evaluating everything around her, perhaps from jobs that required her to constantly wait on people's needs.

But when she smiled and laughed, all that melted away. Her eyes danced and she threw her head back. She had the most elegant neck, one I could kiss all the way down to— And that edgy hairstyle. She'd looked like a pissed-off Tinker Bell yesterday, but today, she was rocker chic in a fucking fluffy pink sweater.

Was that sweater as soft as it looked? And how could those boots both conceal and reveal the curviest legs I'd ever seen?

The discomfort of an impending erection had me shifting in my seat. I grabbed my phone. We had work to do on our short trip, and unfortunately, it was going to make me more uncomfortable. "Bring up the Couples SOS app."

She did. "Does Dr. Herrera have a better name? It limits the impression that it's only for when a relationship hits the rocks."

"I agree. That's one of her sticking points, from what I've heard."

Eva clicked through the app. I tried not to think of her

reading the headings. Frequency. Roughness level. Favorite stimulation. A hint of pink brushed her cheeks.

Wait until I told her that for the sake of research, we were now a couple in need of an SOS. "Both devices are logged into my account. We need to play around and get a good understanding of the range of the app."

Her gaze was steady, but the blush deepened. "Some of these are already filled in?"

Shit. I hadn't deleted all my information from when I'd tested the program earlier. "I played around to learn about it."

A dark brow arched. "Frequency: three times a week. I'm disappointed."

"I travel a lot," I said more defensively than I'd meant to.

She tossed her back as she laughed. "Sorry, I didn't realize these answers were for real."

"I used previous experiences as a starting point." Since they'd all failed, it was a good example for what the app was for.

"Okay, we'll go with that. Roughness. Oh my God, look at her rating scale. It goes from a feather to a whip to…" She peered closer. "Holy shit, are those prison bars? What do those things have to do with each other?"

"Dr. Herrera claims she accounts for everything, including abusive relationships, and not everyone's honest with themselves about it. She's going to separate them into different categories so bondage doesn't get confused with assault."

"Whoa. Um… You went with a feather. Let's see. Scream level. Yours or your partner's? Oh, there's two parts. How noisy you are—five out of ten, I see. And how loudly you can make your partner come." She rolled her eyes toward me. "A nine out of ten?"

"I didn't want to be conceited." And eleven hadn't been an option.

"Post-glow snuggles. You rated that a two out of ten."

Zero was an option, but that had seemed too...honest. "I have it so you can see my profile. You enter your scores and then the program runs the answers through their algorithm and comes up with recommendations."

She chewed on her bottom lip as she went through and entered scores for her profile. I couldn't take my eyes off her plump lips, or the flicks of her pink tongue as she answered. I jerked when she grinned and looked up, catching me staring in the process.

"Done."

"Hit the rose petal button that says 'SOS' and we'll both get a readout, since our profiles are linked."

A list popped onto my screen. It was broken into two sections: witty, sometimes snarky observations of how our answers differed and a second section, an honest, clinical evaluation.

Eva giggled again. I was going to buy this company just to hear her delight. "I put five times a week for frequency and the feedback is that one of us needs to learn how to count or drop the side candy. That's scandalous. I wonder how she accounts for masturbation."

The flush hadn't left Eva's face and she wasn't meeting my gaze, yet she was still open and honest with her comments. And how was I feeling so comfortable testing this program with her? "There's a secondary heading in the premium plan that accounts for devices used."

Eva shifted and crossed her legs. Now they were dangling in front of me. If we were a real couple, I'd tell the crew not to bother us. Then I'd unbuckle and drop to my knees, crawl toward her. Those boots would stay on, but those leggings would get rolled down.

But we weren't a real couple. We hadn't even decided if we were pretending.

"Dr. Herrera thought of a lot of stuff." She flicked her gaze up, then back down to the tablet. "I can see the appeal. Since our answers differed in the roughness, frequency, and afterglow snuggles, she recommends…"

The same report was on my device, but I wanted to hear it in her words. "What? What's it say?" My voice was thick, gruff.

"That, um, after we do it again, regardless of orgasm, we each tell the other one thing we liked about the experience."

"Just one?"

"It might've been more if I'd rated my partner's ability to make me scream higher."

"It's an eleven. I downgraded to a nine."

She flipped the tablet around and showed me the fake rating she'd given me.

"Three? Low blow, Chase." I sat forward. "I can get my partner to hit nine without taking any clothes off."

Her lips parted, but she quickly covered her reaction with a skeptical look. "News flash, King. All guys think that." She flipped the tablet around. "Surprisingly, the generated advice at the end is considerate and encouraging."

Her blush was permanent. I settled back, hoping she'd give up soon and put the tablet down. If the word "masturbation" came out of her mouth one more time, I'd be begging her to join me in a real live trial of the app that had nothing to do with our fake arrangement.

CHAPTER 7

va

I GRIPPED the armrests as the plane bumped down. My first plane ride. What an eye-opening experience.

Beckett was either really cocky, or he wasn't joking about getting a woman to scream. I'd only known him for a little over twenty-four hours and yes, he was cocky. Justifiably so. When I extrapolated to the bedroom, I meant.

I'd had good sex in the past. Really good sex. Not the kind I couldn't walk away from when the guy turned out to be a douche though. Yet I had a feeling New York heiress Cara thought about Beckett when she fucked that pop star she was currently dating.

I had a feeling I'd think about Beckett the next time I fucked someone else too.

The attendant came around with a big smile. "How was it?"

"So smooth. Are commercial flights like this?"

She laughed. "They can be, but you're elbow to elbow with complete strangers."

Like a limo compared to a bus. Got it. I had ridden in a limo before. During a time in my life that I didn't care to think about, for a reason that continued to keep me up at night.

Beckett ushered me out. His hand hovered over the small of my back, but he didn't actually touch me. I appreciated his restraint. He hadn't talked about the marriage proposal, and while I had plans for him that weren't good, I needed space and time to wrap my head around the possibilities.

A private car was waiting for us. Beckett studied his phone. Probably more of that damn app, which I couldn't take. My traitorous body had calmed down, but I was sitting close enough to be warmed by his body heat. I couldn't go into my first meeting with my new boss, turned on beyond all discomfort.

The driver stopped in front of a trendy office building that was all windows, with a large landscaped pond in the front. Beckett led me along the paved walkway around the water. Koi darted around in the depths and I was tempted to tell Beckett to go on ahead. I'd sit by this oasis and pretend I was in the wilderness.

But I followed him to the door he held open for me and inside to the sprawling waiting room. A few other couples were scattered throughout the area. One young couple had their heads bent together, their bodies angled toward each other. So why were they here? A middle-aged couple had one empty seat between them as they each thumbed through their phones—the reason for their presence was a little more obvious. And there was another couple closer to my age that I wasn't certain were actually a pair, but from the way she glared at his back from across the room, it was a good guess.

Beckett checked in with the receptionist. "King. We have an appointment at three."

The receptionist hit me with a reassuring smile. "You two can have a seat. She'll call you in a moment."

While he was at the desk, I chose a seat, thinking he'd put one chair between us like the middle-aged couple. He planted himself right next to me. His proximity overwhelmed my senses. The fresh aftershave or cologne he wore was intoxicating. Or maybe it was a special millionaire musk the dry cleaners spritzed his expensive business suits with.

He leaned in and it was all I could do not to turn my face toward him. We looked like we were about to make out in public, like the young couple.

"The rest of the staff doesn't know about Dr. Herrera's side business."

Interpretation: We'd have to pretend to be a couple in therapy while we were in the waiting room. I shot him a flat look. "Okay, *dear*."

A faint smile touched his pouty lips and he straightened in his chair, pulling his phone out. He dropped his voice even lower. "I have all calls going to voicemail. Tomorrow, I'll quit forwarding your phone to my temporary assistant."

He had a temporary assistant? This was news to me. I hadn't seen any more employees other than his driver.

"She's from an online staffing company," he explained. "All she's doing is taking calls that require scheduling and forwarding the rest to me."

I intentionally raised my voice above a whisper because this opportunity was too good to pass up. "Why didn't I know about her?"

The glaring woman swung her hostility toward Beckett.

Beckett's eyes flared before narrowing. "Well played," he breathed. He spoke a little louder. "I'm sure I told you, you just weren't listening."

I sucked in a gasp and repressed the grin that fought to break free.

A door clicked open and a tall woman I guessed to be in her mid-forties stood in the opening. "Beck?"

Her voice was as rich as her appearance. I had thought my boots were expensive, but hers were the softest shade of brown suede, and she'd skipped the leggings. If I had mile-long legs like hers, I would too. She wore a deep red cowl-necked sweater and black leather A-line skirt. Her gaze was pleasant enough, but keen, and when she glanced from Beckett to me, I wanted to hide behind him. This had to be Dr. Herrera. Could she read minds? One arched brow from her and I swore she knew all about Beckett's crazy proposal and my need for revenge.

I empathized with everyone in the room waiting to see her. Whoever worked with her wasn't going to be able to hide from the real problems in their relationship.

She navigated the maze of corridors with military precision until we arrived at an office with a plush couch, two additional sofa chairs, and a desk. Since we weren't keeping up a ruse with her, I skipped the couch and chose one of the comfy chairs, pulling up the notes app on my iPad. Beckett chose the chair next to me. I couldn't interpret the expression in his eyes. He was congenial, but cool. Like he was evaluating the therapist as much as she was studying him.

Dr. Herrera rolled her desk chair across from us. "So nice of you to meet me today, Mr. King. My biggest question is, what can you do for me that I can't do for myself?"

Right then. She wasn't going to waste time on trivialities. I wanted to be Dr. Herrera when I grew up. From her perspective, she held all the cards and wasn't going to let Mr. King know any differently. Beckett had the finances, but I bet if I went out to the parking lot, I'd find an Audi registered under her name. She didn't need the money. She wanted her app to get into consumers' hands, and she could do it herself if she damn well pleased.

"I can give you the most valuable resource of all," Beckett countered. "Time."

My fingers flew over the tiny keyboard as Beckett outlined the capabilities of his marketing team, the financial push he could put behind a launch, and how he'd assigned a special crew to study the market they planned to target.

Dr. Herrera considered his words, nodded every once in a while, and finally said, "It's not about the time. My son designed the app. And if I sell, he'll be essentially out of a job." She spread her hands. "So you see, this is a passion project for me, no pun intended, but more so with my son."

"He could stay on as lead programmer if he passes a background check." Beckett spoke like it wasn't a big deal, but I nearly choked. He had to vet the man who'd literally constructed this app from the ground up? And there was still a window to shove the kid out of if he didn't measure up to Beckett's standards?

Dr. Herrera lifted a defined brow. "You'd run a background check on my son?"

"I don't allow anyone into the company with a questionable past."

Tense silence filled the room. I was afraid to look between them, but I chanced a glance. Dr. Herrera appeared deep in thought as she studied Beckett. Beckett had deeper pockets. It'd be an uphill battle for Dr. Herrera to release her app and deal with tech issues and continuous upgrades, even if her son was in charge. Selling out would be cashing in. Beckett's team would do all the work, he'd take all the risk, and Dr. Herrera and her kid would reap the bennies.

"Mr. King, let me tell you about my son. He grew up with a single working mom. It took a long time to build this business and it required what you accurately said was valuable.

Time." She paused, and pain and regret flashed through her golden eyes. "It wasn't lost on me that my boy acted out because I worked too much, but what could I do? I had rent to pay, sports fees to cover while hopefully building character, yada, yada, yada. But he got into trouble, found drugs, and it wasn't until a few years ago he accepted the help he needed so much. When I told him about my idea, he ran with it. This program helped him through recovery. He could've been found in a gutter, dead of an overdose. Instead he's home, coming up with new ideas and new designs."

Beckett sat forward, his hands clasped loosely in front of him. "I understand." His tone said the opposite. It said *we're done here.*

I gaped at him. I had a brother who was so deep in depression that I couldn't see him coming out of it. The concern for him was eating a hole in my stomach. Dr. Herrera's story was so moving. The kid had made mistakes and Beckett was ready to write him off?

Beckett went ahead and proved my fears. "Unfortunately, I can't afford to employ an individual I can't trust, or one who has a past that can tarnish the image of my company."

My eyes widened more. I couldn't hide my disbelief. He'd said the same to my brother. Beckett had done one of his coveted background checks and found that Adam had done time. And he'd walked, like he was doing now.

Dr. Herrera gave me a comforting smile. My problem with this situation must've been rolling off me in waves. I tried to school my features to neutrality, but my disgust was impossible to conceal.

She rose and smoothed her skirt. "Well, I'm glad I had a chance to meet the infamous CEO of King Tech. Thank you for coming all this way."

Struggling to be the adept professional she was, I did the same, but I couldn't look at Beckett.

We said our goodbyes and there was more professional bullshit between them, but I couldn't stand it. I stormed out of the office, through the waiting room, and outside. Sucking in deep gulps of air, I stopped by the fish. Nature had always calmed me. Perhaps the concrete jungle I'd grown up in was the reason I'd been a high-strung and wild kid.

Beckett didn't rush after me. At least we'd protected Dr. Herrera's confidence with one last impression that we were a couple with severe problems. Several moments passed before he caught up with me, and he probably only stopped because his car hadn't pulled around yet.

This bastard had destroyed my brother over a history he knew nothing about. If he did, I certainly wouldn't be here. His precious background check couldn't catch everything.

I didn't look at him, glaring instead at the large orange and white fish that looked like it stole food from all the other fish.

"Wilma didn't agree with my business acumen either," he said.

"The more I hear about her, the more I like her."

"These kinds of things can destroy a company, Eva."

Crossing my arms, I faced him. "Recovering addicts can take down a billion-dollar business? I would think that's on the CEO."

"I have no idea how bad Dr. Herrera's son is, or how much of his life he threw away to get a fix, but I refuse to be the one the cameras hunt down if he relapses and hurts someone."

"Yes," I said with as much sarcasm as I could muster. "I can see the headlines now. 'King Tech owner and CEO gave troubled addict and ridiculously talented programmer a second chance.' It would be horrible."

Beckett's hands were in his pockets and his hard expression almost scared me into looking away, but I rallied my courage and lifted my chin. He'd obviously been hurt at some point. That had to be why he was this rigid. But unlike him, I would give him another chance to show me he didn't have to stomp on other people's dreams just because they'd made a mistake at some point in their life. And if he failed, I'd give zero fucks about taking his money and kicking him off his pedestal.

"Have you ever thought of what your rejection would do to Dr. Herrera?" I asked.

The crinkle in his brow was a clear no.

"You pull your interest. Maybe another company that's interested in acquiring her program finds out why, or has decided that any company you pass on must be too risky, so they back off. And Dr. Herrera is left without a dime to help her launch her game. It flounders. Her kid blames himself, thinks he's the loser everyone labeled him as, and goes back to his former destructive way of life."

His mouth twisted. "And I would be to blame? That's a stretch, Eva. People need to be responsible for their own actions."

"A hand up makes a huge difference. You don't know what he's been through."

The drone of an engine approached, but Beckett didn't look away. "I donate to charities, I give to the needy. I'm not risking my entire company just because a working mom feels guilty."

The ride to the airport was full of mutinous silence. I tried to tell myself to break the ice, kiss a little ass, really sell the employee-to-fiancée-to-wife gig. But I couldn't. This trip had unearthed my own guilt. Anger at myself for what had happened to Adam. He'd glowed like a kid on Christmas when he'd told me about King Tech's inquiry. He'd even taken me out to dinner that night and we'd gushed about how life was going to be afterward.

We'd be the ones with drivers. We'd travel. He'd design more apps and I could finish school.

Beckett must've learned that Adam had done time for petty theft and breaking and entering and pulled his offer. No, can't have a criminal like Adam working for him. A bighearted monster like my brother who'd tossed his life into the gutter so I could have a future. Only, I'd told myself at the time that he could get back what he'd lost. He could go back to college, finish his degree, and get a good job. Find a wife to trust with the real story behind his jail time and grow a happy family.

Then King Tech had dropped him. The other tech companies sniffing around knew Beckett's risk-free reputation and they all pulled out. We didn't have enough of our own resources to do a proper launch. It all sank, taking our savings with it. I never thought I'd see the life drain from someone's eyes, but I lost Adam that day.

Fucking Beckett King. When I tore his whole empire down, then *he* would know what it was like to be denied a second chance.

CHAPTER 8

eckett

SITTING AT MY DESK, watching the clock tick down, wasn't how I'd pictured my morning starting.

It was 7:58. Eva hadn't arrived yet. I refreshed my email every minute, but there were no new message notifications.

Nothing, not even a *fuck off*.

Her reaction toward my strict policy about who the company associated with had been surprisingly strong. Why had I bothered telling her that Wilma had disagreed? My former assistant had known the reason behind it, and she'd disapproved because she thought I should forgive in order to move past what had happened. This *was* me moving on.

That'd never happen. Just like I'd never forget what it was like to find my broken mother after the attack.

A soft ding sounded from my phone. Someone had entered the office.

I was up and around my desk before I could slow myself

to a less frantic pace. I was the fucking boss. Justifying myself to my assistant wasn't part of my job description. *She's more than that* drifted through my mind.

Yeah, a fake fiancée, but we hadn't reached that point yet.

I rounded the corner.

Eva was at her desk, nudging a pink bag under it with her foot. If the outfit she'd worn yesterday had sucker punched me, today's was worse. It was like she'd taken fashion tips from Dr. Herrera. Instead of yesterday's damn boots—which had almost required a cold shower—today she wore black ankle boots with black tights and a cream and gold dress that hit just above her knees. The combination made her toned legs look a foot longer and accentuated the flare of her waist. Her hair was styled like yesterday. Edgy sophistication. It went with her attitude. The same attitude I'd been brooding over not two minutes ago but was now glad beyond all relief to see again.

She glanced at me, her smile small and not reaching her eyes. "Morning, Mr. King."

Mr. King. So formal.

"Morning, Eva." I didn't go back to my office. With Wilma, we'd have a quick meeting each morning while I covered my expectations for the day. By the end, Wilma had known them better than me, but it was like a tradition and of course we talked about our families. It was what I missed the most about her. In the few months since she'd retired, I had adapted to exchanging messages with her. And that was done already.

Eva and I had no such tradition. Yet, here I stood. Unwilling to leave. "I switched the phone calls so they won't get forwarded anymore. I'll let you get settled and then we'll go over my employees, where they're working out of, and why they'll be calling."

Eva tapped on her computer. "Actually, I already got a call

from Matt Lamar with Eye in the Sky Security. They're having some issues with upgrades in the program and it's sending out false alarms to their dispatch company. He said he wanted you to be aware of it and will be available if you need to call him about it."

"Thanks. I'll contact him later." She'd already taken a call and not batted an eye. Why hadn't she gotten a job that offered pay and benefits before now?

She sat down and logged in. "Would you like the notes I took yesterday emailed to you, or would you like them stored in a shared document?"

I could access her devices if I wanted to see them. "Keep them as they are. I doubt we'll be moving forward." Dr. Herrera wasn't going to ditch her son for money she didn't need. The buyout would've been for her kid's confidence, not for her profit margin.

"Very well," she said brusquely. "What other details do you require beyond scheduling and answering phones?"

"That's a start. I have a meeting in Richmond later next week and if you're still here, you'll have some preparations to make before we fly out."

Her pretty pink lips turned down. "If I'm still here? Have I done something wrong?"

"No," I said quickly. "Not at all. After yesterday, I wasn't sure you'd return."

"Oh." Her impossibly bright eyes turned luminous. "I'm sorry I was late. I didn't want to take the call on the light-rail. People pretend to mind their own business, but I know every word would've been overheard."

"You weren't late. You didn't drive here? The parking's free for employees."

She shook her head. "I don't have a car."

"But it's getting cold out." How far did she have to walk to catch the rail? The morning temperatures would fall below freezing soon.

"I have a coat." Again, her smile was pleasant. And fake. It shouldn't bother me.

My gaze swept down her tights-clad legs and it was impossible to mask my appreciation. "Do you wear snow pants as well?"

A blush kissed her cheeks. "If I need to."

"Rick will pick you up from now on and take you to and from work."

"Oh, no. That's okay. The light-rail is fine."

"Eva. Rick's been complaining about getting paid too much for doing too little. He's a good guy. It's why I keep him on."

"Doesn't he have a family? Kids he should be seeing off that early in the morning?"

"Rick's divorced and his family lives in Wyoming."

"And you pay him a ton because he's lonely but he's free whenever you call."

Ouch. She made it sound callous. "He's a good driver who likes to work. He'll pick you up at seven thirty."

Eva's hands paused over the keyboard. "What if I don't want a driver?"

Did she have something to hide, or did she like freezing her ass off during her commute? I rarely experienced failure, but it was seeping into all my cells now. The driver thing shouldn't become a standoff. I didn't want her to commute through the cold, dark streets.

But before I could muddle through a response, she spoke up. "I'm sorry, Mr. King. I'll be ready for Rick at seven thirty." She continued tapping into programs. "Wilma left a large file covering the who's who of King Tech. I can read through that instead this morning, if you prefer."

Wilma had done what? My old assistant was like a

beloved aunt, but right now, I disliked her. Why'd Wilma have to be so efficient at her job? The morning I'd planned to spend at Eva's side was now shot and I'd make her uncomfortable if I pushed the issue.

"Perfect," I lied. "I can get some work done."

Another functional smile. "Thank you."

I was wandering back to my office, nursing the unfamiliar feeling of being dismissed, when she stopped me with a surprise question.

"Why first names?"

Turning around, I struggled to keep my eyes on her face when her legs were crossed and the bottom hem of her skirt was hitched up. I shook my head, trying to figure out her question.

She clarified. "People call you Beck. I'm not Ms. Chase. Rick's not Mr.—I don't even know his last name."

"Because Mr. King is my father. I imagine that, like me, you find being called Miss Chase... odd."

"No. Miss would be fine, though *Ms.* Chase would be weird as hell and you struck me as a Ms. person, not a *Rick, Wilma, and Eva* type guy."

Somehow conversations with Eva never went how I expected. "I like to have some informality. I'm supposed to be a millennial, after all."

"Are you? But you're here before ten a.m. and I haven't seen one avocado around." The first genuine smile of the morning graced those lips that would star in my dreams.

"Careful. You're one too."

"You saw what I was wearing when we first met."

Had I ever. How a hoodie could fit that snugly was still a mystery I didn't want to figure out.

Satisfied I wasn't on rocky ground with my potential fiancée, I went back to my office and called Eye in the Sky.

I managed to while away the morning without bugging

Eva every five minutes like I wanted. Normally I wasn't this distracted at work, but I'd been putting in some long days and without Wilma, I didn't do much chatting that wasn't related to this company. My life was work and then I went home alone. My friends had started settling down but going out each night to find a willing partner was getting tedious. I'd rather go home, work out, and get some sleep while not evading promises to call later.

The clock dragged toward lunchtime. I was running through dinner options, trying to predict what Eva would like, when the office buzzer went off and a woman's familiar, commanding voice drifted into my office.

Grams.

Dammit. I shot up, my chair rolling back into the wall, and darted out of the office.

She was already at Eva's desk, her gray hair cut in a bob that rounded her head like a helmet. She wasn't tall, but she wasn't diminutive either. Sometimes when I stood next to her, I was startled by how much shorter than me she was. Emilia Boyd carried herself with the swagger of a six-foot-four linebacker, but she wore her rust-colored power suit better than any Wall Street tycoon.

Unfortunately, Dad was with her. Had he hitched a ride, hoping to be a buffer in case Grams did something like show up with a justice of the peace? Under ordinary circumstances, I'd be pleased he'd shown up at my office. But now I had to spare him from the farce of a marriage I'd asked Eva to participate in. Grams would be delighted, but I couldn't let Dad find out. I needed to handle it better than Aiden had.

Only unlike Aiden, who was, amazingly, still with Kate after his year of marriage and thirtieth birthday had passed, I'd be signing half of my fortune over to Eva. But it'd be amicable and that should be enough for Dad.

Or maybe my younger brother Xander could do something dramatic to take the scrutiny off me.

Dad shot me an apologetic look. I shook my head like it was no problem. A young and polished Kendall was at his side, her honey-blond hair draped over her shoulder. The three of them were facing down Eva across the desk. Dad's and Kendall's expressions were of polite greeting, but Grams's brows were lifted and her head tilted as she studied Eva. Shit, we weren't ready for this yet.

Eva's shoulders were rigid. She hadn't seen me yet, but her voice was polite and professional as she offered to call me. She had to be uncomfortable, wondering how we stood with the fake engagement and marriage.

I stepped behind her, my hand on the back of her chair, a move that did not go unnoticed by Grams. Her smile widened.

Dad's smile tightened. "Beck, apologies for the drop-in."

Grams muttered, "Grandmas don't need an appointment." Her smile grew serene, but it had a purpose, and an edge. "Hello, Beck."

This was the woman who wielded her mineral rights like a boss and had launched an oil company with Grandpa. She'd never been the warm, fuzzy grandma who baked us pies and recorded school programs. I wouldn't be surprised if Dad said she'd rocked me and my brothers to sleep while researching oil prices.

"You guys are always welcome," I said smoothly. "It's lucky you caught me in the office."

Grams's eyes narrowed as if telling me she'd hunt me down anywhere. "I'm sure your time's been freed up, since you have a new assistant."

"Yes, Eva. Meet my grandmother, Emilia Boyd."

She beamed toward Eva. "*Grams* is fine, Eva. We'll get to know each other really well."

Good God. She was already starting in. If Dad weren't here, I could invite Grams and Eva into my office and have a private chat over the details of the trust and what we needed out of Eva. But I didn't want Dad to look at me like he did Aiden, like he wondered what the hell he'd done wrong.

I could tell Dad exactly what he'd done wrong. He'd stomped on Mama's memory and ignored us to sow his wild oats for fifteen years until Aiden had duped a nice girl into marrying him. But that would only make me feel better temporarily, and it'd hurt his new wife, whom I was slowly warming to because of moments like these. Kendall's gaze lit on me with flashes of sympathy and a cringe over Grams's Cheshire-cat grin.

Eva took out the Bluetooth plugged into her ear. "I knew who she was as soon as they walked in." The strain in her voice was obvious. Why couldn't Dad have called first? "Just like I figured you must be Gentry and Kendall King?"

Did Kendall feel weird? She'd been one of those candidates once. Grams had sent her to Denver, hitching a ride in the jet with Dad. Thankfully, a storm had waylaid them and she hadn't made it to the interview before she'd grown too close to Dad.

"My reputation precedes me." Dad grinned. "Should I be worried?"

Kendall nudged Dad. "Depends on which rumors she heard." She turned her grin on Eva. "Nice to meet you."

Dad laughed and Kendall snaked a hand through his arm. "Ms. Chase, is it?" Dad asked. "You don't mind if we steal my boy for a while, do you?"

Eva's gaze brushed over me like she was unsure why he was even asking her. I knew why. He was trying to whisk us away from Eva and leave her be instead of giving Grams a chance to set her up to marry me.

Grams charging in here to scout out the newest candidate

might scare Eva away. The whole plan might seem too outlandish after being faced with Grams, and Eva could decide the drama wasn't worth it. It was why I'd been letting her get to know me.

As if she'd do it for me instead of her cut of the hundred million.

"Not at all, Mr. King," Eva said to Dad. "Enjoy your lunch."

"Oh, you're more than welcome to join us." Grams leaned over the desk. "Beck won't mind."

"Thank you for the offer, but I have plenty of work to do." She reverted to her polite self like she had around Rick, the airplane crew, and Dr. Herrera. She was a watcher, used to being dismissed as the help, like I was about to do. *Thanks a lot, Grams.*

Grams wasn't done with her matchmaking though. "Really, it's no—"

"Order whatever you like delivered, Eva." I gave Grams a hard look. I should've just called her and told her that my trust was secure and not to worry. But it wasn't, and I wanted more time with Eva. More time to get her comfortable with the idea. "Tell them to bill me. Any place nearby should know the drill. Block out my afternoon for a meeting."

"Yes, Mr. King," she answered.

"Still just Beck." I smiled. "Mr. King is on the other side of the desk." I hated leaving her behind, but I walked out with Grams, Dad, and Kendall.

Grams waited until we were settled at a nearby cafe before she started in. "I see you've hired your own choice." She studied the menu, her face tight. "Not at all what I assumed you like."

"Eva's competent."

"Mm. Have you asked her out yet?"

"She just started working for me this week."

Grams's silver brow ticked up. "But you want to ask her out?"

"Yes." I could say I answered so quickly for Dad's benefit, but there was no one else I wanted to ask out. Besides, it'd get Grams to lay off.

She drew back and I took pleasure in catching her off guard. "Then do it, and quickly."

"Emilia—"

Grams jabbed her index finger into the tabletop. "The Cartwrights have always been after our money, blaming us for every bad thing that ever happened to them because of *their* laziness and stupidity, including that drunk of a son. They will not get a dime because Sarah was too naïve and nostalgic."

"And I've said that I agree with you," Dad argued. Kendall's gaze darted back and forth between Dad and Grams. The way her arm was angled under the booth, she was probably white knuckling his hand. "But I don't want my sons to sacrifice—"

"It's for a year, Gentry," Grams hissed, leaning over the table, her hazel eyes flashing steel. "And a hundred million dollars. Or at least fifty, but if a nice girl like Kate can walk away richer than ninety-nine percent of the world's population, who loses?"

Well, the Cartwrights. That was the point.

Grams hitched her shoulder as if to block onlookers from seeing us. "But if Beck doesn't give up a little over a year of his life, then Danny Cartwright will use that money to make all of our lives a living hell. He'll snatch up land, he'll bribe, he'll interfere."

Dad scoffed. "Danny's not smart enough for any of that. He'll drink himself into the ground."

Grams narrowed her eyes until they were slits. "Are you

willing to bet your job on it?" She pointed her finger at Kendall. "Or better yet, *hers?*"

So Grams wouldn't just leverage Dad's position, but Kendall's too? God, she'd probably agreed to hiring Kendall for the sole purpose of using her to get Dad to do what she wanted.

Grams sat back. "Anyway, there's his daughter. That's a girl with a brain in her head, as long as she can stay away from the vices. I'd like her if she weren't a Cartwright."

I'd seen firsthand how much Bristol despised us, but I expected no less. She'd grown up hearing the stories about how my grandparents had scammed hers out of oil rights and then built an empire from it. I'd be interested to know if she'd heard how her grandparents had used their own scam to steal land from Dad's parents.

Dad's expression shuttered and he reclined back. Kendall's worried gaze flicked up at him. His gaze filled with resolve. "This argument always turns out the same, Emilia, and I'll still support whatever Beck decides."

Gratitude welled within me, but then I looked closer at Dad. His shoulders hung like he carried the weight of ten thousand oil barrels and Grams had just heaped on a few more. His eyes were pinched, and even more worrisome, he looked his age.

I'd already made my decision, but I needed to make sure now more than ever that it played out like I wanted it to. "I have time, Grams. Don't worry."

The intensity she'd aimed at Dad rounded on me. She considered me for a moment and I raised a brow in the cockiest way I could manage. "Fine. No more talk of it. Let's enjoy lunch."

Lunch was tense and it turned out there wasn't much to talk about if it wasn't about my trust. I ordered an appetizer so my food would arrive faster. Excusing myself once I was done, I left.

Walking back to the office, I couldn't escape the feeling that I should've handled lunch better. I should've stepped in for Dad. He had two more sons to get through Grams and the trust business after me. Dawson and Xander and I didn't cross paths too often, but as of Dad's wedding, they'd both been inexorably and happily single.

Naïve and nostalgic. I had been young when Mama was killed, but she was still Gram's kid. She'd had a reason for setting up the trust that had nothing to do with fond memories. Whatever they were, if I didn't hold such a heavy grudge toward them, I'd deliver the check myself.

But they were the reason Mama was dead, so I needed to finish this fiancée business.

Eva's brows lifted as I walked in, a sandwich in her hand. She chewed, swallowed, and set it down. My mind was riffling through the restaurants that would've delivered such a plain-ass sandwich when she asked, "Everything all right?"

I slumped on the edge of her desk, nearly bumping the printer off with my butt. "Just Grams doing what Grams does." Was that bologna? Her sandwich sat on a clear plastic baggie. Another baggie with carrot and celery sticks rested next to it. "You packed your lunch?"

She nodded and opened the veggie bag. She held it out. "I didn't want to be presumptuous that you would buy me lunch every day."

I snagged a celery stick. "We go and talk shop and write it off. No big deal." The fresh crunch of the celery was strangely satisfying. My five jumbo Sriracha shrimp weren't as filling as I'd hoped. "Wanna go out tonight?"

Eva was about to pick up her sandwich, but she left it there. "Another meeting?"

"No. To decide if we're getting engaged or not." I pointed

out the door. "You know how Dad met Kendall? Grams hired her to work for me. I nearly hated Dad for a while, but then he met Kendall. I didn't trust her at first, but then... I saw how they were together." I wanted that. Would I be the one making the sacrifice for the money? "Now she works for King Oil and Grams is threatening both of them."

Surprise flickered in her eyes. "That's hard-core villain stuff."

I lifted a shoulder. "Like all villains, she thinks she's right. I dunno. Maybe she is. It's hard to say when I don't have all the facts."

"Why'd you hate your dad?"

After the lunch I'd had, I wasn't ready for the heavy topic. I never talked about what Dad had been like unless it was me bitching with my brothers. I found myself telling Eva anyway. "After Mama died, he grieved, then set about sleeping with every woman in town. He'd leave for long weekends, or weeklong ski trips—in the Alps—with a near stranger and miss homecomings, football games, and parent-teacher conferences. As an adult, as long as I was making my own money, he was never interested in my job."

"And Grams?"

The corner of my mouth lifted. She'd said "Grams" and not "Mrs. Boyd." "You can probably guess after meeting her what she was like growing up. She'd call and check in, but now I wonder if it wasn't because she was monitoring my marriage prospects."

"I'm sorry." The words were simple, but sincere. My exes wanted me to pour my soul out, but I never spoke about my family. With Eva, I was brutally honest and she was matter-of-fact.

"Thank you, but I guess that brings us to the engagement."

"No marriage?" She wore a small smile, but her eyes were shrewd.

"Like most marriages, it would depend on how well the engagement goes."

"We'd still need to get our stories straight." She pulled out the other half of her bologna sandwich and offered it to me. I accepted it and took a bite. I'd grown up with money, but Dad and Mama had made us work and live like a normal family, which included T-ball and school plays. Sometimes that meant bologna and white bread sandwiches for supper. I'd forgotten how good they tasted.

She was blank faced, perhaps studying my reaction to her food, but she said, "But I can't meet tonight. Maybe tomorrow?"

Tomorrow was Friday. It'd be like a real date night, but I didn't want to take her to a noisy club or an expensive restaurant that we couldn't relax and talk in. "You can come over to my place."

She paused midchew, her gaze turning wary.

I waited for her to finish her mouthful, my gut churning that she was going to turn me down. Negotiating a marriage sucked.

"Since I don't drive, and I don't want to be dependent on Rick for a date, can we meet somewhere?"

I shrugged. "I can pick you up."

"No." By now her refusal shouldn't surprise me, but the vehemence was unexpected. "I... If this doesn't, you know, work out, I'd like to keep my home life separate."

"You mean you'd still work here if we decided not to get married?"

"Yes?" She worried her lower lip between her even teeth and I couldn't take my eyes off it. "Would I get fired if I didn't marry you?"

"Of course not." I should've made that clear up front. "Would you be comfortable staying here while I hunted for a future fiancée?"

Her eyes narrowed and my pride grew. She didn't like that thought. "I kind of like the work." She sighed and stared at the remnants of her sandwich. "Fine. Rick can pick me up at seven."

"Pack an overnight bag." She blanched and I chuckled as I pushed off the desk. "Just kidding. If it's seven, why don't you just ride home with me? I'll have some food delivered and we'll talk—outside of the work environment."

"Just don't call Silver Eats Catering." At my questioning look, she explained, "The caterer I used to work for. It'd be weird."

"Don't want them to see you with a personal life?"

"Don't want them to think I'm a haughty bitch. I might need that job back."

Not if I could help it.

CHAPTER 9

va

I WRUNG my hands together and stood in the hallway. Adam was playing Xbox, no big surprise. I'd just gotten home from work, reeling from my conversation with Beck about my date tomorrow night. Meeting his family had made it clear this was about more than me and Beck, and he had a lot more people surrounding him.

I had to tell Adam.

He might seem checked out on the world, but he still worried about me—occasionally. The shopping spree, a car picking me up for work, and the late nights would make him ask questions.

I entered the living room, standing off to the side. "Adam, can I talk to you about something?"

"Sure." His fingers maneuvered controls and his gaze didn't leave the TV.

"Can you pause the game?" I knew better than to ask him to stop.

"Just a minute." He must've sensed the seriousness because he actually put the controller down after he got to a stopping point. "Shoot."

His eyes were bloodshot and his shirt hung off his lanky frame. How much more weight did he have to lose?

"You know my new job?" He nodded. I sucked in a deep breath. "I haven't been completely honest about why I accepted it, or who it's with."

Adam scrubbed his face and sat forward. "Everything okay?"

Moments like these made the guilt almost unbearable. Adam was withering away in his own pain. He'd given up college for me. He'd lost a major buyer because of me. And yet he was still willing to peek out of his depressive hole to check on me. I was a shitty sister and I needed to make it all better.

"So... I was downtown the other day and happened to run into Beckett King."

The first major emotion I'd seen in months flashed through his eyes. Actual anger. "Did he do something to you?"

"No. He offered me a job." The story spilled out of me. How I'd gone looking for a way to get revenge and how the target had dumped himself in my lap. It all sounded so idealistic and naïve.

But telling the story made me wonder why I'd want to be responsible for hurting anyone. I was only aiming to harm his professional reputation, but that was what had happened to Adam. Would I really be okay if that happened to someone else? Because of me?

Adam stared at me, horror in his gaze. "You're not whoring yourself out to that bastard."

"I don't think he expects me to do, like, wifely things with him." My face burned. Any wifely tasks with Beckett wouldn't be a hardship either. "Just play the role, get the money, and go away. But it'll give me time to find out how we can publicly humiliate him like he did to you."

Adam snorted. "It wasn't public. It was all very polite and hush-hush. All prospective buyers just backed the hell out and blocked me like malware. Eva." He shook his head. "You can't do this. His family is rich and they can crush us."

"Look around, Adam. There's nothing to crush." Adam's gaze swept our shabby apartment with its bare walls and water-stained ceiling. "He's paying me a shitload for the next four months. Worst case, I decide not to do the fake fiancée gig and don't get married, and I don't find a damn thing on him. At the least we've paid our rent for the next year. Best case, he has a skeleton that the entire tech industry will spurn him for and he'll be the one no one wants to associate with. Or even better case... I stay married to him for a year, divorce him, and walk away with fifty million. I wouldn't find better odds in a casino."

Adam didn't look convinced. "He's hot, Eva. And loaded. I know you're not usually that type of girl, but these guys don't rise to the top because people can't stand them. These kinds of people aren't the type to hand over millions to someone they just met, even after they've spent four hundred and ninety days together. What if you fall for him?"

He was attractive. I couldn't deny that. But it'd never happen. If I didn't hate him after our year was up, then that would be an improvement. "I know better than that."

Adam was quiet for a while, his thoughtful stare on the TV screen. He wasn't losing interest, but he also wasn't losing his temper. "Do you think he's done anything that would hurt his career?"

"Honestly? I don't know." I crossed my arms against a sudden chill. It was getting colder out and I could turn the heat up. We could afford it now. Adam hadn't noticed the temperature change. He was numb. "But he's willing to fake a marriage to get some trust fund that'd go to the neighbors he hates. A guy who would do that has to have some skeletons." I hoped.

"You think you could hide your relationship to me and marry this guy?"

"For fifty million, I'll find a way."

Adam let out a slow exhale. "So he pulled out on a deal just because that lady's son was in recovery?"

Nausea cramped my belly. It was an identical situation. "Yep."

"That's harsh."

"Yep."

His gaze swept down my new outfit, then back around the crappy apartment. A decision was being made and I couldn't guess what it was until he said, "Do you at least feel safe around him?"

That was the old Adam, worrying about me first. "Yes. And if he's a squeaky-clean choirboy, then I'll have made enough to cover bills while I look for a better job. Surely I can rack up some skills that another CEO looking for a fake wife would need."

Adam's smile was faint, an echo of past Adam. "Be careful, Eva. I don't like it. I know our finances are tight, but the money isn't worth it. And the revenge thing? I mean, whatever. I'm over it. Don't go exposing yourself to harm because of me."

"I'm worried about you," I blurted.

He blinked. "I'm worried about me too."

"Do you need to see a doctor or something?" Please.

"Nah. I keep skimming the help wanted ads. The right job will turn up soon."

The right job that would hire him with a record and serious lack of job history.

But at least I'd made progress. I wouldn't have to sneak around and rush out the door before he saw Rick pull up. He'd accepted what I was planning, but he was stuck in his status quo and wouldn't lift a finger to help.

I made my way back to my room. The dishes and laundry could wait for the weekend. A shower, then bed. For some reason I didn't want to look into, I looked forward to tomorrow.

∾

"THAT PLACE IS HUGE." Gaping out the window, I compared my apartment complex to Beckett's mansion. I think his was larger.

"You make it sound intimidating." Beckett drove around the back. He'd taken his own car today, a Mercedes, to save me from facing Rick while I went home with Beckett on a Friday night.

"It is." There was not one chimney, but two. The house was multilevel with a boxy look, though rock accents and soft lighting lessened the hard edges. Shrubbery lined actual rock walls that made up the porch and walkway to the home.

The house didn't get smaller from the side as Beckett looped into the garage.

I snorted out a laugh. What'd I expect, an empty four-car garage? He had a pickup that probably cost close to six figures, a freaking golf cart because this was country club land, and a boat.

"Not the reaction I was expecting." Beckett killed the engine. The garage dimmed as the door closed us in.

I tipped my head toward the boat. "I mean, it's not a yacht."

His eyes crinkled at the corners. "No, that's in storage at the dock." My mouth dropped open and his lips curved. "Just kidding. I like to fish. I don't need a yacht to fish, just something I can hook to the truck and take off."

"Do you camp in that thing? Oh wait, the mountain cabin."

His smile died. Apparently he didn't like a have-not pointing out all his haves. "Yes, but I don't get out there as often as I'd like."

There was a story there, and since we were beginning a fake relationship, I was going to keep asking. "Why not?"

He slid out and led me into his house. Mausoleum-level silence greeted us. The arched ceiling made the snick of the door closing and my clicking heels reverberate in the emptiness. His walls had forgettable, anonymous decorations that didn't mean a thing beyond aesthetics.

Beck's voice echoed as he answered. "My younger brother used to visit more, but now he's traveling the world. My older brother is married and runs the company with Dad. That leaves Dawson, the youngest, who runs the ranch."

Didn't the guy have friends? Girlfriends who liked to fish? Hell, if he asked, I'd kick off my heels and go fishing barefoot.

I'd kick off my heels for a lot less. "Can I take my shoes off? My feet are killing me."

He glanced at my black chunky heels, a total splurge I'd excused because it was hard to find heels that went with thick leggings and a long belted lilac sweater. His gaze drifted up my legs, something I'd caught him doing all day. I was short. My legs getting attention was novel, but then I rarely bothered to wear heels.

"Why do you wear them if they hurt?" he asked when his

gaze reached my face. He shrugged out of his suit jacket and loosened his tie.

Fuck, that was sexy. I wanted him to keep going. Drop the tie on the floor, undo the first few buttons. Then all I'd have to do was run my hands up his toned abs and slip his shirt over his head, maybe lean in and kiss—

Oh, he'd asked a question. And that's not what I was here for. "Asks the man undoing a tie he was probably dying to get out of all day."

"Ugh, I hate them. The shoes too."

I chuckled and we both stepped out of our shoes. "I don't get the impression your other footwear is cowboy boots though."

None of his decor had a Western flair. Odd for a country boy. The articles I'd read on him before we'd met gushed about his upbringing. Sure, they had hired hands, but Gentry King had made his boys work without pay to teach them what hard work really was. It hadn't helped that the article had come with a photo of the brother who ran the ranch on a horse, his cowboy hat pulled down low, cattle kicking up a dust cloud in the background. No doubt a flock of women had run to King's Creek, Montana, to net themselves a King. I was practically one of them.

He grimaced. "No more boots for me."

"You wear that when you go home?" I gestured to his suit.

"I've only been home for Aiden's wedding and Dad's wedding since I left."

Our light conversation had taken a serious turn. I couldn't imagine having family and shunning them. They could be gone in an instant. "That bad?"

He sighed and looked away. We were still standing in the entry and I felt safer here, less lost than the massive house already made me feel. "Since you read up on me, you know my mom passed away when I was twelve."

"Yes, I'm sorry. Are you upset that your dad didn't abstain for years, or that he did what he did in the house?"

Beckett's jaw tightened. "Yes."

"But more so the house." I didn't have to ask. The way he talked about his mom—he adored her. I tried to think of how I would've felt in his place. What if my dad had survived and moved on? The way I'd rebelled after they died, I couldn't imagine that I'd be accepting.

"All those women." His voice was ragged and as much as I didn't want to, I softened toward him. His pain was clear.

"You have reason to be upset with him, but I don't think it's really his bed count. Your dad was disrespectful to your mom's memory and ignored how you and your brothers were dealing with her being gone."

Beckett studied me for a moment. "Yeah. That's definitely it. I guess it was one thing to know they married young right after they learned she was pregnant, but another to know that maybe she wasn't the love of Dad's life."

"But he loved her nonetheless. And his kids."

"True." He seemed to give himself a mental shake and ushered me into the… I don't know what it was called. The ceiling soared overhead. To one side and down a few steps, there was a plush living area with puffy couches and chairs. Straight ahead was a flight of stairs and another cove that I guessed housed the entrances to more rooms, though the bedrooms must be upstairs. Then to my left a huge kitchen and sprawling dining room took up half the floor.

"Everything's so shiny." My words lingered in the air. This place was not homey. A chill ran through the place, like there was no reason to make anyone comfortable because no one was here.

"I can't tell if you're giving me a compliment again."

"Just a comment." I wasn't going to lie. I'd rather be tucked in the fluffy couch with a blanket, catching up on the fall TV lineup. The hard floor was at least warm. "Oh my God, is the floor *heated*?"

His smile was slight as he crossed to the island, where a stack of to-go containers waited for us to dig in. I sniffed. Shouldn't there be savory smells too? Was this place just so massive that delicious dinner smells had no chance to permeate? That was kind of sad.

Beckett pulled out a bowl of salad and containers with fluid sloshing inside. Next was a tub of breadsticks. Soup and salad came next. He glanced up to see my perplexed face. "Is this not to your liking?"

"You're feeding me. I'm not going to complain about free food." But the former rancher didn't strike me as a soup-and-salad guy. "It's not what I expected, but then I'm used to greasy bar food."

"I go vegetarian one meal a day. I let the caterer know to deliver enough for two. I didn't mention that she could change it up."

"Vegetarian?" Was there such a thing as a vegetarian rancher?

"It started in high school to piss my dad off. What can I say? It stuck."

I laughed, but quieted as he finished doling out the food. Perhaps Adam was right to warn me. Beckett was becoming a real person underneath his cool business exterior, and his feelings were real. Didn't mean I understood them. The part about losing his mom, yes. That hit close to home. I knew the loss of a parent all too well.

But Beck hadn't lost as much as I had. His home was cold, but expensive. My early "luxurious" years in a small house with vacations to local parks had morphed into tiny apartment living and multiple jobs to keep it, and I was worried about how long Adam would be around.

There. All better. I could do this and not fall for Beckett King.

We were both in socks as we sat at the island. With the lid off the soup, I could finally smell the beer cheese. My stomach rumbled as I dug in. I ate over my bowl, dreading the enviable spill that always accompanied soup. Beckett was next to me, his body angled toward mine until our knees almost touched. I was on a stool eating a fancy version of a soup that I'd had countless times in the bar, but Beckett's kitchen was more extravagant than any place I'd ever worked.

He passed me a second breadstick. By his dish, the bag was empty. I might've been absorbed in my meal, but I didn't remember him having another breadstick.

"Who the hell sends three breadsticks for two people?" I ripped it in half and gave him one piece.

He broke into a grin. My heart stuttered. The man smiled and it was devastating. His deep laugh prompted my own smile, but I couldn't take my eyes off him. He'd gone from unattainably sexy to sitting right next to me. All I wanted to do was crawl into his lap.

"I guess she's used to my ex shunning all carbs."

Supermodel ex-girlfriend. And he was back to unattainable. I wouldn't get closer than pretending. I didn't want to get closer than pretending.

But he was hot.

I shifted in my chair while bringing a spoonful to my mouth. A drop clung to the bottom of the spoon, then spilled off, right onto my brand-new sweater dress. "No!" I swiped a napkin—cloth of course—and dabbed at it, but the grease spot remained. "I knew this would happen. I should have drunk this damn soup from a cup."

I slid off the stool and went to the massive sink. The faucet had a motion sensor and a spray nozzle in the high arching faucet head. It was the most complicated sink I'd ever seen.

The dish soap was harder to find. "Do you have any Dawn? Or Ivory? Never mind. Found it." I doubted Beckett even knew it was stored in the tidy area underneath the sink with the garbage bags and dishwasher tabs. Putting a dab on the soup stain, I flipped the water on and leaned over the edge to rinse as little of the sweater as I could. Everything I'd bought on my shopping spree was machine washable. No dry clean only, no thank you. I didn't have time for that, nor did I care to waste money on the service.

Searching around, I couldn't find a rag of any kind. "Okay, now a dish towel?"

I started opening drawers without waiting for an answer. Again, I doubted he knew where they were. I didn't bother to look at him. How embarrassing, but I'd never set out to impress him. Finding the towel to dab at the area proved harder than the dish soap, but after the third drawer I found a pile of pristine, cornflower-blue plaid towels. There, lingering-grease-stain crisis averted. I glanced up. Beckett was staring at me, a bemused expression on his handsome features.

"What?" I asked.

"I felt like I was watching *MacGyver*."

"Over a soup stain? Please, that was easy. Dump some marinara on that shirt and I can save the day." Weird that he thought this was crazy inventive. But as I scanned the house that looked like it had been staged for an open house, I shouldn't have been surprised. This place was little more than a hotel room. His meals were catered when he was home and I was sure he had a cleaning crew. All his clothing, down to his socks, were probably dry clean only.

Beckett followed my gaze around his home. "What you're thinking is written all over your face."

I blanked my expression. He was paying me a ton, feeding me, and yeah, I might be planning his professional demise, but I didn't want to be rude. "Oh?"

"'Big, empty, and I don't know where anything is.'"

Pulling my lower lip in, I worked out what to say. Did I deny it? "If I took you to my place, you could see how an entire carpet looks with grease stains. And the bathroom could fit into your coat closet. It's a real treat."

He chuckled. "I don't spend much time here. I sleep, work out in the gym downstairs, and go to work. There are so many people in and out of here cleaning and cooking that I don't even do any work at home. My office is more secure."

"You have a home gym?"

"Wanna see?"

Did I want to see where he got all hot and sweaty? Yes, please. "Lead the way."

Trying not to be self-conscious of my wet spot, I followed him down the stairs. I paused at the bottom of the stairs to wiggle my toes in the cushy carpet.

He caught me. "It's good quality carpet."

"Hell yeah, it is." My apartment's carpet had been through several tenants and had the wear and tear to show for it.

"I can't say I've ever had a woman ooh and ahh over my rugs."

My cheeks flamed. Probably because his women weren't broke as hell and had never been destitute.

"Hey." His shadow cast over me as he closed the distance between us. "I was kidding."

"I know, but it proves a point. We're from different worlds and no one is going to buy that we're engaged."

"They will once they see you."

I jerked my head up, wondering if he really meant it, but his hooded gaze stole my breath. His eyes were on my lips, his body close. "I…" I swallowed, my own gaze stuck on his

87

mouth. That pouty lower lip. Without thinking, I reached up to stroke it.

His eyes narrowed, like he was the hawk and I was an itty-bitty mouse that was going to get pounced on. But I couldn't stop. Other than brushing across each other in the office, I hadn't touched him. I didn't want to stop now.

He flicked his tongue out to lick my finger. I gasped and snatched my hand back. He caught my wrist and brought it down to my side, using his other arm to pull me into him.

"I've been dying to know what kissing you is like." His low tone rumbled over me.

A bloom of heat exploded in my belly, sinking lower until I was uncomfortably turned on. "This was only supposed to be pretend."

"The engagement would be pretend, Eva. Wanting to fuck you is very real."

My lips parted with a sharp inhale. He wanted me? I could use this, but if we took it to the physical level, well, I wasn't stupid. There was nothing about him that said he'd be bad in bed. He treated me with respect and I could stare at him all day. Throw in the high-class lifestyle and how could I play along for a year and keep my heart protected?

Those thoughts were wiped out as he lowered his head and captured my mouth. My hand was still in his, curved behind my back, as I sank into his embrace. His kiss started soft, searching, but when I opened for him, his tongue moved in and I was swept away. Licking, nibbling, exploring, he plundered my mouth, all while holding me in place. We didn't move, but my heart slammed against my ribs and an echoing throb resonated through my core.

Eventually, he splayed his hand along my ass and released my arm. He snaked both arms around me and hugged me against his hard body. I angled my head to taste him better and twined myself around his broad shoulders.

An alarm bell was going off. This was too hot, felt too nice. Kissing like this? He wouldn't just be good in bed, he'd be epic. He wasn't an eleven, he was a fifteen, and his hard length promised pleasure that I'd never known—and I wanted to know so badly.

I should stop.

He skimmed his teeth along my lower lip and nipped his way down my neck. Scrunching the fabric of my dress in his hands, he was drawing it up, and oh God, were we going to fuck at the base of his stairs?

Did I care?

We'd only met less than a week ago. I should care. But I didn't.

"Eva…" he growled. "I want—"

I wanted it too, but it was a bad idea. Too fast, too much. My mind was scrambling and I had to be clear-headed around him. All those months internet stalking him had done this to me. Beckett King in real life shorted out all rational thought. He seemed to be waiting for an answer.

What did I do? What should I say?

A musical chime rang through the stairwell. The tension between us drained. I knew that tune. They played it all the time in the bar.

The chime sounded again. "'Drunk on a Plane'?"

"Yes," he growled. "It's my brother's ringtone."

He released me and grabbed his phone from his pocket, flipped it to vibrate, and shoved it back in again.

"You should answer that." Because his brother had saved me and I wasn't sure I was strong enough to resist if he kissed me again.

"I can call him later."

The dull buzz of his phone went off.

"I've been with you long enough to know that no one

89

keeps calling when they can't reach you. Is that what your brother's usually like?"

He looked like he could commit murder, but he answered the phone. "What."

He listened a moment, his expression dropping from irritated to grim. He straightened and turned his back.

"How bad?" He shook his head and cut his hand through his hair, leaving it there. His body was tense. "What? Now? Yeah, I know. Fine. No, I'll make the arrangements." He disconnected but stood there, staring at the phone.

"Beckett? Is everything okay?"

"Dad collapsed. He's in the hospital."

I put my hand on his hard shoulder. "Is he in Montana?"

"Yeah, he was home. This weekend is the big cattle drive. Dawson wants me out there so one of us can be at the hospital and the others helping. I guess Xander is flying out."

"Oh... Okay." My professional mind took over. "I need a key for the office, but I can field all your calls. Just keep your phone forwarded. If I have any questions, I'll just bundle them and we can catch up once a day so you can concentrate on your family."

He turned to me, his brows low, his eyes questioning. "Come with me."

I cocked my head. Surely I hadn't heard him correctly. "Hmm?"

His hands were on my shoulders, but his touch wasn't sexual. The news of his dad had kicked him off-center. Understandable, but wouldn't he rather be with his family?

"Fly with me. We wouldn't be gone more than a week. Moving cattle to the winter pastures takes three days and by then we'll know what's going on with Dad."

Panic was crawling up my throat, the soup curdling in my belly. A week away. "What will I do? Work from Montana?"

"Be my pretend fiancée." He clenched his jaw and the

muscles in his cheeks jumped. "It'll help— It'll help take the stress off the old man."

I was two seconds from saying fuck the fake fiancée gig. It had been different when I could walk away whenever my conscience decided I was a good girl. No harm, no foul. Beckett would never know that he'd had someone like me working for him. But I hadn't signed on to fool a sick dad. If I hadn't met Gentry King, I might have felt differently, but I had. He was a real person, not a face on a website.

"I…" How could I leave Adam for a week? He'd be a skeleton sunk into the couch with a controller in his bony hands by the time I got home. And Kitty? Could she mouse and keep her strength up?

Maybe I could call Adam every day. If I picked up groceries before I went and stocked the kitchen with ready-to-eat meals, even stacked some snacks and water bottles right next to him, he should be all right. I could leave Kitty extra food and maybe, just maybe, Adam would be willing to set a can out on the doorstep after a few days.

But the real question was, Did I want to go?

Yes. Except for being there for Beckett, my reasons were several and selfish. To fly on a plane again. To go to freaking Montana and hang out on a real cattle ranch—not just any ranch, but the Kings'. To see a little bit of the world other than downtown Denver.

And if I was going to do this, really do this, to find out as much as I could in the place Beckett had spent most of his life. Nothing was buried in this tomb of his house, not even his secrets.

"I'm sorry." Beckett started to turn away, his expression dejected. "You can't just leave town for a week."

"No!" I hadn't meant to shout, but he stopped. "My brother lives with me and he's not the best with self-care. I just need to get some groceries and talk with him before I leave. And pack."

Beckett stepped closer and stroked a thumb down my cheek. "I'll have Rick take you to the store and home to grab your things. Then he can take you to the airport. The jet should be ready by then."

CHAPTER 10

eckett

DAD COLLAPSED.

I glowered out the window at the spots of bright lights on the countryside as the plane circled for a landing. Oil wells. All from King Oil. *The doctor hasn't come out yet, but I think it's his heart. He's been complaining about indigestion since he arrived, but he kept blaming the tacos or some shit. He listens to Kendall about everything, but even she couldn't get him to go to the doctor.*

I'd just seen Dad and he didn't complain about anything. He wouldn't. But I'd seen the stress weighing on him. I should've—

I rubbed my eyes and exhaled a slow breath. He was still around, and Eva and I were flying to Montana. There was nothing more I could do.

Before the call…the way she'd kissed… Our attraction was off the charts. A strong love/hate relationship was warring inside of me. Without the trust, I wouldn't have Eva in my life. But because of it, I had to rush a pretend engage-ment and wouldn't have the chance to date her for real. We wouldn't be able to take things slow.

Eva was curled in the chair diagonal from me, watching our descent with a blanket over her lap. I hadn't sat beside her. Too many thoughts running through my mind. But I couldn't be far from her either. Leaving her behind to work hadn't been an option. I don't know why. But bringing her home was going to kick this plan into high gear.

Other than a few high school girls that I'd dated, I hadn't brought anyone home. After the first girl I'd been serious about—the daughter of the local newspaper's editor in chief —had wanted to know the gory details of finding my mother, I couldn't bring myself to trust anyone else's motivations.

What did Eva know about Mama's death? The paper had left out specifics and I hadn't shared them with anyone other than my brothers. I hadn't even told Dad, but he probably knew, had likely been informed by the officers when he'd been interrogated.

Dad getting interrogated had been as scary to us kids as Mama's death. Most murders were committed by the people closest to the victim...unless some relapsed druggie was let out of jail early and hit his meth stash hard. Then it was completely, heartbreakingly random. Except for my neigh-bors' role in the ordeal. I'd never forgive them.

I should've tried harder to find someone to marry. I couldn't let the Cartwrights get a dime.

And now that I had Eva, I might even be able to return home without sleeping in the barn. Would the nightmares that had plagued me before I'd moved away come back?

She was the spring-fed pond this country boy needed. I liked her. A lot. She intrigued me more than anyone because I could have a real conversation with her. She didn't play coy, she didn't flirt, and she wasn't shy about expressing her opinion, whether it was written across her delicate features or coming out of those lush lips.

It felt right, coming home with her.

The reason I was on this plane came rushing back. What if they couldn't find out what was wrong with Dad? What if they did and Dad ignored their medical advice and kept up his high-stress lifestyle? Kendall had chided him more than once to slow down.

What if he passed away and my brothers and I scattered to the four winds? I wouldn't have a reason to visit. Dawson and I were close enough, but we could catch up on the phone just fine. That way, I wouldn't have to revisit the past when I walked through the house. With Xander, it was always a game of Where in the World Is Xander. And Aiden... He was hard to talk to. He never used to be, but I didn't see that changing in the future, especially if he had to take on more responsibility at the company.

The flight attendant came through to prepare us for landing. Eva smiled and chatted about the quick flight, how long the attendant had worked, and what the most exotic place she had flown was. All it took was a question or two and the flight attendant, Shirley, was spilling her guts about her entire career, even diving into her family. Must be that bartender effect. Eva's first impression was tough and abrasive, especially now that she was back in her Toms and blue jeans and that fitted hoodie. But she was genuinely interested in who she was talking to and the world around her.

When was the last time I'd struck up a conversation with Shirley? She was newer, but I'd gotten to the point where I ignored the staff around me. I didn't want to encourage more interaction in case I had to fire them one day, or in case it was a young woman and she thought I was interested in dating. It was why I hadn't replaced Wilma. Initially, setting those professional limits had made me feel like an asshole.

Except with Eva, who I'd hired with the intention of marrying.

Eva was the exception to more than a few rules.

The plane bumped down and we taxied in. King's Creek airport was as tiny as a small-town gas station. Three hangers dotted the property and were more for agriculture planes and little two- or four-seater Cessnas. But it handled the family jet—Dad donated enough to make sure of it—and it was close to home. Dawson sent a message saying he'd left a vehicle here for me and the night clerk would have the key.

The luggage was waiting at the bottom for us. With no driver and a limited flight crew, I took both my black suitcase and Eva's purple one. She had a worn backpack slung over one shoulder.

She shivered in the brisk wind and folded her arms across herself, but she seemed captivated by the surroundings. "It's so bare here."

In so many ways. "Welcome to Montana."

Vegetation in eastern Montana wasn't lush and we needed a lot of land to graze cattle. King's Creek was in the middle of nowhere. Billings was the closest large town, and that was hours away. No buildings marred the countryside, and the dull glow of King's Creek's city limits didn't light up more than a minuscule slice of the sky. Smaller pinpricks of light came off the oil wells that had funded my trust. Old-timers in the area bitched that they ruined the horizon, but they'd all signed the papers when the oil company had come calling. Having a well on the property meant a lot less stress when cattle prices dropped. Dad and Aiden were the most gossiped about villains, but also the local heroes.

An older man with shaggy blond hair rushed out. "Beckett King, as I live and breathe." He jingled a set of keys. "Dawson left these for ya."

"Thanks, Herman." I accepted them and my eyes

narrowed. I knew this keychain with its metal horseshoe stamped on a teardrop-shaped flap of leather. *Fuck you, Dawson.*

"Heard about your dad," Herman said. "Let him know we're all pulling for him."

"Will do." I had to get away. Herman had said similar words at Mama's funeral. *Sorry about your mom. We're all pulling for you kids.*

I ushered Eva to an obnoxious charcoal-gray pickup littered with flame decals. It was equipped with a lift kit—all the better to go muddin' with—and Eva would probably need a ladder to get inside.

Stopping in front of it, Eva glanced at me and blinked.

"I'm ashamed to say this was my high school pickup," I admitted.

She sputtered a laugh and walked around it. "Oh, my gosh. This is like the teenage boy version of peacocking, isn't it?"

"At its finest. Wait until you hear the pipes on it." Good thing it was dark, or I might get caught blushing. "They rattle the windows when I pull up."

Her smile got wider, then slowly faded. "Are you going to the hospital first?"

"I'll get you settled before I head there. It's late." I winced. "Or early, actually. The sun will be coming up soon." It would've already if it were still summer.

"Whatever works for you." She squeezed my arm and went to the passenger side.

I rushed to open the door and she crawled in without a problem. The delight in her eyes was enough to make me grateful that Dawson had spared this gaudy beast from the sales lot.

After I threw the luggage in, I hopped in and fired up the engine. Eva chuckled at the noise rumbling out of the tailpipes. I was transported back ten years to late country nights heading to a bonfire, only instead of roaring out of town, I was coming home.

"This is so not like the Beckett King portrayed on the gossip sites," she said.

Ordinarily that comment would make me bristle, but her light tone took the sting out. I'd worked hard for my fairly spotless reputation in the press. "Beckett King hasn't been like this in many years."

"Can you picture Rick driving this?"

A laugh burst out of me as I pulled out of the lot. "He'd be thrilled."

I pointed out landmarks as I drove to keep the silence from locking me into my own head with thoughts of Dad. "All those oil wells are ours." I gestured from the lit wells toward the glow of King's Creek. "The town is named after my dad's side of the family. Kings have ranched here for generations." But it was Mama's oil legacy that fueled the town. "We won't be going through town. Our house is about fifteen miles away."

"Can you see the mountains when the sun comes up?" She sounded so wistful, I hated disappointing her.

"No, we're too far east. Our land is in the Yellowstone River Valley. Flat, but just as beautiful in its own way."

As I left the main highway and hit gravel, she settled in her seat and watched the scenery fly by. The horizon was lightening enough that the trees in the river bottom were a dark contrast against the pastures and fields lining the river.

My childhood home came into view long before we wound our way there on the gravel road. The wraparound porch lights were on, making the house a beacon in the dark. Dawson usually kept them off, but with my arrival, he'd left inside and outside lights on.

I pulled right up to the door instead of circling around

back to the big garage. Dad and Mama hadn't held back when they built this place. It was bigger in square footage than my home in Denver, but all on two levels, with a cellar underneath because Mama had liked to preserve food from her bountiful gardens. None of us had kept her plants going, instead suffering through what the cooks Dad hired had made and raiding the packaged food when Dad started sleeping with the staff and they quit in a huff when he moved on to greener pastures.

Killing the noisy engine, I hopped out to grab our bags. Eva's feet hit the dirt and as I rounded the corner, a shadow was at the door.

"Beckett? That you?" Dawson called.

"Who the hell else would it be driving this piece of crap?"

His laughter echoed through the early morning hours as he opened the door.

Eva stuck close to me as we approached the house. Dawson was in his usual cowboy boots, jeans, and solid-colored, button-up, long-sleeved shirt. He wasn't wearing the beater of a straw cowboy hat he preferred, but only because he hadn't yet left the house for the day. His dark brown hair swept over his brow, longer than I preferred to keep mine.

"Up early or late?" I asked as we climbed the four stairs to the porch.

"Early. Aiden is at the hospital. I came home to grab a few winks and check on things. I'll head down later today." Dawson's gaze landed on Eva, appreciation written across his features along with more than a little surprise. "Hello."

She smiled, but her attention skipped over Dawson to gape at the rest of the house and the surrounding property that was slowly getting highlighted by the dawn.

"Dawson, this is Eva Chase. She's my assistant." Saying the next words were surreal. "And my fake fiancée, but to Dad she's the real deal, so play along."

Eva stiffened. I wrapped my arm around her slim shoulders and steered her past a stunned Dawson and into the house.

He whistled, closing the door behind us. "And you're okay with it?" He gave her another once-over, as if it suddenly made sense that she wasn't my type and I was still marrying her.

"He pays better than bartending," she said and hitched her backpack higher.

My jaw tightened with her honesty, but…it was true. "Grams keeps trying to intervene, so she agreed to help me and deter any future women Grams tries to send my way."

Dawson blinked, then grinned. "She's been doing that with me too. Suddenly thinks I need extra housekeeping and office help. I don't even let them through the door. But I can't imagine it getting bad enough to sling a deal. I've been dying to see how she gets to Xander."

That was probably why Xander never stayed in one place too long. I clapped Dawson's shoulder. "You have a couple years yet. Just wait. You might even be willing to marry Bristol Cartwright herself to keep her from getting all of it."

The humor drained from Dawson's face. "I'll never be that hard up."

Eva was looking back and forth between us.

"The neighbor girl and Dawson's sworn enemy," I explained. "Though she was a little sweet on him through school."

Dawson's lips flattened. "There's nothing sweet about Bristol. She's as prickly as a pear cactus and as impulsive as her deadbeat parents. And she ain't getting my money." He tipped his head toward Eva. "And I'm glad she's not getting yours."

"Just remember—Dad needs to think it's real."

Dawson shook his head. "You think he really cares as long

100

as the Cartwrights keep their hands off our green and their cows out of our pastures?"

"Aiden."

Dawson winced. "Yeah, I've never seen Dad disappointed like that. Not even when I buried the tractor halfway in the mud cutting silage. And the way he went cold turkey with sex? Like the ghosts of hookups past couldn't make him a changed man until his behavior had warped Aiden."

"He doesn't need the stress. Especially now of all times."

"True enough. Does Grams know?"

"Not yet. I should've called right after she appeared, but I wanted to let her stew awhile." Dad would've been suspicious if Grams had suddenly turned sweet as honey pie. "I have to figure out a way to spin it to Dad since I just saw him and now I'm engaged. It'll be more believable if Grams is just as stunned."

"They don't know when we met," Eva offered. "All they know is that you were turning assistants away. You can say that we'd been dating and then I...was laid off or something."

"That would work. That would so work." I was private about my private life. Dad might actually buy it.

"All right, that's settled." Dawson whistled low. "Glad it's you and not me, bro. I'm guessing that you two aren't in the sharing-a-room stage of this plan? Aiden's here, so he's using his old room, and my old room is full of storage. Do you want Eva to take Xander's room? Who knows when the hell he'll show."

I wasn't going to use the excuse that there wasn't enough space in order to make Eva share a room with me. That didn't mean I felt right tossing her in a strange room that belonged to another man, even if that man was my younger brother. I wanted her to be comfortable here—in my home.

But the only other place was a spare bedroom in the housekeeping wing. Back in the day, Mama had insisted on having it in case any visitors got snowed in. That was her excuse anyway, because she invited anyone and everyone out. I think it was for the company. Four boys under five this far out of town, she brought the company to her. But the room was across the house in a lonely corner and no longer had a bed. Dawson had turned it into a game room with a pool table he never used.

Besides, Xander's room was right next to mine so it sounded like the best option. "If you think Xander's not showing up anytime soon."

Dawson snorted. "God only knows where he is. I had to leave a message and a text and a hundred missed calls. Idiot should tell us where he's going, especially if it's somewhere without cell service."

"Is he done backpacking through Europe?"

"Yep. He's somewhere in Asia."

Dawson had become our unofficial hub. He and I got along the best, and Xander and Aiden got along better with each other than anyone else, but since Dawson was the owner of the house we'd grown up in, he was the one we naturally checked in with—*if* we checked in.

"Go on and do chores. I'll get Eva settled and get to the hospital."

"You might as well get some rest," Dawson said. "They're running more tests this morning and the nurse said doctors will be in and out. Kendall is prepared to deal with all that—I doubt she's prepared to deal with Aiden hovering, but he seems to like our new stepmom and will probably take it easy for once since she hasn't left Dad's side."

Of all of us, I'd thought Aiden would be the hardest on Kendall, but when she appeared on Dad's arm, it was like he'd had dreams for a long-lost sister and they'd just came true. Either that or he hoped she'd be a stabilizing force in Dad's high-strung life.

"Is Kate here too?" Aiden's wife was probably my favorite thing about him. Sweet and congenial, she had all the personality my brother lacked, and she would ease any awkwardness for Eva as a stranger in a family home.

"Couldn't get off work. She'll come down this weekend."

I nodded, happy to let Aiden do what he did best and run Dad's life. Now he had help. "I'll catch up with him over lunch." I tipped my head at Eva since my hands were full of luggage. "Want to follow me upstairs?"

She murmured, "It was nice meeting you," to Dawson. Her silence didn't worry me as we went up the stairs and down the hall, then around the corner to where my bedroom was. I knew her well enough by now to know that she was gawking at the place.

It was impressive. Mama and Dad had intended it to be. The home was a giant log cabin with expansive windows and skylights to let in the sun's rays or offer a glimpse of the stars. Peaked ceilings arched over the living area. At the landing above the stairs, the entire main floor of the place was visible. The open kitchen flowed into the dining area and the living area with the big screen TV and fireplace. Those areas were functional, but for show. A small movie room with reclining chairs, a couple of offices, the guest bedroom, and the laundry and cleaning closets were under the family bedrooms. They took up more space than the main areas, which gave the family bedrooms above plenty of square footage.

The master bedroom was on the first floor, opposite the laundry area and hidden from view. Dawson had moved in there.

The four bedrooms and bathroom for the family were on the second level. We reached the door to Eva's temporary room and I set her bag down.

"You sure you're okay with this?" I asked. If I hadn't

known she'd been up all night, I'd still think she was radiant, her eyes luminous.

"I'm fine. I'll call my brother and get some sleep. Is there a space where I can work when I wake up?"

"Downstairs there are two offices. Pick the one that doesn't have piles of paper falling off the desk."

"You sure Dawson won't mind?"

I chuckled. "He's the most easygoing of all of us."

"As long as my last name isn't Cartwright." She smiled, and it wasn't the dreamy-eyed smile a lot of people got around him. Thank goodness.

"Exactly." The urge to give her a goodnight kiss was strong, but I resisted. I didn't know what that earlier kiss had been about, but the phone call had put a pause on finding out. "Good night, Eva."

CHAPTER 11

va

THE ALARM on my phone went off obnoxiously early. I
squinted at the screen. Noon.

With a groan I sat up before I fell back asleep and rubbed
my eyes. I wasn't in my bed or in my apartment. I wasn't in
my city or my state. Hello, Montana.

Adam.

I had the phone dialed before I was fully awake. Before I'd
crawled into bed, I had texted him a reminder to have a
protein bar or something for breakfast.

"Yo," he answered.

"Hey. I'm in King's Creek, safe and sound. How are you
doing?"

"What's it like?"

I thought of calling him on his evasiveness, but maybe he
really was just curious. "Nice. I haven't seen the ranch in the

daylight, but the house is unreal. It's like a log cabin and a mansion had a baby."

"Figures. Some people are born with it all."

We'd had it all, everything but money. Sure, we'd feel down when we couldn't go to Disneyland like our friends, but those moments had been fleeting. But I guess in the end, so was time with my parents.

"Did you eat yet?" I asked.

He sighed. "Yes, *Mother*. I ate one of those bars that tastes like cocoa and chalk had a baby."

"And a bottle of water?"

"Eva." His exasperation was clear, which was a good sign.

"I know. But you get wrapped up in your game and forget to take care of yourself."

"I'll look at more jobs today."

Are you ever going to do more than look? "Sounds good. Fair warning, I'm going to call you after supper and I want to hear all about the delicious food you ate."

"You mean the lunch-meat sandwiches you made?"

"And what kind of chips you picked. I also left carrot and celery sticks."

"I saw that."

A beat of relief hit me. He'd been off the couch and actually to the fridge. Maybe being away from Adam wouldn't eat a hole through my stomach lining after all.

"I'd better get to work," I said. "Talk to you later."

"Hey. Take pictures would you? I want to see what that rich bastard grew up with that made him so sanctimonious."

I chewed my lip, afraid that would set back any progress Adam had made with his depression. But where there were cows, there was cow shit, right? I didn't have to take pics of the most opulent parts of the ranch. "Sure."

Hanging up, I tossed the phone on the nightstand. Daylight streamed through the window and lit up the room.

What had once been Beckett's brother's room was now a tastefully decorated guest room. At one time, there'd probably been sports decorations, or half-nude women, or gaming posters, or whatever teen boys hung on their walls. There was no longer any sign that a Xander King had grown up here.

The paint job was a light gray, offset by trim that matched the exterior log wall. I ran my fingers over the wood, if that's what it still could be called. It'd been treated and shellacked to within an inch of its life, but perhaps that was necessary for it to last decades as a home. The square window was bigger than any bedroom window I'd ever seen and it overlooked the barn and shops and whatever the giant metal buildings were. Beyond those, I caught a glimpse of the river. How many miles away was it?

My suitcase was on a storage bench at the foot of the bed. The pillow-top mattress had taken me a moment to get used to. Springs didn't creak when I sat on it and if I thought too hard about how nice it was to sleep in, I might decide to answer calls and reply to emails in bed.

Tugging out my laptop case and my work phone, I set them on the bench. Once I delved into work, I might not come up for hours and I wanted to be situated where I could work and not be standing in a T-shirt and underwear to take a message. I was still new at my job and had enough pride to want to earn my money.

I couldn't believe he'd told Dawson. At least we didn't have to pretend to be a real couple around him, and probably not around Aiden or Xander either. It was sweet how they wanted to protect their dad. I was softening toward him too, just because he seemed to care more about his kids being happy than these supposedly awful neighbors getting money they hadn't earned.

I gathered my shower kit and some of the clothes I'd

packed last night. Regular jeans—an old thrift-store pair, but with a cable-knit sweater. Wearing my new office clothes had seemed overkill in the middle of the night while I was packing, but in this place, I would've blended. Would Beckett keep the same style?

I tried to picture him wearing what Dawson had on. The warmth blooming through me made me think of that kiss and how far it would've led.

So not the time.

At the door, I peeked down the hall. Could I make it to the bathroom without being seen? We'd kissed, but that didn't mean I was ready for Beckett to see me in my underwear. And risking running across Dawson dressed like this seemed a little rude. They were worried about their dad and I didn't need to be running around in my tighty-whities.

The bathroom was on the other side of the hall and two doors down. It was open. I scurried into it and clicked the door closed behind me.

I had been in here last night, but that didn't stop me from gaping around the room again. A bathroom for four boys had a corner shower, a whirlpool tub, and a double sink with a floor-to-ceiling cabinet. This was no tidy, enclosed water closet. Natural light streamed in through the skylight in the ceiling, brightening the space enough that I didn't need a light. The room was done in various shades of gray with only a couple of pictures hanging up. I squinted at them, recognizing the views from out the window.

Humidity hung in the air. Someone had recently been in here. Good, then I wouldn't keep anyone waiting.

I ran through the shower, staying only long enough to wash the product out of my hair and run a washcloth over my body. After drying off and brushing my teeth, I was in my bra and underwear, dancing to get into my pants when the door swung open.

"Eva!" Beckett's brows rose in surprise and he backed out. "I'm not used to—sorry."

The shock was too much for my balance. I danced around on one foot and landed with an *oomph* on my ass, my back toward the door.

The door swung back open. "Shit, I'm sorry. Are you okay?"

Strong hands wrapped around my arms and hefted me up like I weighed nothing more than a stack of towels. I was too aware of my boobs bouncing in my bra.

"I'm fine." Without looking at him, I stuffed my other foot into the jeans and dragged them past my ass without too much wiggling. My sweater was on the edge of the counter… by the door.

"You sure? That was a hard bounce."

My cheeks burned that he'd witnessed it. I was about to bite his head off, but when I looked over my shoulder, all I saw was his back. He had a hand on his hip and the other running over his hair.

I turned around, and not knowing what possessed me, I stepped close behind him and reached for my sweater. "My butt has enough padding. It didn't hurt."

He jerked and almost twisted to look at me, but caught himself. "Your butt has just the right amount of padding."

The low rumble of his voice sent prickles over my skin. I shrugged into the sweater, taking way too much time. Why wasn't he leaving? "You can turn around."

My sense of self-preservation shouted *turn back!* But I just stared. So *this* is what he wore in Montana. His blue dress shirt hung open, his chest and abs just as spectacular as they'd been last night. His slacks were on, but the button undone.

"No suit today?" I croaked as my mouth went dry and my body heated up.

His gaze didn't leave me. "No suit. Not while I'm here. I'm just wearing this to the hospital, but I'll change into a country boy when I get home to help Dawson."

"How's your dad?"

"Doing well and back to himself. Aiden said he's cracking jokes with the staff and begging Kendall to bust him out." His jaw flexed, one of the few signs of how much his dad's health worried him. "Mild heart attack. The rest of the day will be scheduling follow-up visits and repeating some labs to make sure his levels are going down. Sorry I rushed you here."

"Don't be. It's better to rush than to be too late."

The faint smile was back. "Now I'm stuck until we move cattle."

I glanced at the paintings. "I wouldn't call getting to spend your days in the great outdoors being stuck."

He shifted closer. "You've made similar comments before." He was looking down at me, but not touching me. "You like the great outdoors."

"I've never been out of Denver. The idea of running off to a mountain cabin or to a ranch to rustle cattle or whatever you call it…" I looked away, wistful. "Sounds amazing."

He caressed my cheek with the back of a finger. "It's sweaty and dusty." A soft smile. "And maybe a little exhilarating. And frustrating, depending on how stubborn the cows are."

"I, for one, can't wait to see you dressed like your brother and on a horse." I leaned into his touch, wanting to forget about depressed brothers, engagements, revenge, and sick parents.

"I dressed like him all my life until graduation. I was raised on a horse. Her name is Black Gold. Want to ride her with me?"

My lips parted with a gasp. "Really?"

"Not while we're working, but after we can go trail riding. Tomorrow?"

I nodded and he drifted even closer until I was pinned to the sink counter. This thing between us was spinning faster than I could've imagined when I'd stood outside of his office building. Had that been only a week ago? Since coming to Montana, it felt like I'd known him longer. All the reasons why and why not didn't compare to how much I wanted him.

I licked my lips and forced myself to be responsible. "Don't you need to get going?"

"Soon," he murmured and lowered his mouth to mine. I arched against him and would've smiled at his groan if my lips hadn't been busy.

The kiss heated up faster than last night's. He licked into my mouth, hot and needy. I met him swipe for swipe, our tongues clashing, our kisses getting sloppy as our desire escalated. Releasing me, he laid kisses down my neck and skimmed his hands under my sweater. Why had I bothered getting dressed?

Right. Because we weren't dating.

Except I felt like I knew him better than my exes.

His big hands caressed my back and up my ribcage, until he circled around and cupped my breasts over my bra. It wasn't enough. I ached for his touch. Circling my hands around his neck wasn't enough either, not when his shirt was hanging open.

How could a guy feel this good? Was I daring enough to brush my fingers over the trail of dark hair leading under his waistband? My palms were splayed over his chest, his defined pecs teasing my skin. He was so hard. Everywhere.

And he surrounded me. He was taller and wider and bent over me until I knew nothing but his taste, his touch, his smell.

Just when I thought he'd carry things farther, he pulled

away. My lips were swollen, my body was flushed, and my skin ached so bad that it hurt when he took his hands off me and gripped the counter.

"I swear, Eva, I'll never forget how you look half naked."

My heart slammed and it was hard to catch my breath. He was inches away, his chest close enough to land a kiss on. I didn't want him to stop. I wanted him to close us into this bathroom, lock the door, and undress us both.

And if I wanted that, then I had to rethink everything I was doing here.

"I don't want to stop," he murmured and pressed a kiss to my temple. "But I don't want you to feel cornered."

He couldn't be concerned about me. He was supposed to be a heartless jackass. I closed my eyes and nodded. "How can we pretend to be engaged if we don't stop? Seems confusing."

"I don't want anyone else to be my fake or real fiancée, but I want to explore this thing between us." He stroked my face. "I knew the moment I saw you that I couldn't let you get away."

Oh God, he was sweet too. I was toast. Dropping my gaze, I tried to think of something to say, some way to rewind this to the beginning, when I'd had a clear goal of what I wanted.

What did I do? I was really starting to like him and the chemistry between us was unreal.

"Eva?" He spoke so softly, I looked up. It was my undoing. I wanted him, and I didn't want to leave. For the first time in years, I felt like I was living a little. This thing with me and Beckett could still help my brother. It wasn't selfish.

Was it?

Was it such a smart plan to destroy one guy just so I could go back to my dingy apartment and feel smug in my invisible monkey suit while catering another minimum-wage event between low-tipping bar shifts? Or was it smarter to just help Beckett and earn good money to take care of Adam? Forgiveness went farther than revenge—for both me and Adam. I might've started out with revenge in mind, but I couldn't ignore the relief washing through my veins at the thought of giving it up.

"I want to explore this between us too," I finally said.

"But?" He could read me well enough to know there was more.

"But I want to keep it between you and me." Faking the engagement was one thing. But it was quite another to face speculation about whether people believed we were a real couple. Seeking revenge hadn't made me feel as vulnerable as this. "We can pretend to be engaged for your dad and Grams, and when your birthday nears, we'll figure the rest out then."

My thumb was resting at the corner of his mouth when he smiled. My stomach fluttered. His smile was his secret weapon. "Between us then. Everything else is the same but this." He planted another kiss on my mouth that made me wonder if I'd end up naked after all.

But he ripped himself away, leaving me sagging against the counter. "I gotta get going. I'll show you where the office is before I leave." His lopsided grin was reminiscent of the wild boy he must've been. "But first, I need to grab the lint roller I came in here for."

There was still the matter of my brother. What would Beckett do when he learned who I was related to? And not only that, but that I'd known exactly who he was when we met? Things might not get that far, and if they did, by then, I should mean more to Beckett than his reputation. If things didn't get that far, then I could still help out with the trust and walk away. Adam and I would be set for life and Beckett would never have to know about the connection.

Either way, if the time came, I'd be honest and deal with the consequences. No one would need to save me this time.

 eckett

I WAITED for Eva to come out of her room. All I wanted to do was spend the day with her. I'd never had a hard time walking away, not when I had important work to get to.

I just equated Dad with work, and that's exactly what this felt like. Show up, be a good son, make him feel better, and try to talk to the marble statue that used to be my brother. Like all of us, Mama's death had hit him hard. It was like an emotional switch had been flipped to off and melted there by Dad's philandering. Maybe that was why he had embraced Kendall as family. Once she'd entered the picture, we'd gotten part of our dad back.

Whether the old *Aiden* ever came back was a mystery.

Eva emerged, her gaze flaring, then sweeping over me.

Struck by self-consciousness, I stood for her perusal, cursing myself for changing clothes. After my talk with Eva, a weight had lifted. The drive to set high expectations for myself had lowered to a more comfortable level. It just seemed weird to wear a suit to the hospital I'd been born in. Plus, I had to help Dawson afterward. It was just efficient.

"Whoa" was all she said.

"Is it that different?" I adjusted the jeans hanging off my waist. Good old Wranglers. A pair from when I'd come home for Aiden's wedding and they'd tried to recruit me as a ranch hand. Dawson was shameless in getting us all back on a horse. He kept clothing in all our sizes on hand.

"Different, yes. But not bad different." Her gaze trailed over my long-sleeved, striped snap shirt, down to jeans that had never seen an iron, and stopped at my worn boots. The shirt and pants were new, but my brown square-toed boots were the last pair I'd bought since high school. I might've filled out after graduation, but the boots still fit.

It was on the tip of my tongue to say this was the real me, but that wasn't exactly true anymore. The Beckett King I'd created after leaving Montana was also me. I loved my job, but I couldn't deny that I'd missed being home. The longer I was away, the easier it was to forget how I'd found Mama—and then months later, how I'd found Dad walking out of his bedroom with our nanny.

Despicable. He could've waited for at least a year, or hell, gotten a hotel room. Everyone dealt with grief differently, but he'd waltzed women in and out of the house. When the maid Mama had been close friends with had walked out of his bedroom one morning, I'd decided to move out the day after graduation. That seemed so long ago now.

Eva leaned back and crossed her arms. I don't know why being out of my business suit was such a big change. She was a mix of office and off-duty Eva and still looked as sexy as always. Both styles were just her. On the job, she was proficient and direct. Outside of work, she was cautious, yet blunt.

"I can see it." She wiggled her finger toward me. "Cowboy Beckett. I can picture you doing whatever you do on a ranch now."

I swaggered closer to her. Her pupils dilated and I knew exactly how she felt. I leaned down close and she tilted her head to the side. "You haven't even seen me in my hat, darlin'," I drawled.

A subtle shiver coursed through her. "I never thought 'aw, shucks' would be my type."

"It's not. 'Aw, shucks' is the innocent country boy. I'm not innocent." I grinned and folded her hand into mine. "Do you have what you need for the office?"

She patted the black tote slung over her shoulder. "King Tech stationery and an extra notebook, pens, and the tablet. And of course, my work phone."

We started downstairs. "How's your brother?"

She paused for a moment. "Okay, I guess. I only have his word, but as long as he keeps answering the phone, I'll try not to worry."

"If you don't mind me asking, what's going on with him?"

She shrugged as we hit the landing. "He's had a rough go. Our parents died when I was in middle school. He was in college and he moved back home to raise me."

"But he kept going to school?" Respect for her brother built. If we'd lost Dad, none of us would've been old enough to take care of each other, but as the oldest, Aiden would've dropped everything to try.

"For a time. He had to quit to raise me but he had a promising career. Then he...ran into some bad luck. A major career move didn't pan out, and he just hasn't bounced back." The melancholy in her voice tugged at my heartstrings. I didn't normally get invested in my dates' families, but with Eva I wanted to know more. If her brother got well, she'd worry less.

We went downstairs and I led her toward the office. I gestured toward the kitchen as we passed. "Help yourself to anything. Disclaimer: I have no idea what Dawson eats, or what's growing in the fridge, but if you find something good and edible, go for it. He's an awesome cook, but it's like he can barely run a microwave when he has no one to make food for. I can bring some food home."

"I can always beg a ride and pick up my own stash."

What did she like to eat? She said she wasn't picky, but what did she enjoy? There were no food restrictions, no requests for dressing or butter on the side, and no sending food back to the kitchen. *I* wasn't even that chill when ordering. To Eva, it was normal, but to me, she was like taking a unicorn out to eat.

I skipped the biggest office that Dad had used whenever he worked from home—at least until all of us had been born. After that, he'd insisted it was too loud at home to risk a business call. Dawson had taken it over and it looked like a paper recycling dumpster threw up in there. Mama had done the books for the ranch in her own space. The other office.

The door was half open. I led Eva inside, trying to swallow past the lump in my throat. I hadn't done much more than walk past here when I still lived at home. The last time I'd been back, I hadn't come near this wing.

Mama's decorations were still in place. The rest of the house was high-end, rustic Western, but there was an undeniable Mama flair in here. The pictures were still of the land, but close-ups of various flowers that she had grown. Roses. Lilacs. Cone flowers. The paint was a softer cream tone and any extra touches like vases, candles, or lamps had deep pinks and purples coursing through them.

"This is nice." Eva strode in and spun around. A few boxes lined the walls, labeled with the last few years. Tax documents Dawson had shoved out of his way. One wall had spare computer parts. I had advised him to save a few things, but he'd held on to it all. I'd have to go through that mess before I left and wipe hard drives, find new homes for some of the screens, and recycle the rest. It'd be easier to haul it to Denver with me than find a way to do it all in King's Creek.

Eva crossed to the walls and inspected the art. "Was your mom the photographer?"

"How'd you guess?" No one had asked before. They assumed we bought everything because we had more money than most, but Mama had run the ranch and often worked it, teaching us more each day. Hired help came and went, but all of us knew the inner workings of this place and what went into it. Dad spent the weekends he wasn't traveling working cattle and stacking hay. He still did, actually. For all his faults, he was around to help Dawson.

"The bathroom photos were of this place. And these," she peered closer at the roses, "these have heart. Like these flowers aren't just pretty, but effort went into them and the photographer knew it."

"She used to tend a huge garden." I laughed. "She made us weed all fucking summer until we prayed for haying time."

Eva turned away from the wall, wistfulness in her eyes. "Sounds wonderful. Potted tomatoes sitting on a concrete pad just don't grow the same. Especially when the neighbor keeps picking tomatoes off it when I'm at work."

She dropped her bag on the desk and emptied it. First her tablet, then she placed her King Tech stationary, notebook, and pen off to the side.

I didn't want to go. Being in here didn't hurt so much with her. "I'll be home for supper. What do you want to eat?"

"What do you guys normally have around here?"

"Meat."

Her full lips twitched. "And potatoes."

"Any starch will do as long as it goes with steak. I'll find out what Dawson has planned." I forced my feet to walk out the door, but I couldn't leave without one last glance behind. Eva was planted behind the desk and she looked so damn comfortable that my chest ached.

Mama used to have the same look. Peaceful concentration. I would play on the floor with Aiden while the younger two napped until Dad got home from work. Then he'd take us outside to work and give Mama some peace. I could think about that without a wave of grief crushing me to my knees.

On my way to the front door, I dove into the coat closet and pulled out my sand-colored Stetson. The cowboy hat was my runaround hat and I hadn't worn it since moving out. With Eva here, I was sinking more into "Cowboy Beckett" and less into "Beckett King, CEO of King Tech."

And it didn't bother me as much as it should have.

Stuffing the hat on my head, I went out the door—only to stop and glower at the obnoxious pickup waiting for me. "Fuck you, Dawson," I muttered and got inside.

The engine started with a roar and I was off. Clouds of dust billowed behind me as I flew toward town. Yesterday, it was private planes and personal drivers. Today it was my high school ride with the lift kit. The plane and driver helped me get more work done. I tweaked apps and read through contracts on long flights and took calls while in the vehicle. Aside from Eva fielding my calls and scheduling meetings for after this week, I wasn't getting any work done.

And that didn't bother me as much as it should either.

I was twenty-eight. I couldn't be burning out already, could I?

Maybe it was the lack of vacations. Real vacations. Not meetings in exotic places.

I relaxed the more I drove. The countryside was brown this time of year. Rolling hills broke up the landscape and my family's cattle dotted the view. Black Angus surrounded me.

To my left was the golden cornfield Dawson had already cut into silage. On my right, a stock pond glittered deep blue in the sunlight, a stunning color against the crisp vegetation.

Some people thought the mountains were the only beautiful part of Montana and wouldn't think of eastern Montana as picture-worthy like Mama had thought. But it was. The view melted my stress away like no other, and I'd been to some beautiful places.

King's Creek approached. When I was little, it hadn't seemed ridiculous to be surrounded by everything with my name on it. My great-great-grandfather had founded the town and kicked off the entrepreneurial spirit in the next generations.

The town, however, had never grown as large as our aspirations, but there were no truly big cities in Montana. King's Creek had peaked at twenty thousand during the oil boom of the last decade but held steady since then. There were probably more cows than residents.

I wove through the minimal traffic to the three-story hospital. Not bothering to see if I recognized anyone, I went straight for the elevators and up to Dad's floor. The place hadn't changed since Mama was in here and I hated that I knew the route so well.

The elevator doors opened to a quiet floor. Nurses bustled through the halls but spoke softly to each other. Maybe I passed doctors, but everyone wore scrubs and I couldn't tell them apart.

I found room 312. The door was closed, but that was probably because Dad insisted on privacy. Inside, Aiden sat in a padded metal chair, using Dad's adjustable side table as a desk. Kendall was sitting next to him, watching a show on her phone, and Dad had the head of the bed up and was reading the *Wall Street Journal*. A *King's Creek Daily* was folded on the white linens draped across him.

And fuck, it was hot in here.

Aiden didn't do more than glance up and go back to his work. "Beck. You made it."

Kendall smiled and shut her phone off. "Glad you could come." She stood and laid a kiss on Dad's lips. "I'm going to grab some coffee."

He clasped her hand and his expression was as serious as when he'd told me he was marrying her and I'd better respect the hell out of her or he'd wonder how he failed as a father. "Don't come back until you get some rest."

She whispered, "You're not my boss in here." She winked and walked out.

"My type seems to be gorgeous and stubborn." Dad snapped the paper together and set it down. His gaze was as sharp as ever and his barely graying brown hair was brushed into its standard *Mad Men* style. Except for the off-white hospital gown he was wearing, he looked like he could go right from the bed to the boardroom. "I heard you got in this morning."

I nodded and chose the other padded metal chair next to Aiden. Being away from the office was probably killing him more than being gone from his wife.

"I wanted to get Eva settled," I said, dreading the lie that was coming next.

Dad's brows popped. "Your assistant came with you?"

I took a deep breath and went for it. "I didn't want to say anything with Grams around, but I've been seeing Eva for a while. She took the assistant position after she was laid off, then agreed to help with Grams. But she's really good. And… we're engaged."

"Oh?" He narrowed his eyes on me, and I felt ten years old again, trying to explain how Xander broke his arm if we were "just cleaning" the barn.

I ignored the dubious look Aiden shot my way. He was a

smart guy and he knew me better than Dad. He'd figure it out. "I thought Grams was going to scare her away. I'd already bought the ring and everything and was planning the proposal when you all showed up."

Dad continued to study me. "Why didn't you tell us about her?"

I lifted a brow and flattened my tone. "The trust. I didn't want her to think that was the only reason I was getting engaged. And I didn't want anyone to pressure me. Like Grams." I shrugged. "Besides, I don't tell anyone about who I'm dating."

The last comment clinched it. His face relaxed into a smile and delight shone in his eyes. "Congratulations. I only met her for a few minutes, but she seemed delightful."

"She's the one, Dad." Was this really going to work? I leaned in and winked. "I haven't even told Grams yet."

Dad blinked a few times as he comprehended what I was saying, then he laughed. It helped with the guilt. "That's my boy. Let her wait it out a little longer." Dad's smile faltered when his gaze slid to a still-working Aiden. "Perhaps your brother will pass down your mother's wedding ring set." A pregnant pause. "Since he didn't give them to Kate."

For all of Dad's faults, he believed in true love, enough to fool himself that we were marrying the loves of our lives when we had a deadline and a price. That was why Aiden hadn't proposed with Mama's rings. I wanted to believe he loved Kate. She certainly loved him with all her generous heart, but he'd be just shy of soulless to pass on his rings to a woman he'd duped. He'd never said as much, but his rigid silence when I'd asked was enough.

"Jewelry is a personal choice, Dad." Aiden's standard answer.

I strove to change the subject. "Eva's working from the

house. I think she might be a country girl trapped in a city slicker, so after I'm done here I'll give her a tour."

"Oh, yes." Dad nodded. "Show her on horseback."

"She can probably see just as much from that damn pickup Dawson's loaning me."

That actually got a snicker from Aiden. "If that didn't scare her away…"

"It almost scared *me* away. But I bet I can still drive it out of the mud patch in the north field."

Aiden scowled at me, but a smile played across his lips. "If you had stayed out of the mud, you wouldn't have had to prove your pickup could get out."

"A cow was stuck."

"And you scared it to death with that thing."

I laughed. Yeah, I'd probably taken a few years off the heifer's life. "So what's going on here?"

Aiden paused long enough to update me on all things medical. Because Dad was either in denial or didn't want to be reminded of his mortality, he started in on oil and cattle prices.

Dropping all my work and rushing here had turned out to be unnecessary, but I couldn't bring myself to regret it. Eva was at my family ranch. And I had a ring to buy.

va

I HAD HALF a ton between my legs.

"Still doing okay?" Beckett asked from his own horse beside me. He'd come back from the hospital and offered to take me for that horse ride earlier than expected. I'd gotten through as much work as I knew how with what I had access to and had jumped at the chance to spend time in fresh air.

"Y-yeah." As long as Fool's Gold did everything, I would be fine. I held the reins like Beckett showed me, but it was mostly for looks. This beast would go wherever Beckett's black horse went.

I thought of getting a picture of my Toms shoved into stirrups, but I didn't know how Adam would deal with me having the time of my life with the man who'd destroyed his. He'd be relieved to know that I was no longer striving to get one over on his old nemesis, but would it be worse for him to know that I'd lied about not falling for Beckett?

I hadn't been smarter than that. And so Adam was added to the list of people we would tell a different story to about us.

Grams got the engagement. Neither Beckett nor I cared if she believed it was real or not. She probably wouldn't even ask. Gentry got the true love story. The fake-engagement excuse was for the brothers, including mine.

What story was I telling myself?

Looking at Beckett didn't help. He was sinful with his cowboy hat pulled down to block the low-hanging evening sun. His strong body rocked in time with Black Gold's gait and his powerful thighs flexed and gripped as needed. This couldn't be the same prick in a suit I had met on the sidewalk.

There were no buildings in sight other than his house, the red barn, and three large rectangular buildings. We were in the pasture, riding away.

"What's over there?" I pointed in the direction that Beckett had been intermittently glaring in. I had a guess.

His eyes glittered. "The Cartwrights are over the hill. Too damn close if you ask me, and they didn't when they planted their shack on the edge of our land."

"Is there a King-Cartwright line I shouldn't cross?"

"Yes. They'll probably lift all your valuables off you like the garbage they are, and then blame it on you."

I tensed. My horse's brown and white ears flicked, and I loosened my grip on the reins. His words hit too close to home but there was no way he knew why. "Oh?"

"Bristol Cartwright runs the ranch now, but they got the land because her grandfather tricked my grandfather—Dad's dad—after a night of drinking. Promises were made, papers were signed." He made a disgusted sound. "Her dad is even worse than his old man ever was. I think he drinks himself into a stupor most nights, given the way he smelled every time I've had the misfortune to come across him in town. He's run off all his wives."

"And Bristol?" I couldn't help but have empathy toward the unknown woman. Bristol might be just as bad as her family, but with a dad who treated his wives so bad, my experience with drunks at the bar said he probably treated her poorly too. Only, unlike the wives, she'd never known better.

"She's a hothead like her old man. She's a couple years younger than Dawson, and from what I remember, she was always getting into fights and logging more than a few hours in detention. And now she's in charge because her pops is worthless. But enough about my shitty neighbors. What were you like as a kid?"

The pasture was wide open and Beckett rode close enough for our knees to touch.

"Pretty tame." I'd saved the wild for after graduation. "I worked through high school, so it's not like I played any sports or anything. Were you and your brothers the apples of the teachers' eyes or hell on wheels? Because I've seen your wheels."

He chuckled and that full smile was back. It was becoming a daily occurrence. "Yes to both. Mama did a lot of volunteer work once we were all in school, and Dad liked talking to everybody. We didn't give the teachers problems and they appreciated it."

Had the school's faculty taken pity on him and his family because of their mom? My school had been too large for anyone to care and I sure hadn't talked about my heart getting ripped out of my chest and living each day with the feeling that what I had left would all get yanked away from me too. So I'd taken from others. The thrill of feeling alive. I should've gotten that out of my system in high school instead of working.

I planted my gaze on the grasses in front of me. The mooing of cattle ricocheted around me. One would moo and another would answer. The light breeze was cool enough to warrant the spring jacket I'd packed, and the whole outdoor package came together to calm me.

"I got the rundown on Dad." Beckett's smile had faded and he was staring straight ahead, like I had been. The only sound besides the cows was the crunch of the dried grasses beneath the horses' hooves.

"Does he make a good patient? You've said a few things that made it sound like he was a workaholic when he wasn't screwing around."

"His job is stressful anyway. Then he has Grams to deal with. With both Kendall and Aiden sitting on top of him, he'll be a good patient." Beckett fell quiet but I got the sense he wasn't done. "I don't know what he's going to tell everyone, but I doubt he'll confess to a heart attack. He'll want to protect his privacy as much as possible in a small town and, therefore, protect the company." He squinted into the fading sun and wispy clouds. "Hey, I have something for you."

A spike of excitement hit me, but I squashed it. We'd only kissed. It wasn't like he was going to come bearing gifts.

But when was the last time I'd gotten a gift? It'd been two years at least. Before Adam had sunk into his depression.

He reached into his pocket and pulled out a velvet bag. "I told them to keep the box. It was too bulky. I know it's just for pretend, but I hope you like it."

He dumped a sparkling gold and diamond ring into his palm and handed it to me. My gaze was stuck on his hand.

A ring. We were going to look legit engaged.

He lifted a shoulder. "I know it's not very romantic, but there's no manual for how to fake propose to the girl you actually want to start dating."

His words drained the awkwardness out of the situation…until I slipped the ring on. Its band was warm from being in his pocket and the way it glittered… I frowned. "Is this real?"

"Why wouldn't it be?"

I stared at him, thankful my horse followed his horse's pace. A simple square-cut diamond sat on the band, but its clarity and shine was no cubic zirconia. "I'm sure those manuals wouldn't recommend buying a real diamond for a fake proposal."

"I wanted it to be believable."

It was the first time I suspected he wasn't being completely honest. Was he too proud to buy a fake rock? Beckett seemed so grounded in who he was, but then he did run in a circle of people who could sniff out imitations.

"We should head back before it gets too dark." He showed me how to turn Fool's Gold around.

On the way to the barn, the horses kicked up the pace and Beckett chatted about his dad's treatment plan and how Dawson wanted the next few days to go down.

"The herds in the farthest pastures will get rounded up and brought closer to the house. Some will go in this pasture, actually. And we'll use the horses and four-wheelers."

It'd be cool to see but I didn't dare ask to spectate. I would end up under hooves or in the way of an ATV. "Leave me a list of what you'd like me to do beyond the usual."

His penetrating gaze hit me, warming me against the bite of the wind better than my thin jacket. "You don't have to work, you know. Most things are still on autopilot."

I slanted my gaze toward him. "Most things are being done by your online assistants, you mean."

"You're still in your first weeks."

"I had a lovely conversation with David Kim about the concept behind *The Bubble Game*. His firstborn is due next month and I've already made a note to send a card. This afternoon, I asked DeShawn Gorman how the weather was where he lived and long story short, I'm invited down to Georgia next month for the launch party of his workout app."

"He didn't invite me."

Fool's Gold huffed at Beckett's horse, kind of like I wanted to. "My point is that I spend more time chatting up your clients than I do actual work."

"That's still important. Wilma was the personal touch in the business, not me."

I shot him a wry grin. "You don't say."

He shook his head and chuckled. "Only she lacked the sarcasm."

The ride home finished quickly. Beckett took my reins and led Fool's Gold to the barn. When they stopped, I swung my leg over the horse's broad back and slid down. I followed Beckett's lead, taking the tack off. The smell of horse sweat surrounded me, but it wasn't unpleasant. It was better than many odors I'd come across in the city.

The whole process of storing gear and brushing horses was new and interesting, and after the short ride, I could see why vacation dude ranches were a thing. Not that I'd lurked on any sites and wondered what it'd be like if I could ever afford it.

"Go on inside," he said. "I'll finish up out here and see what Dawson has for supper."

"He mentioned throwing in a meatloaf and potatoes earlier."

"If he cooked, then it'll be good. The guy could go to chef's school if he got sick of ranching."

My stomach growled. Home cooked food. I should be homesick. I should be worried about Adam, but being here and working without fretting over bills, going on a quick trail ride, and getting fed was the best vacation I'd ever had.

~

After the best supper I'd had in a long time, I lay in bed, staring at the ceiling. I couldn't fall asleep. It was relatively early and I was prolonging the inevitable.

I rolled over and grabbed my phone. It rang until voice-mail picked up. The message was an old one, from when Adam had had actual inflection in his voice. I tried again.

He picked up on the third ring, his greeting slurred. "Sh-ello?"

My heart pounded. "What's wrong?"

A grunt and a sigh. "Nothing. I was sleeping."

"Oh." My anxiety drained away. Without me there, he had nothing to keep him awake. "But otherwise everything is okay?"

"Yep."

Silence. Well, he'd eaten when I called him earlier so even if he'd skipped dinner, he should be fine. I'd save my nagging for tomorrow. Relieved that I didn't have to talk to him about my new direction with Beckett, I said, "I'll let you get back to getting some rest."

The trip to the kitchen must've really taken it out of him. I chastised myself for the sarcastic thought. He was hurting. Sick. I couldn't be bitter about the way he was acting any more than I could if he'd had a coughing fit.

"Night." He hung up.

Worry snaked through me until my throat clogged with emotion. *Please be all right, Adam.* I couldn't lose him too, and it had nothing to do with the guilt that was as much my fault as Beckett's.

Dressed in only a T-shirt and underwear, I snuggled into the blankets like I could hide from the world. For the night, I would.

What would it be like to sleep with Beckett? To curl next

to his big body, feeling safe from the world, having his support in the physical sense even if he would kick me out once he learned my secrets? After we got married, would we sleep in the same bed?

We were engaged and in different rooms.

This was confusing on so many levels. Would it hurt his dad to know the engagement was fake? Beckett was oddly protective of how his dad felt on this subject.

My eyelids grew heavy and I must've drifted off because the next sound I heard was the snick of a door. A slit of light shone briefly across the room and disappeared when the door shut. Without city lights surrounding the building, the room was dark, nearly pitch black.

Bold move, Beckett.

I'd just been dreaming of how nice it would be to snuggle with him, but I wasn't ready for him to come on in. Was I? Guess I was going to find out.

Soft footsteps padded toward the bed. Clothing rustled and hit the floor. He wasn't going to neatly fold them and set them on the dresser? Beckett didn't do messy, but then I'd never seen his bedroom.

Should I say something or did he want this to be a surprise? Did I even like that he assumed he was welcome?

The covers lifted and the bed dipped under the weight of a solid body. I stayed under the blanket but rolled toward him. His scent hit me and...that was different. Being from Colorado, I knew the difference between patchouli and pot, and at least the sheets weren't going to smell like weed. Before the wrongness of the odor registered, an unfamiliar voice cut through the night, only inches from my face.

"Well, now," he drawled. "I'd surely like to snuggle, but I'm guessing you're expecting one of my brothers."

I let out a shriek and rolled back, sliding through the covers until I hit the floor with a *thunk*.

"Whoa now." He soothed me like Beckett did the horses. More bedding shifted like he was hopping out of bed. "No need to be scared. I imagine my surprise is a little more pleasant than the one you got."

The smile in his voice became real as he flipped the bedside lamp on.

A man as tall as Beckett, a little lankier, with just as many abs, grinned at me. All he wore was a pair of navy-blue boxer briefs. His dark hair hung nearly to his shoulders, but his features were all King.

"Nice," he said as he got a good look at me. His dark brows waggled. "To meet you. Nice to meet you." His grin was unrepentant.

The door burst open. Beckett rushed through and stopped when he saw his brother. He swept his gaze around the room. I was on the floor between the bed and wall, my head sticking above the mattress, my hair probably in all different directions.

"Xander, what the hell?" Beckett slept in the same attire. Boxer briefs. My adrenaline was still pumping. Being caught in bed with a strange man was a new experience and now I was facing off with two very hot guys, both with their shirts off.

"I swear I didn't know she was in here. Dawson's texts said you brought a woman, but I thought she would be in your room."

I stayed down, my legs out to my side like I was the Little Mermaid. But I was also braless and pantless, so here I'd stay until Xander turned around.

"Did you get hurt, Eva?" Beckett rounded the bed, holding his hand out to help me up. He stopped when he saw my bare legs. "Wanna give us a minute?" he asked Xander.

"I ain't had a proper introduction yet." He acted like he was taking off a cowboy hat to bow. "I'm Xander King, wayward third child of Gentry and Sarah King. You would've figured out I wasn't Beck as soon as I blew you away with our first kiss."

"Xander," Beckett barked.

Xander's grin widened. "The girls always said I was better than you."

"That was Emily, and she was drunk when she slept with you."

"Doesn't mean I wasn't better." His smile turned lopsided. "And she wasn't drunk. She just wanted to get away with sleeping with both of us."

My mortification should be turning to awkwardness, but I was enjoying Xander's teasing. "Nice to meet you, Xander. I'm Eva, Beckett's assistant and fake fiancée."

"Fake is the best kind of fiancée." He glanced at Beckett. "Pretending for Dad's sake?"

Beckett nodded and they exchanged a knowing look. "You saw how he was with Aiden. But Grams is relentless."

Xander shook his head. "I see what I have to look forward to for the next year. Anyway, I'll wait outside so she can grab some pants."

We both watched him saunter out the door.

"He's not like you or Dawson," I said.

"God, no. And he smells like weed."

"Patchouli," I said and rose. "Thanks for coming to my rescue. I might be too wired to sleep now. Um," I tugged my shirt down and hunched my shoulders as I went to my suitcase, feeling exposed in the soft lamplight. Digging out a pair of sweats, I wished it wouldn't be so awkward to put my bra on with him in the room. "Where should I sleep?"

Beckett's gaze drifted down to my breasts and back up. "You can have my bed. I'll go down and take the couch."

"Doesn't Dawson have an old room up here?"

His features went taut. "It's full of Mama's stuff."

Her artwork was all over the house, but her personal items were too much for him? Had he avoided coming home because of her? If that was the case, sleeping in Dawson's room would be torture. I hated displacing him. "I can stay in there."

"I doubt the bedding is fresher than my high school jock-strap. Don't worry about it."

When was the last time Beckett King slept on a couch? He was willing to do it for me. My next suggestion was only spurred by the fright of my life a moment ago. "We can just share a bed. I'm sure we can be...adult about it."

Beckett's gaze turned molten, sending the flush from my face down to ignite a throb between my legs. "I'd be way too adult about sharing a bed with you."

He grabbed my suitcase and hauled it next door. I slipped out behind him. Xander was good to his word and nowhere to be seen. Darting into a room that was nearly identical to the one I'd just left, the first thing I saw was the rumpled sheets and the blankets flung back. He'd rushed out of bed to come check on me.

"Good night, Eva." Beckett pressed a kiss to my temple. I refused to look at him. He was so close and so shirtless, and those boxers...

"Sleep tight, Beckett."

He was gone, clicking the door shut behind him. I stared at the bed. I didn't want to be alone. How could I go from a kiss to wanting to sleep with him so quickly? Crawling into bed, I burrowed into sheets that smelled like him and all I could think about was how he was sleeping on a couch in a cavernous open-concept living room for me.

CHAPTER 14

eckett

TALK about a rough night's sleep. Hearing Eva scream as I was drifting off hadn't accelerated my pulse as much as seeing her in nothing but a T-shirt and pale blue underwear had.

I'm sure we can be...adults about it.

Oh, dear Eva. My thoughts about sharing a bed with her were so adult.

Somehow I had kept my wits about me. Keeping this growing relationship between us from everyone else would be a lot harder if we shared a room. But it was sweet of her to offer.

So damn sweet, like how she'd taste if I pulled down those panties...

Groaning, I opened my eyes and made sure the blanket was still over me. The couch wasn't half bad and I usually slept on my side anyway. It was almost long enough so I didn't have to do an hour of yoga to straighten myself out.

My gaze landed on a pair of assessing eyes and I jerked. "Aiden, what the fuck, dude? Have you been watching me sleep?" I should be honored. He never even put down his laptop to gaze at Kate.

"What the hell is this engagement about?" he snapped.

Yep, he'd figured it out. No way would he believe any one of us could fall madly in love within days. "You know exactly what it's about and it's for Dad."

"Grams was the one trying to set you up. Why pretend and not just tell him this woman will marry you for the payout?"

I bristled at his tone. Yes, I'd told Eva she'd get half, but unlike Kate, I wanted her to know she had an out. "So I can keep my status as less disappointing son."

That got nothing more than an eye twitch. "Gooder."

I ignored the use of my old nickname. "Besides, I heard Grams threaten both him and Kendall. This way, Grams is off his back and he doesn't blame himself."

Aiden's matter-of-fact nod shouldn't piss me off. He was so analytical. Like a sense of humor had skipped the first-born. "You don't want to stress him."

Like you did. Dad loved Kate and probably thought she'd be able to chisel down to Aiden's gooey center. Hadn't happened. "How bad was his heart attack? Really?"

I caught a glimpse of the pressure Aiden was under. Fatigue gathered in the corner of his eyes and his black suit was rumpled from his bedside duty. His tie was loose to the point of *why bother keeping it on* and his short hair had been run through a few times. "If it hadn't been for Kendall, he'd be gone."

"I guess she's not a gold digger then."

"Even if she were, he's a better human when she's

around." He sat on the plush chair across from me. "He'll be on blood pressure medicine and a low-fat diet. Kendall will make sure he goes on long walks."

"He'll hate that." Dad was like a little boy jumping from toy to toy. Running and ranching helped focus his energy.

"He won't with her. She's slowing his life down and bearing some of the burden. How'd you meet Eva?" Idle curiosity wasn't why he'd asked. I was going to get interrogated.

"She was outside the office. I thought Dad had sent her, but we got to talking and I offered her more than her current employer to work for me."

Aiden's brow ticked up. "If you carry through with the marriage, you'd better prenup the hell out of it."

"Is that what you did with Kate?"

Annoyance crossed his face. "None of your business."

"Then how is Eva any of yours?"

He stared at me, but he eased further into the chair, his interest more focused. "Kate signed a prenup."

"She doesn't know that she can leave you for a cool fifty million?" I shouldn't have said it, but Aiden had a way of making me feel challenged.

"No one's forcing her to stay with me." That would be a no. It made me wonder why he'd never divulged the fact. Did he want Kate to stay with him? I looked at him with new eyes. Tired, worn out, and probably burned out. Maybe Kate was the eye of his storm and no matter how much he told himself he'd married her for the money, he might be wrong. Would he ever admit it?

It wasn't my problem to solve. Someday, he and Kate would have to work those answers out themselves. "Are you finally getting some sleep?"

He nodded, but didn't get out of the chair.

"Xander's home."

He didn't look surprised, but he leveled another stare at me. "Then Dad's going to want to throw the party he's been planning since you told him you were engaged."

I sat up, no longer concerned about morning wood. "What? What kind of party?"

"An engagement and welcome-to-the-family and no-you-heard-wrong-I-wasn't-sick party." Aiden sighed. "I hope this Eva knows what she's signing up for. Dad's going to welcome her with open arms and Grams is going to sink her claws in her until you turn thirty."

"You think the Cartwrights know about the trust?"

"Talk gets around and if it'd be a stick in the side, Grams would make sure they heard rumors."

"True." I rubbed my face. What a mess. I didn't want Eva to be escorted around town like a prize pony. She was more than a ruse. "When does he want this to happen?"

"He's getting released this afternoon, so I'd guess tomorrow."

"Already?"

Aiden shrugged, as if I should know the answer. "People might hear he was in the hospital and wonder. He has to make a good show of it before investors start to worry."

"And he can use the excuse that we're working cattle soon so we'd better have the party." I shoved the blanket off and stood. Aiden looked like he could sink into the chair and become one with it. How long had he been awake?

Self-recrimination passed through me. A foreign emotion. I should've seen how hard it'd been for him. He'd picked up Dad's slack and just when he was finally getting some help, Dad dropped. Since his help was Kendall, she was going to be preoccupied at Dad's side.

"Go get some sleep. You look like hell."

"You always say the sweetest things, Beck."

Another glimpse of my brother beneath the marble. It

was almost worth an engagement party looming over my head. "I'd better go warn Eva."

"Warn me about what?"

I looked up and couldn't look away. She was running her hand along the railing toward the stairs. As she descended, I thought seriously about changing my dress code to casual. Those jeans hugged her legs, she wore her Toms, and her pink hoodie was a little less frayed than her pale blue sweater but appeared no less comfy.

I caught Aiden's reaction out of the corner of my eye. His brows ticked up as he assessed her. Like everyone else who knew me, he would comment about how she wasn't my type. Her hair wasn't styled, but it wasn't messy. She looked like a garden fairy had decided to land on Earth and work for me. Her entire outfit probably cost less than any of my exes' pairs of shoes.

He rose and stood beside me because being a refined businessman had been bred into him. For some reason, I wanted to know what he thought. I'd never cared before what my brothers thought about my dates.

"Dad's throwing us an engagement party."

She paused halfway down, looking like she'd sprint back up and disappear. "How big of a party?"

"The whole town and possibly much of the county," Aiden replied and I elbowed him. The asshole snickered.

Color drained from her face but she descended the rest of the way. "I guess it's on, huh?"

When she approached, I introduced her. "Here's the brother you haven't met yet. Aiden."

He extended his hand. "Eva."

She gave him a perfunctory shake and part of me eased. I never worried about my brothers as competition. If I had to worry about them, then my date wasn't worth it. But Aiden was the oldest, the one we all looked up to even if none of us would ever admit it. He was also the one the girls our age would ask about. His demeanor had screamed untouchable since he could walk.

"Nice to meet you. How's your dad?" She looked between us, her gaze dipping to my bare chest.

"Hounding the doctors to finish the paperwork to release him." Aiden straightened his suit as if it wasn't wrinkled and unbuttoned. "If you'll excuse me, I'm going to catch some sleep in a real bed before my wife arrives."

"You'll like Kate," I said. "She's nothing like Aiden."

Aiden shot me a glare, but his lips twitched. "It's one of her best qualities." He disappeared up the stairs.

Eva looked at me as I watched him go. "You're worried about him."

"I am." It surprised me to admit it. Aiden would be in Dad's shoes by the time he was fifty and if he ran Kate off before then, who'd be around to save him? Maybe I should come home more. "I'll go get cleaned up. Mind making two of whatever you're having for breakfast?"

"Dawson sent me—you—a text on your work phone. There's a blueberry french toast bake in the oven. I just have to start it. It should be done by the time you're finished."

Dawson and his food. "He used to slide a chair up to the counter and help Mama whether she wanted him to or not."

Eva smiled. "I doubt she minded."

"Oh, sometimes it was tough for her. But by the time he got over breaking eggs all over the floor and counter and quit starting the mixer at maximum speed when it was full of flour, she looked less frazzled."

Her laugh was exactly what I wanted to wake up to every day, though I hadn't known it until now. "Better get the bathroom. It's getting full in this house."

It was. I liked seeing all of us coming and going. Two weddings in the ten years since I'd left home weren't enough.

140

I trudged up the stairs and was about to turn into the bathroom when Aiden popped out. He had stripped down, wearing nothing but black satin pajama bottoms.

He saw my doubtful gaze on them. "Shut up." His expression sobered and he glanced toward Dawson's old room. "Dad and Kendall are going to stay here. Dawson offered to give up the master suite, but I think the thought of Kendall and Dad messing around on his bed freaks all of them out."

My mood darkened. "So we'll need to clean up Dawson's old room."

Aiden's jaw tightened. "I thought we should do it before they get back."

Keep Dad's stress level down. And throw Kendall a bone. She wouldn't want to sift through Mama's stuff. I hated admitting how considerate she was, but *if* she was as genuine as she seemed, then it'd be hard for her to shove Mama's things aside and move in.

"Fine. I'll start after I eat."

Aiden nodded and went into his room. I stared at the closed door of the room I'd be tackling in an hour. I'd survived entering Mama's old office. Eva may have had something to do with that. But cleaning out a room full of Mama's treasured possessions would be torture. Then I'd remember what it was like before. What I was like before. I'd start to do something stupid like wonder if Mama would like Eva.

And I wouldn't have to think about the answer.

Yes, she would've.

I CUT into my french toast bake. Dawson might need to give me some chores to do to work this off.

Eva was sitting next to me at the giant rectangular table I

used to eat breakfast, lunch, and dinner at. She moaned and the sound went right to my gut, curling in on itself until I pictured her moaning under me like that. "This stuff is just naughty."

"Just like Dawson." I shoved a bite in my mouth, but even the explosion of creamy sweetness couldn't lighten my mood. "Are you going to work after this?"

She nodded and fiddled with the ring on her hand. I liked it there way too much. "Unless you have something for me to do."

I just liked that she was going to be under the same roof. "I have to clean out Dawson's old bedroom for Dad and Kendall."

She put her fork down. I should tell her to pick it up. To take another bite. Give me another moan. But I couldn't. "Do you want help?"

"No, it's fine. Xander might wake up and jump in with me."

She nodded and we finished our meal. No more sexy sounds came from her, but when she got up from the table, she came to me. She laid the softest kiss on my lips. "Let me know if you need help after all."

I watched her hips sway as she turned down the hallway that'd take her to the office. Why was she different?

Because she saw me as a person and not as a King, or Aidan's little brother, or the owner of a big, fat bank account. Eva was the real deal and I hadn't realized that was the trait I'd been looking for.

I cleaned up my area and covered the food. The heavenly smell would draw my brothers down soon.

Trekking upstairs went way too fast. Should I have brought anything with me? Would I need boxes or trash bags? I didn't remember what Dawson had shoved in there.

The house had stayed Mama's until we'd all moved out and it had become his.

Had he cleared Mama out of the house by himself? I should've been around to help, but I'd found a college so far away that it gave me a good excuse not to return home.

Opening the door, I peered inside like I was looking at an oil spill and I only had a mop. That was a no to boxes. He'd already packed items away but had stashed the boxes and plastic bins haphazardly around the room.

Entering, I flipped on the light. My eyelids drifted shut and I inhaled. Mama. Vanilla and lilacs. When was the last time I'd seen the lilac bushes that lined the main yard bloom?

Everything was packed, but I could haul the boxes to my room so Kendall and Dad wouldn't be sleeping with Mama's ghost.

Since when did I care? Apparently Dad's heart attack was a wake-up call for more than just him.

I crossed to bins of various sizes that had been dumped on the bed and stared at them. *Just pick them up and move them to my room.*

But I opened one instead.

Pictures. I let out a soft laugh. The top picture was of me and Aiden when I was about three and he was four. We each wore tiny chaps and nothing else. Our expressions looked like we'd won the lottery. Our own chaps.

Sitting on the bed, I sifted through the pictures, lingering on some before flipping to others. Mama had been a scrapbooker, and most of the boxes were probably filled with her creations.

A soft knock at the door caught my attention. Eva lingered in the opening. "I couldn't quit thinking about you."

"Come in." I scooted over and handed her the first photo I had seen.

She let out a delighted gasp and covered her mouth. "Is that you?"

Pointing to the one that was me, I nodded. "The other is Aiden, and I need to make sure Kate gets a copy." I fell quiet as she went through the same photos I had just looked at. "She used to scrapbook."

Eva stopped and looked around. "You think that's what most of these are?"

I nodded. "If I start opening them, I'm going to lose entire chunks of time, and then I'll never get done. But I can't bring myself to just move them." I sighed. "It smells like her in here."

She put her arm around me and rested her head on my shoulder. "I can help you move them. When you're ready."

"Thanks."

Neither of us moved, but then she lifted her head. "What happened? No, never mind. Today is already hard enough—"

"Eva." I twined my hand through hers. Sharing the story meant she was more than an assistant, and that mattered to me. "Dad took us out to a movie so Mama could get some work done. I don't even remember what we saw." I stared at the wall as that night came flooding back to me. "I was the first to run inside and she didn't answer. So I went searching, calling for her." My throat grew thick but with Eva's arm around me, I could continue. "She was in her office, on the floor. She'd been beaten."

Her soft gasp cut through my memories. "By who?"

Anger seeped into those memories. The rage I'd been living with since then was staggering. "Some meth head out on probation. Fucking Old Man Cartwright hired anybody that'd work for shit money. Sex offenders. Hitchhikers thumbing rides off the interstate. People with major problems who had no business being near children. We'd warned him after some of his hires had stolen from us and vandalized our vehicles and barns. We'd told him that someone was going to get hurt, that it'd be serious, that it could even be his own daughter. But he didn't listen. He went and hired some guy who got high and broke through the back door of our house, looking for cash to get more drugs. Mama got in his way. She died at the hospital. Her head trauma was too severe."

A warm drop landed on my shoulder. She was crying. I twisted to face her.

"Eva, baby. Don't cry." She'd lost both parents and she was crying for me. I wiped her cheeks.

She shook her head. "I'm sorry, I'm fine. It's just… You were only twelve."

I'd ask how she knew, but Mama's obituary had been in the paper. Simple math would deduce my age. The story hadn't been in the paper. Grams and DB hadn't wanted our business leaked all over the state, not if they couldn't leverage it over the Cartwrights. Dad still felt the same. If we'd hated them before, it was nothing compared to how we felt about them now.

"Yeah." I was ready to put this room-cleaning thing behind me. "And now I have a stepmother who's thirty. Funny how life changes. I'd better get the boxes out."

Between the two of us, we made quick work of the job. When I came back from the last round, she was stripping the bed.

"Those should be clean," I said.

She looked over her shoulder, but I had the most delectable view of her ass. "I thought they weren't any fresher than your high school jockstrap."

"I took good care of that jockstrap." Picking up all the bedding and grabbing the sheets she'd just pulled free, I went down to the laundry room.

She trailed behind me to the main floor laundry across

from the office she worked in. "Am I getting to see Beckett King do laundry?"

"Ha ha. I can even run the machine."

"Now, this I have to see."

I made a big show of stuffing the sheets into the washing machine and adding detergent.

She crossed her arms. "I'm impressed, Mr. King."

Either it was the release of pressure that had built from being here, or I'd been wanting more and more of her with each day that went by. I grabbed her around the waist and swung her up and around to pin her between me and the washing machine.

She let out a yelp that I swallowed with my mouth. She melted, wrapping her arms and legs around me. She was all things warm and soft and so responsive that it wasn't long before my jeans were uncomfortable, my cock pushing at the seam.

When she gave me a little wiggle and one of those moans I'd wanted more of this morning, I shifted my hips. I rubbed into her center, and there was too much fucking denim between us.

"Beckett," she murmured against my mouth. "God, Beckett."

"I like how you call me Beckett." It was special. *She* was special. "I like how you moan when you eat my brother's cooking. I like how you look with no pants." I ground harder against her.

"Beckett, yes." She was straining against me. "I need more."

"Me too." Could I come like this? It felt like it. The machine was filling with water, but soon it'd be rocking and it might be enough to push me over the edge, but what about her?

Our position made it hard to reach anything, but I was

able to roll her sweater up past her plain beige bra. Her bras were so simple and understated and so her. I liked it. I liked everything about her.

But that damn bra was hiding creamy breasts from me. I pushed it down and the loveliest tits I'd ever seen spilled out. They were a perfect handful and would be an even better mouthful.

I went to work, hitching her higher so I could lick across her nipples and draw one into my mouth without losing contact with her core. She hugged my head to her and arched against me.

I nipped one tight bud and got the moan I was looking for. Going to the next breast, I knew this wouldn't be enough. Gently unwinding her legs, I knelt in front of her. Her sweater was still bunched up around her armpits and her rosy nipples still glistened from my attentions.

I was hard to the point of hating my jeans, but her pleasure was paramount. Unbuttoning her pants, I rolled them down while holding her gaze. Her lips were parted and her cheeks flushed.

Next was her underwear and she was bare before me. I leaned in to land a kiss on her navel and work my way down.

"Holy shit!" Xander's voice cut through my passion. "Did Dawson bake again?"

Eva recoiled and shoved her shirt down. I spun around to make sure she hadn't been exposed to my brother yet again. Standing, I stayed in front of her and listened for him.

"He's in the kitchen," I whispered over my shoulder.

"I hope he stays there," she hissed. She was moving behind me, covering up those pretty tits and that part of her I wanted to taste so badly.

Once she was covered, I went to the door and peeked out. No Xander. "All clear."

"I'm going to the office." Her face was flaming, but I caught her around the waist before she left.

"I plan to pick up where we left off as soon as possible."

"Make sure none of your brothers are around." She scowled at me, then broke into a smile. She stepped into the hallway and peered down toward the kitchen. Then she snuck across the hall to the office.

Smiling, I went nowhere. It was going to be a few minutes before I was presentable.

CHAPTER 15

va

MY BODY HATED ME. Beckett had promised to pick up where he'd left off, but we hadn't had a chance. Kendall had insisted on helping ready Dawson's old room and when she'd found out—thanks to Xander and his not-so-subtle comments—she was all about passing around scrapbooks.

It was late in the evening and Gentry refused to go to bed. He was regaling his new wife with tales of his rowdy boys instead.

Kate had arrived a few hours ago and I'd instantly liked her. She wasn't as outgoing as Kendall—okay, Kate was a wallflower. Kendall was comfortable with herself, happy to visit with everyone. If she needed to command a room, she could. Kate, however, was content to observe, though she had an air of familiarity about her that made everyone comfortable around her. And the way she'd looked deliriously happy to see Aiden made my heart melt until I noticed

149

that he'd barely looked up from where he'd parked himself with his laptop at the kitchen table. I'd dislike him, but fatigue hovered around him like a fog. Had he been this exhausted before Gentry's heart attack?

Kate and Aiden had retired to bed an hour ago—after Dawson had coerced him into helping with cattle a day early since it was supposed to rain midweek.

"Still taking pictures, Xander?" Gentry asked. Beckett's dad didn't look like he'd been in the hospital for three days. He was dressed in plaid pajama pants and a T-shirt that made me doubt he had to start a workout routine from scratch. Were fifty-year-olds naturally that cut?

"Here and there." Xander tossed a book with horse cutouts on it to Beckett. "Here's your I Love Me book."

Beckett opened it. The first thing was a blinged-out birth announcement. Sarah King had done one for each boy. From the number of scrapbooks she'd made, each kid would've had fifty apiece by now if she hadn't died.

I leaned closer to see, the side of my body pressed up against his. He shot me a discreet, but searing look from the corner of his eye. I wasn't the only one with finishing what we'd started on my mind.

"What are you doing other than kicking around the globe?" Gentry's voice held a note of censure. Even Kendall pinned her husband with a hard stare.

"Traveling, Dad," Xander answered. "It's hard to learn about the world from a private jet."

"Learning about it's one thing, but are you ever going to do anything about it?"

Xander rolled a shoulder like maybe he'd consider it one day. Beckett scowled at his brother.

"Didn't you do some relief work in Eastern Europe?" Beckett asked, a vexed edge to his voice like he wondered why Xander didn't mention it himself and get Gentry off his back. I wanted to hug him for sticking up for his brother. Maybe he'd understand when he found out about mine and what I had planned to do for him.

Xander rolled his eyes. "Now Beck, that doesn't fit the middle-kid-syndrome stereotype. I just fuck around on beaches and party all over the world."

Gentry frowned. "Language, Xander. And that's for the youngest. Dawson runs the ranch, which is a family business going back decades."

Xander laughed. "Right. Sorry, Kendall and Eva. I'm sure your ears are going to bleed, you poor little women." He slapped his knees and stood. He wasn't dressed quite like Beckett and Dawson. Cowboy boots and jeans maybe, but his hemp-woven eco-friendly hoodie was one I saw around Denver all the time. "I'm still fighting jet lag. Night, y'all."

Beckett draped his arm around my shoulders and his thumb rubbed a steady circle on my upper arm. The move was through my shirt, but he might as well have cupped my sex in the middle of the room. My body was humming.

With Gentry and Kendall here, we were going to have to share a room. I looked forward to it, but at the same time I was terrified. On a normal date, I'd never want my guy's family overhearing me being intimate. But only Gentry, and probably Kendall, had to think we were real. If I moaned too loudly, the others would know this wasn't fake.

What would they think? Would they think I was sleeping with Beckett just for the money and hold it against me? Or be relieved that Beckett and I would most likely cross the one-year mark if we were intimate?

None of that seemed to matter when his thumb stroked its steady circle.

Or wait…was he pretending? Was this a show?

I was in over my head if he was only acting.

"Way to go, Dad," Dawson said dryly as he paged through his own I Love Me scrapbook.

"The kid has got to learn to earn his own way through life." Gentry sounded unrepentant and all dad. I'd missed out on this. Sorrow fought to the surface, but no, this night wasn't about me. "You have the ranch. Aiden has the oil company. And Beckett made his own empire. Xander has a lot of catching up to do."

"Why worry when he's going to get a windfall when he's thirty?" Dawson sounded exactly like the youngest, egging his dad on.

Gentry scowled. "The way you boys have been cutting it close, I don't think I'm done with Grams."

Dawson snorted. "She's not done with us."

Kendall stroked Gentry's arm. "I think Xander's doing just fine, but I know you can't quit being a dad and not worry about him. It sounds like he's been doing good wherever he goes."

Gentry's expression went from disapproving parent to besotted fool in a second. "You're right. You're always right. I'm worrying too much."

She giggled. "Then on that note, you won't argue when I tell you it's time for bed." She got up and collected scrapbooks. I reluctantly pulled myself away from Beckett's side and helped her, and Beckett joined in.

Dawson rose and gathered a couple of boxes in his arms. "Beck, why don't you show your fiancée the Montana stars? It's as clear as a horse's ass out there."

I chuckled. "I can't imagine what level of clarity that is."

Dawson's grin was mischievous. "If I said cow's ass, you'd know you could barely see the sky for the shit-covered clouds."

Gentry was halfway up the stairs, but he stopped. "For God's sake, Dawson. Language. I didn't raise wildebeests."

Dawson laughed and he ran up the stairs past Kendall and his dad. I looked at Beckett.

He shrugged. "If we drive out far enough, there won't be a ton of light pollution."

Stargazing and a chance to have Beckett to myself? "I'll grab my coat."

"Nope. Blankets." He disappeared into the laundry and the thrum that started between my legs reminded me exactly where we'd left off.

He came out with an armload of blankets. When he got outside by his pickup, he wrapped one around me and kissed the tip of my nose before loading me inside. We were alone. This wasn't acting.

He shoved the key in the ignition, but before he turned it over, he said, "It serves Dawson right if I keep him up." With that he started the engine.

It roared and he pulled away, but instead of taking the road, he aimed for a pasture. I watched as he stopped, got out, opened a gate I didn't realize could open, then got back in. He drove through and stopped again, then went out and shut the gate.

"We're driving through the pasture?" I asked.

"The middle of nowhere is the best place to look at stars."

The drive was dark. All I could see was what the headlights lit up. But he was right. As I looked out the window, the stars were clearer and more brilliant than I'd ever seen.

"Wow." My breath puffed across the glass.

"Wait until I kill the lights." It was a few more minutes before he stopped on the rise of a hill. Air bordering on frigid wafted across my cheeks when I got out.

Beckett opened the box and spread two of the blankets out, then helped me up. We stretched out on them side by side, and I covered us both with the blanket that had been around me, then he draped another blanket over that one. It wasn't the most comfortable. The padding under us did little to soften the hard metal ridges running down the pickup bed under my back. I positioned my head so it was between ridges.

His heat radiated into me, encouraging the ache that'd been frustrating me all day. The stars were brilliant. We could see the thicker belt of stars that was the Milky Way. It was astounding.

"It's so quiet." I never left the city. Had I heard this level of silence before?

"No traffic. Sometimes the cows get vocal but they're on the other side right now."

The moon was waning; otherwise we'd be draped in utter darkness. But I wasn't afraid. All that was out here were cows.

"And once in a while, you'll hear the coyotes howling."

I swatted him. "Don't scare me."

He chuckled. "I'm not trying to. They won't bother us. Even though Dawson's dog died last year, and he hasn't had time to train a new herding dog, the coyotes won't bother us."

"Herding dogs are still a thing?"

"Get between a mama cow and her calf and they can save your life." We fell quiet, listening to the crickets when he rolled toward me. This whole night had been like all the shows I'd grown up watching on TV. Idyllic family life. Food on the table. Laughter, and maybe just a touch of conflict. Gentry loved his kids. That much was clear.

Adam and I had missed out on all of this.

"Eva, I want to finish what we started."

I turned my head toward him. "I do too. But out here?"

"I can keep you warm."

I didn't doubt it. Just thinking about how he'd knelt in front of me earlier was enough to stoke my inner furnace.

But I wasn't naïve. If we did that, it'd lead to the rest. "Earlier, in the living room, were you just pretending?"

I felt him tip his head toward me more than I saw it. "I don't have to pretend."

"Me either."

He hugged me tighter. "And that bothers you?"

"It's...confusing." I didn't want to turn into a flirt just because Gentry walked into the room. I didn't want to question whether Beckett meant it when he kissed me. The money issue wasn't one-sided. Fifty million was riding on the line for him too. He might already be rich, but that was a lot of money.

I could lay here and debate it for hours, until we both froze. Or I could find out how real our chemistry was.

I rolled into him. "Do you have protection?"

"In my wallet." He leaned close. "A King's always prepared."

He gave me a long kiss, then disappeared under the blanket, leaving me breathless. A cold draft followed him, but I was quickly warmed once his hands landed on my hips.

He was starting right where he'd left off. Staying under the covers, he rolled my pants and underwear down and gently wedged himself between my legs. I stared up at the stars but slipped my arms under the blanket. I had to touch him.

He kissed a path up one thigh and down the other, killing me slowly. Beckett King was between my legs and we were going to have sex tonight—out in the middle of a pasture at his family home. There was no way he was the horrible man that had destroyed my brother. He had a scrapbook.

Those thoughts were obliterated when he parted me and stroked his hot tongue across my clit. My hips lifted. I could come in no time.

He was a master. He licked and when I was about to

155

explode, he backed off pressure until I was grinding against him for more.

"Beckett." I sounded whiny. I was close to begging. If it weren't so chilly, I'd throw the blankets off and ride his face until I exploded.

His voice was muffled. "I've wanted to do this for too long. I'm not rushing it." Another lick. I twisted my fingers in his hair and it wasn't easy. The short strands slipped through my fingers.

When he slid a finger through my wetness and pushed inside, he turned ruthless. His tongue showed no mercy and he plunged in and out of me.

My back bowed and I cried out, long and loud. I came so hard I couldn't see a single star with my eyes wide open. He continued to play me, to string it out until I didn't think I could take it anymore.

I wiggled away from him and reared up. He emerged from the blanket and wiped his face off. "That was amazing, Eva." He settled over me, but kept his weight off me. His expression was shadowed, but the awe was clear in his voice.

Still trying to catch my breath, I only smiled and stroked my hands along his chest. That *was* amazing. Chemistry like that couldn't be faked. It was a base, something we could build on.

Starting now. It was too cold to unbutton his shirt, but I tugged it out. "I hate to say...that was an eleven-out-of-ten scream."

His laugh rumbled through his chest. "I never lie." He pressed a kiss to my lips. I could taste myself on him. He was over me, I was getting his body heat, but I wanted him in me.

I undid his belt, then his pants, all while keeping our kiss going. How could I get worked up again so soon?

He shifted to the side and reached behind him. Getting the condom out, he ripped it open and rolled it on.

"I wanted to do that." I couldn't see a thing, but I'd get to touch him. To see if he was as big as he'd felt earlier. To see how he felt in my hand.

"I don't want you getting cold." When he moved back over me, he tried placing his arms in a couple of places. It'd either slip off a ridge, or he'd grunt as his elbow got caught between them. "Are you really uncomfortable?"

"I mean, it's not every day there's a metal ridge running up my ass."

Keeping me covered, he maneuvered to his back and dragged me on top. My sweater was twisted around me and I had no idea where my pants were, but this would work. I shifted until my knees had purchase, then centered myself over him. Reaching between us, I palmed him.

He was as hot and hard as I imagined. The latex did nothing to detract from the feel of him, like petting a velvet-covered metal rod.

Like him, I took my time. As each inch filled me, his hands gripped my hips like a life raft.

"Fuck, Eva."

I rolled my hips and he groaned. Another inch.

"Take me. All of me."

"I want to take my time," I said, partly teasing him for earlier and partly wanting to draw this out, to relish it. To remember it. Because I could lose more moments like this in a heartbeat.

Those long hours looking at his picture, swearing I hated him, were revealed for what they were: as close to obsession as I'd ever been. I'd thought I was better than that. But he was hard and under me and I wasn't better.

I pushed down and he was buried completely. We were connected and all I knew was him and this pickup box. Anchoring my hands on his chest, I started riding him. At first it was for his pleasure, but then my own built, and we were moving in synch. I pushed down as he thrust up. We moved as one. Our breathing and our bodies slapping mingled together with the crickets.

At some point, the blankets fell off my shoulders, but I didn't care. The peak was close and I wanted to find it. Beckett was holding back.

"Touch yourself," he growled. I obeyed him. There wasn't much I wouldn't do at this moment if he asked me. "Touch yourself with the hand wearing my ring."

My breath caught, but I did it, my index finger landing on my clit. A long moan left me. "Beckett."

"You're coming with me." He covered my hand with his. "We're coming together."

My hips rolled and bucked. It didn't take much pressure and I was flying apart, shattering into as many pieces as there were stars in the sky. I shouted his name over and over.

He cried out mine and went rigid. A flood of heat filled my body.

Collapsing on top of him, I buried my head against his chest. He was coming to mean so much to me. It scared me as much as the thought that he'd ditch me in a hot second if he knew my past.

BECKETT STOOD NEXT TO ME, a proprietary hand around my waist. We were in a back room at a restaurant called Hogan's. I was nursing a long neck, the same kind he had. I wasn't a big drinker, but the bottle helped me blend better. I'd rather be back in the middle of a pasture than here.

The party Beckett had warned me about was in full swing. We were putting on a show for his dad's sake, and the whole family was putting on one for the community. We'd been tasked with proving the rumors of Gentry's heart attack were false, even though they were true.

Beckett chatted with Dawson. Both were dressed in crisp white shirts and black jeans. Xander listened on, probably more interested than I was in the ranch discussion. His khakis and white shirt weren't nearly as crisp. But he wore cowboy boots. When all four brothers had gone out to move cattle, I'd witnessed a mirage so hot it'd seared my retinas. All four brothers in boots, worn jeans, cowboy hats, and weathered, plaid, button-up shirts, sauntering out the door, laughing at some stupid joke Dawson had made. I'd thought about taking up scrapbooking just to have an excuse to take a million photos.

Grams approached me on the other side. Even socializing, she was in a power suit. I gave her a polite smile, but inside my cells iced over. "Mrs. Boyd."

"Now, Eva. I asked you to call me Grams. Congratulations on the engagement."

"Thank you."

"Awfully good timing." She smiled like she was a cat pinning a mouse and leaned closer. "Well done. Gentry bought the whole thing."

"Thank you?"

She shrugged. "But if you two really have a thing, then... welcome to the family." She sauntered away to work the crowd.

Welcome to the family. Did I want to be part of *her* family? It'd been me and Adam for so long, but even if I married for just a year, Grams and Beckett's dad and brothers would become family during that time. *My* family. Because they might never know about Adam.

Beckett and Dawson had slipped into talking cattle and even Xander had gotten involved. Minerals and feeds and breeding schedules and it was all interesting for the first few minutes until I got hopelessly lost. And here I'd thought cows were just cows.

Across the room, at Aiden and Kate's table, a woman I'd briefly been introduced to as having gone to school with one or all of them slid next to Aiden on the other side of Kate. He politely finished tapping out something on his phone and chatted with her. Poor Kate had to angle her body around Aiden to be involved. She was too good for him.

I took a drink of my beer to keep from staring at the three's-a-crowd effect. Beckett was treating me better than Aiden treated his wife, but would it stay that way? Kate didn't know she was married for the inheritance. This ruse was as much for her benefit as Gentry's. If our lie got out, it could hurt two people now, not just his dad.

I scanned the room full of good ol' boys talking up Gentry and classmates of the brothers milling about. Some had spouses, others were acting like they never crossed paths in this small town.

On the way here we'd passed the Cartwrights' ranch and it had been an eye-opener. Ratty fences, worn barns, diminutive cattle. But the most startling part was the house—a trailer home that looked like it was better off with plywood over the windows and a condemned sign.

True, thieves used what they stole or fenced it quickly. And smart thieves avoided looking like they'd come into a sudden cash flow, something I knew all too well. You didn't steal a diamond necklace and then wear it the next day, or sell it and strut around in a new watch. Bristol's pickup had been sitting outside and she wasn't cruising through town in a truck even half as flashy as the high school bro-mobile Beckett had.

If they were the den of thieves Beckett accused them of being, then they were the wiliest crooks I'd ever seen. Yet somehow I doubted there was much extra flowing the Cartwrights' way.

The venom Beckett aimed toward Bristol bothered me. I was more like this mysterious Bristol than I was like him.

My throat was suddenly tight and I couldn't stomach the last tepid swallow in my bottle.

I nudged Beckett to get his attention. "Want another?"

"I can go with—"

"I have to use the restroom too." I hadn't meant to interrupt him, but I needed space to breathe. After last night, we'd crept back into the house and gone our separate ways to sleep. He'd been up and gone early in the morning and I'd only caught that glimpse of him and his brothers leaving.

"Nothing for me."

His arm slipped off of me and I wound my way out of the room. The din of conversation dulled with the closing of the door. I skimmed the perimeter of the bar and grill to get to the restrooms. People stared, some discreetly, others blatantly. The small-town stare, Beckett called it. I breathed a sigh of relief when I hit the darkened hallway. If anyone knew me at all, it was as Beckett's fiancée. Tonight was the night we'd shared our good news.

I felt like a fraud in so many ways. I was still way more put together than usual. My look was as fake as the lady Aiden was talking to.

And call it silly, but once I'd roamed outside during my lunch break, I'd spotted a few barn cats slinking between buildings and gotten homesick. How was Kitty doing? The food I'd given her was probably gone. Adam might feel up to feeding her, but when I called him earlier, he was despondent and claimed I had woken him from a nap.

Did you eat?

Eva, you're not my mother.

I had wanted to scream, *Then take care of yourself!*

But I'd just hung up. I had to get home soon. Once we got home, would things between Beckett and I change? This thing between us was just blooming. When we landed in Denver, would it wilt or blossom?

I was about to push into the restroom when someone came out.

"Oh, excuse me." I made to go around.

"You're Beckett's fiancée." It wasn't a question, the rich voice direct.

A woman about my age towered over me, studying me. Waves of light auburn hair fell to her shoulders. She looked like she was a brush 'n' go girl. Her green eyes were shrewd and she wore what the guys had worn earlier—worn jeans, a button-up emerald shirt with her sleeves rolled up, and I didn't have to look down to know there was a set of dusty cowboy boots on her feet.

There was nothing soft about this woman. Her gaze was hard and her face was angular. She was like a cut diamond without the sparkle. Not one stitch of makeup, but it wouldn't suit her. She was gorgeous.

My first thought was that she needed more laugh lines. I didn't get the impression she laughed nearly enough in life. But who was I to talk?

Oh, she'd asked me a question. "I am. Did you go to school with him?" I'd been introduced to so many people that it became a default question.

She shrugged. "Sort of. I'm sure you've heard of me." She arched an auburn brow. "Bristol. *Cartwright*."

I didn't sense hostility. More like a resigned *get it over with*. "Am I going to burst into flames talking to you?"

The corner of her mouth twitched. "The Kings will do that to me if they learn I'm talking to you."

I cocked my head, only more curious about her. "Why are you then?"

"Might as well get it over with or you might accidentally be nice to me and then get in trouble."

"I can talk to who I want to."

She gave me an *are you sure about that* look. "Right. I won't be waiting by the phone for a sleepover invite. But congrats."

A shadow fell over us. "Bristol, what the hell are you doing harassing Eva?" Easygoing Dawson had morphed into an uptight asshole. Bristol's jaw tightened and I swear she winced at his volume. I recalled her history and guessed her dad probably bellowed around the house.

She whipped around to face him, but she also tensed as if preparing herself. "Dawson King, do you control the use of public areas too?"

"We wouldn't want you to pass on fleas."

She winced. "It was lice. Get your insults straight if you're going to bring up shit from when I was eight." She pushed past Dawson. Beckett was behind him, shooting Bristol another glare.

Dawson turned toward me and opened his mouth. I held my hand up. "If I was in danger, I'd thank you for your interference, but Bristol hasn't done anything to me and I was enjoying talking to her."

"You don't know her," Dawson shot back.

"Do you?" My volume went up. "I hope so if you're going to tease her about getting lice as a kid. Not all of us grew up with money." I gave him a pointed look. "Or parents who weren't addicts, or loaded."

He clenched his jaw, the muscles jumping on either side.

Beckett came to my side. "What Dawson's trying to say—"

"He hates her, I get it. But he doesn't get to dictate who I talk to—or run them off." I crossed my arms.

Beckett's expression mirrored Dawson's. "Her family is responsible for our mother's death."

"The meth-head was," I said quietly. "And she was just a

kid too. You blame her family as guilty by association. Maybe they were just desperate for a hired hand and couldn't afford to be picky."

"He could've passed on a tweaker," Dawson said as if that made it clear. I disagreed. I could spot an alcoholic after working in the bar, but I didn't have firsthand knowledge of what a meth addict looked or acted like. "He could've looked for someone else. And Bristol might've been ten like me, but she sure as shit didn't lose sleep over Mama's death. She refused a ride to the funeral. Neither one of them showed."

I stared at Dawson. He was upset because she'd refused a ride with a family who hated hers? He had no idea how the other half lived. "They say money doesn't buy happiness, but it does buy opportunities. Have you ever had to decide between a one-dollar carton of spaghetti or a buck for a bottle of no-brand shampoo? Because I have. Do I eat for a couple of days, or do I wash my body for a couple of months because shampoo is a better hair and body wash than soap?"

Dawson looked away, his jaw working. I looked at Beckett. He didn't avoid my gaze but he was studying me much like I had studied Bristol.

"I didn't remember the lice thing until she said it," Dawson said quietly. "I wasn't intending to insult her...like that anyway. And she harasses everyone. Why would I think you were different?"

"Do they harass her first?"

Dawson shrugged and gave me a lazy grin. "Well, that'd be fifty-fifty. She doesn't hold her opinion in."

Beckett put his hand on my shoulder. "Are we all right here?"

I nodded. "Did you come looking for me?"

"One of my classmates said they saw Bristol lurking, and since she tried to ingratiate herself into Kate's and Kendall's lives at one time, we were worried about you."

"Yes, she was so terrifying." My sarcasm wasn't lost on them. This Cartwright thing was a war, but I'd won a battle. "I'm sure Kendall took two whole minutes to befriend her."

"She'd probably put Bristol to work spying on Dad's diet. If he so much as sniffs a cheese stick, she's going to know."

I smiled, but my heart still pounded. They'd handled my outburst, but it didn't change a thing. They hated Bristol because they'd been taught to. I didn't know Bristol, but the way they treated her? I was seeing my future.

 eckett

THE NEXT TWO days passed too quickly. I was going to have to get back to Denver. To my empty office. To all my online contacts. Back to interacting only with my driver and the flight crew.

I brushed off my dusty jeans and led Black Gold to the barn. Between the four of us boys and the two guys Dawson had on payroll, we'd gotten the cattle moved in record time with little incident. The bite in the air promised snow flurries once the sun fell.

Finished with Black Gold, I put her back out to pasture and wandered to the house. Dawson was going over instructions with his hired hands. Aiden had already cleaned up and left with Kate. Dad and Kendall were staying for another week, but Xander was flying out in the morning.

He met me on the porch. "You two going to," he threw up air quotes, " 'watch the stars' again?"

I was afraid my brothers would think our nightly excursions were…well, exactly what they were. Fucking Eva in the front seat, backseat, standing up, I didn't care. I'd had to restock condoms and at least we had the fiancée thing to hide behind instead of everyone thinking I was sleeping with my assistant. Which I was. I also wasn't sleeping on the couch anymore, but the house was a no-sex zone.

"She's a city girl. She wanted to see the stars." I guess I lied when it came to Eva.

"Right. She's also not fake. How's this engagement thing working?"

"We'll see when we get home I guess. I have three and a half months before I have to say I do."

Xander whistled. "A four-month courtship. That's a pretty quick turnaround. You two are going to have to be ready to marry for real by then."

I could be ready now. Waking up to her mussed pixie hair was becoming one of the favorite parts of my day. Then there was the way her body clenched around mine. I'd never been so connected with someone. "It'll be a conversation, that's for sure. What about you? You're turning twenty-eight next. A year and two days after my birthday."

Xander's expression went from interested to shut down. "Can you imagine if I don't marry? It'd be just another epic failure in Dad's book."

"He doesn't think you're a failure." At Xander's lifted brow, I clarified, "Yet."

"Exactly. But I don't know, man. Aiden didn't have to look hard. Neither did you. At least Eva's good people if you two go your separate ways. Who am I going to meet?"

"You're rich and you travel the world. Use that."

"I'm not rich," he muttered and I wanted to hear more. Like all of us, he'd gotten a healthy stipend during college. "I work my way through traveling the world. Who am I going to win over when they have to squat in a latrine to do their business, then come out to the field to work for room and board?"

"She's out there. Still writing?"

Xander was an unusual journalist. He wrote for fun on serious topics like the hurricane devastation in Puerto Rico and the ever-shrinking glaciers. "Yes, but I think I'm going to need a pen name. King slams a few doors shut when I'm reporting on the environment."

"A publication doesn't want a piece on wind energy from an oil heir?"

"Pretty much. Or I get the 'We're interested in serious queries only' line."

"Ouch."

He shrugged. "I'll use a different name, no worries. But anyway, I wanted to say that I'm really happy for you and Eva."

"Seems a little premature." I was happy too. The way she'd stood up to Dawson—and me—at the party only made me respect her more.

"I've never seen you this way with a girl."

"Because she's not a girl. We haven't really hung out enough as adults for you to know what I'm like with my girlfriends." Still, I couldn't help but compare. I lived for kissing her graceful neck and eliciting those breathy sighs. I loved how she still called me Beckett when everyone else called me Beck. When I woke up before her, I watched her, though not long enough to be creepy. But the way she slept on her side, her face buried in the pillows and the blankets up to her ears, was adorable and so at odds with the sexy vixen that could ride me until my eyes crossed.

"Beck." Xander's flat expression said he was reading my mind. "You remember when you met me in LA during one of my layovers? You and that Insta-whatever star?"

"Sahara. She modeled lingerie."

"On social media. Anyway, she whined the whole time about all the meat in the restaurant we met at. You said there was a vegan store next door and we'd still be in the restaurant when she got back."

It'd kind of been a dick move, but Sahara's incessant critiques of the food had annoyed me. "So, what's your point? Eva likes steak."

"She's special. Just sayin', I'd rather have an Eva as part of the family than a Sahara. Don't fuck it up."

"Why do you think I'd be the one to fuck it up?"

He rolled his eyes. "Lesson number one, it's always our fault."

Xander's words rang in my ears as I walked into the house. It was so early in my relationship. We hadn't hit any rough patches, unless I counted the hallway at the party. But like Xander had said, she was right. Didn't mean I was extending an invitation to Bristol to be friends, but I'd quit being openly hostile. She'd had a shit life growing up and none of us doubted it.

I stomped the grit off my boots but kept them on. The door hung open a few inches. Eva was behind the desk, her hair slicked off her face. She hadn't worn that style since we'd been here, but seeing her comfortable in my family home satisfied something in me.

She glanced up from the laptop at the sound of my boots scuffing the floor. "Hey. Done so early?"

My brothers and I had put in a few late nights. Getting the Cartwrights' cattle cut from our herd had been tricky. They didn't want to be parted, but me and Dawson had herded them back, then Dawson had called Bristol and hounded her to "fix the damn fence or you're gonna owe us for the tonnage they eat." He'd been tamer than usual, but from the volume of Bristol's voice coming through the phone, the conversation hadn't gone well.

"The cattle are moved." I shuffled into the office, swung the door shut behind me, and plopped in the chair across from the desk. The heavy weight of my limbs wasn't unpleasant. As much as I liked technology and had the mind for it, I missed labor that required more than a mouse click. "We'll be flying out in the morning. Unless you have a pressing reason to go back tonight."

Her expression flickered. Did she need to get back to her brother? "Tomorrow morning is fine. You have a lot of meetings scheduled when we get back, but I lined them up starting next week."

"Good plan." I didn't want to go back to meetings. I wanted to wake up to her for a few more mornings. Would she be open to sleeping over when we got back to Denver?

Our relationship had started here. What was Denver going to be like? Going back to my quiet house? My quiet office? This house wasn't always quiet, but I was content here and it wasn't just because of Eva. But the fact that I was still in a good place with Eva here wasn't insignificant.

I'd never been content with a girlfriend. My mind never stopped blazing through my to-do list, evaluating programs and their viability in the market, who I needed to call to make it happen, and trying not to get lost in the simmering rage left behind after Mama's death.

That last thought gave me pause. I didn't think about Mama most days. Yet when I was in the middle of a deal and found out the other party was begging for a second chance after destroying their own life and others, I had no mercy. But that rage had died down. Two of the scrapbooks she'd made me were packed in my suitcase.

"I hate to bring this up, but Dr. Herrera called." Eva glanced at the tablet in front of her. "She's getting a ton of buzz about her app and she's had some amazing offers—her words, not mine—and she wants to give you one more chance."

"That's bold. What did you tell her?"

Eva smiled, but I detected a hint of sadness. "I said I'd talk to you. I'm not the boss."

"But you know the answer."

She clicked her tablet off. "I do, but I'm not the one who should tell her." The hard edge to her voice told me what she thought of my decision.

"You think I'm making a mistake."

"I don't know about your business or how you make money, but I think that if you're basing your entire decision on her son's history, then maybe that isn't the best strategy."

I dragged in a deep breath. This was a sticking point between us. I pointed to the floor next to the desk. "I found Mama lying there."

Eva recoiled and blinked, her gaze darting to the area I indicated. "Geez, Beckett."

"She was unconscious and I was screaming for Dad. I can't just forget that."

Her eyes glistened but her jaw was tight. "What happened to the attacker?"

"Life in jail."

She nodded once, but the news didn't lighten her expression. "I forwarded Dr. Herrera's contact information."

"Eva…"

"You don't have to justify your decisions to me." She clicked off the tablet.

"It's not that, but your opinion matters to me. I was trying to show you how important this is to me."

"What if…" She trailed off. After a moment, I wasn't sure she'd keep going but she did. "What if your mom had been the addict?"

It was like someone had tied a cinder block to my feet and dropped me through a hole in a frozen pond. Cold washed through me, then anger because how could she say such a thing, and then I forced myself back to the present.

"But Mama wasn't. She didn't hurt anybody and she raised four boys who haven't beaten anyone to death."

Her lips pressed into a line. "Okay. So, I'm done for the day. Is Dawson making supper or does he need a hand?"

The abrupt subject change didn't fool me. She was upset with my decision, but she was still talking to me. I'd gladly take the shift in conversation.

"He's trying to live it up before we all leave and he's back to reheating for one."

She gathered her items and walked around the opposite side of the desk than the one I had indicated.

"I'm sorry I—"

"Don't be." She spun on me and for a moment, the conversation between us was forgotten. Compassion shone in her eyes. "Don't be. You didn't have to come in here. I could've worked somewhere else."

"I've been avoiding this place too long. I mean, if I hadn't cleaned out Dawson's room, then Dad wouldn't have told us stories all night long and there wouldn't be scrapbooks in my luggage."

She smiled and my anxiety drained away. I don't know if I'd ever change the way I was in business, but I didn't want it to come between us. "Which ones did you pick?"

"The I Love Me one, of course. And the one from when I was a baby. I also snuck in the assless-chaps photo."

Her laugh put me more at ease. "Kate still needs a copy."

We left the office. Dawson was in the kitchen. "What'd y'all feel like tonight?"

"You take requests?" I asked.

"Nope, I was just curious." He grinned and turned to rummage through the cupboards. "I'm making spaghetti."

"Pasta from a cowboy?" Eva was heading for the stairs. "You're full of surprises."

"Wait until you see my balls." Dawson straightened and winked. "They're a handful. My meatballs are good too."

She laughed as she climbed the stairs. "Promises, promises."

I jogged up behind her. Before I could ask if she wanted to go for a drive tonight, she glanced over her shoulder.

"I think I'm going to pack. I want to go to bed early for the flight tomorrow."

A pit opened in my gut. Her message was clear. There'd be no stargazing tonight.

va

I GLANCED AT THE TIME. Today was a traditional workday. Beckett was in the office all day. In the last three weeks, I'd flown with him to Providence, Seattle, and LA. Tomorrow, we were supposed to jet to Lincoln, Nebraska, and my excitement about the traveling had faded. Each trip just made me feel torn in two.

Nebraska was because he'd heard about an app designer who was looking for a backer. The designer planned to make an app that would tally discount points and notify the customer of what they qualified for and when. It'd consolidate so many apps that even I was excited for it, and I didn't shop enough to earn rewards points.

Old habits died hard, and other than groceries that were a few Michelin stars better than bologna and my work outfits —like the black jumpsuit I wore today—I didn't shop. The new couch and bed I'd bought were necessities more than luxuries. And I'd bought them both on sale, during the brief spans I was in town long enough to hunt for them.

For once I didn't have to worry about when I could check on Adam. I was going home at a normal time today. I half wondered if Beckett had made up trips to keep me with him. When we were in Denver, I slept at home and I never invited him over.

My phone pinged. Beckett. *Come in here, please.*

It was almost time to go home. Kitty's kittens were moving around and each day I worried that they'd stray farther from their sparse den. My heart crawled into my throat every time I did a head count. Logging out of everything, I told myself that they were fine. I'd go home and there'd be five little fuzzy heads.

"Everything okay?" As I rounded the door into Beckett's office, I slowed. The blinds were drawn. His suit jacket was off and his tie was undone. "I didn't think you did informal Friday."

He leaned back. "I don't. Come here."

My body tingled. The workday was over. Since we'd returned from Montana, he hadn't worked past five on days when we were in the office. He was thoughtful about my family needs, and he'd been asking leading questions that were getting harder to evade.

I walked closer and he patted his lap.

"Mr. King, if I didn't know better, I'd think you were seducing me." I had no doubt I was reading him right. Whenever we had the opportunity to have sex, he'd get that hot look in his eye. His body would relax and he wouldn't have to say anything before my body was wet and primed for him.

"I was Mr. King two minutes ago. Now, I'm 'harder, Beckett, harder.' " He pulled me onto his lap.

It was dark and cold outside and while Rick would give me a ride home, I'd be out in ankle boots looking for kittens.

He noticed my hesitation and paused. "Do you have to rush home?"

Yes. And no. It's not like I was going to swoop in and save the kittens at the last minute. And Adam was stable. No better, but not really worse. The better-quality food had given his mood a small boost. Small, or I was lying to myself because I felt guilty for being gone all the time.

I unbuttoned the jumpsuit. "No, but you'll have to be quick. This outfit isn't one you can just hitch the skirt up on."

"You never wear clothing I can just hitch the skirt up on."

"The time on the plane, going to DC."

"Leggings." He nuzzled my neck. "Always with the leggings, but I like how you challenge me."

I kissed him because it was easier than letting him see my anxiety that I was feeling like two different people. With him, I had to pretend I could leave town as soon as his phone pinged. But I wanted to. I wanted to be with him, to sit on his lap and find out what he had planned for us in his office. Over his desk? Riding him on his office chair? Standing up against the window while Denver foot traffic flooded the sidewalk?

But the other part of me urged me to get home before dark. To check on Adam and Kitty because there was no one else that would. I hadn't even told Beckett about Kitty. It was like she was from that other life I led and if I let Beckett that close to her, he'd discover the rest about me.

He brushed the fabric of the jumpsuit over my shoulders and down my arms. Leaving my bra in place, he scooted out of his chair until my feet hit the floor.

"Lean over the desk."

I did as he said and the sound of his zipper registered. He was making it quick. I was both grateful and frustrated. On our trips, we would get a night or two of lazy sex in the hotel, after which he treated me to meals I thought were for TV only. People like me didn't eat at fancy restaurants on the arm of tech giants.

I shoved my jumpsuit over my hips and it pooled at my feet. He laid kisses across my shoulders and his hands were everywhere until I was squirming and needy.

"Put your hands on the desk."

I planted them wide and spread my legs. He didn't waste time. I appreciated this part of him. When he could steal me for himself, he did. But when he sensed I needed to get home, he kept strict office hours and didn't work late. This would only set me back fifteen minutes, a half hour at the most, and I hated to think about our time together like that.

Rubbing his rigid length against my ass, he snaked his arms around me. His fingers were on my clit and again, he didn't play. I was bucking and gasping within minutes. I mourned the loss of his arm as he positioned himself and thrust inside.

"Beckett." His hard entries always caught me off guard. The sudden fullness, the exquisite pressure.

He set a pace that steadily increased. Leaning over me, pressing my chest into the cool surface of his desk, he plunged in and out. My arms were spread wide and I arched my back into my release, but refrained from calling out his name. Other offices bordered ours and I would be the one everyone gave "the look" to and talked about.

He grunted and slapped his hands next to mine, his left one covering my ring. He had an obsession about that ring, especially during sex. I'd never tell him that I took it off as soon as I left the office or right after Rick dropped me off.

When we were done, he popped into his office bathroom to clean up and I tugged my clothing back into place. It was like nothing had happened. We'd leave this office like professionals.

I turned around to wait for him out front, but found him

leaning against the wall, watching me. His expression was unreadable, and definitely not one I was used to seeing after we fucked.

"Let me take you home."

"Beckett…" The longing in his voice stopped me. He was ready for the next phase in our relationship, and God, I was too. But Adam.

He closed his eyes, nodded, and opened them again. "Rick should be waiting."

I didn't want to part like this. "Okay."

He nodded again and went to grab his suit jacket.

"I mean, okay. Take me home."

He jerked around to face me. "No, if you're not—"

"My brother's not fit for company. But you can…" I shrugged. "Drop me off." Like that was a stellar offer.

But his smile lit up like the Christmas lights already appearing in windows and yards. "I'll let Rick know."

Beckett had been driving himself so Rick could be my ride. We walked out together, looking like a power couple, except the balance of power was not weighted in my favor.

The car he used in Denver was not like his pickup in King's Creek, but the sleek black Mercedes was still all Beckett. I couldn't see him in a flashy sports car, but he wouldn't drive something sedate as Beckett King, CEO of King Tech.

He knew my address from my application. Had he ever done a drive-by? Did he wonder why I hadn't moved yet? I wasn't planning to. Not until I knew he wouldn't drop me as quickly as he had Adam and Dr. Herrera.

"What are you doing for Thanksgiving?" he asked.

"I usually work. This year, I don't know." *Make sure Adam ate.* Was it next week already?

"Want to come to King's Creek? Dawson thinks that since nothing blew up the last time we were all out, he can get us all there again."

"How many days?"

"However long I can get you away."

"Can I think about it?" I wanted to say yes, but we had that trip to Lincoln. Without me, he could fly right from Nebraska to Montana. I couldn't be away that long.

"Are we good, Eva?"

I blinked at him. He sensed that I was splitting in two and couldn't keep going much longer. I should be honest with him, but I couldn't help but think that the closer we got, the less likely he was to leave me.

"We're good." I squeezed his hand. "We're good. I just have some things I'm dealing with."

Streetlights glinted off his dark hair as he glanced at me. "I could help."

I could've laughed. He was the reason for what I was dealing with. He was the reason I couldn't be honest. He was the one I couldn't trust.

But I just said, "It's not only me in this situation. My brother's private."

"Is he at least open to getting help?"

I had no idea. Picturing Adam leaving the house, jingling his car keys in his hand like the old days, seemed like a giant leap. Would his car even start? He hadn't left the house for months and it had been cheaper for me to commute than to pay for insurance.

"I'm going to bring it up," I said. "I've had a stable income for a month so maybe he'd be willing to spend the money."

That was mostly the truth. Would he set up an appointment? He'd talk about doing it. Would he let me do it for him?

We reached my complex. Beckett's gaze landed on our peeling front door. Like the rest of the place, it needed a good scraping and a couple fresh coats.

"Fair warning," he said. "I'm not driving off until you're safely inside."

My heart sank. It was either open the door to my personal life a little more or sneak back out after he left, and that seemed too duplicitous. I gave him a sheepish smile. "I, um, haven't told you about Kitty."

"Who?" His full attention was on me again. At least it was off my low-income apartment. What did he think? I'd never been shy about the circumstances of my life, but having him witness it left an antsy sensation in my gut.

"A stray cat I've been feeding. She had kittens a month ago and I check on her before I go inside." When he did nothing but stare at me, I defended my actions. "I didn't tell you because your family has a thousand barn cats and I didn't want you to think I was an idiot for caring for one stray."

His brows lifted, but he laughed. "Yeah, but you never saw Dawson out there cuddling them. He's like a cat whisperer. We used to tease him about all the pussy he got." He leaned toward me. "Did you know that when he's feeling down, he'll go out there and sit for fun and get all loved up?"

"*No*. Does he really?" My smile was fueled by relief. Beckett wouldn't think I was wasting time and money on Kitty. "I can actually see that."

"Yep. Those cats are skittish of others, but I think he's named most of them."

I pointed out the bush Kitty was hunkered down under. "She's there for now, but the kittens are moving around a little. I'm worried one day…"

"Can you bring them inside?"

"Our apartment is small and Adam is allergic. Even if he wasn't, I'd need to get Kitty to the vet and then there's the supplies."

"And you'd need to be at home to have time for it all when

your jackass boss drags you around the country." He smiled and pulled me closer for a kiss. "Check on Kitty, but I'll wait to leave until you get inside."

"Good night, Beckett."

"It won't be without you."

I fought the urge to dissolve each time he was sweet and considerate. He acted like that in so many important ways, but not where it really counted for us.

Getting out of the car, I buried my hands in the pockets of my new coat that was so much warmer than the secondhand parka I'd bought a few years ago. Kitty was easy enough to find and all her kittens were there. Was she warm enough? Should I get her inside?

No. I was leaving town tomorrow.

Sighing, I went to the front door and made sure to wave to him before I stepped inside. Closing it behind me, I counted to thirty before checking the peephole to see if he'd driven away.

No Mercedes.

"Did he drop you off?" Adam let go of the curtain behind him. Shit, had he been looking out? How visible would he have been?

"Yes."

"Cutting it close." He picked up his controller. "Is this still all pretend?"

"What do you mean?" I knew exactly what he meant.

He tossed the controller down. "You're flying all over with him, pretending to be his fiancée, and that ring? Don't think I haven't noticed."

I clenched my hand into a fist, but there was no point in hiding. "The ring had to be real to fool his dad."

"He's rich. He's good-looking. He bought you a ring. And he takes you everywhere with him. Don't tell me you don't have feelings for him." Adam's expression was clear for once, clearer than it had been for months. He was focused, his gaze as sharp as the mind behind it. I'd always envied his intelligence. Mom had always said his bio dad had been wicked smart, just low on common sense and a commitmentphobe.

"I…" I had so many feelings for Beckett it was hard to sort them.

"Dammit, Eva. I warned you. He likes you too?"

I could only nod and wring my hands. Tears burned my eyes. I wasn't a crier, but when it came to Beckett, emotions I'd never known popped up.

"Let me guess, he doesn't know who I am to you."

Pressing my lips together, I shook my head. "It's going to be ugly, Adam. He's uncompromising when it comes to…"

"People like me." Adam knew me better than anyone, and he'd known exactly what I couldn't say.

"And people like me."

He reclined back with a huff. "I can't believe you did this."

"What was I supposed to do?" It was hard not to shout, but I managed to keep my tone down before Mike You Motherfucker came storming over. His lady friend had let him back in a couple of weeks ago. "We were broke. You say you're applying for jobs, but I don't know. It's all I can do to get you to eat. You shower like once a week. I'm terrified I'll go on one of these business trips and come home and find you dead on the couch."

His expression turned hard. "People won't hire a guy who's done time for stealing."

All my righteous anger drained out. "Of course. I know." But did I? Other people got out of prison and got jobs, right? "Look, I thought that maybe if he and I grew close enough, he'd be understanding."

"Eva… People like the Kings don't want to be bothered with our drama. And this will be drama for him."

"I think he's falling in love with me." Saying it hurt. Never had I thought I'd find a guy like him and that he'd fall for me just as hard.

"And you're already in love with him. Tell him. Just fucking tell him and get it over with." Adam picked up his controller and went back to his game. "Then two of us can feel worthless."

I wanted to argue that it wouldn't turn out like that. That Beckett would forgive me, but the words wouldn't come.

Stepping out of my shoes, I shrugged off my coat. I hung it up and trudged to my bedroom, bypassing supper. My phone buzzed. Flopping down on my creaky bed, I pulled it out.

Beckett. *Just say when and we'll move Kitty and the kittens to my place. I can pay more to have the housekeeper look after her.*

A hot tear streaked down my cheek. Looking around my plain box of a bedroom, my gaze landed on my suitcase. I kept it half packed. Adam didn't think Beckett would stand with me. Why was I seeing him if I thought so too?

I sent a message back to Beckett. *When we get back from Lincoln, think maybe I can stay at your place for a night or two with them?*

Cringing, I stared at the screen. Would he be offended that I was willing to sleep over at his place for the cats but not just because of him? *Don't worry about supplies. I've got it covered.*

A smile crept over my face, then died. At least when I told him about me, the cats would be safe with him. He wasn't coldhearted enough to toss them out in the cold.

It was just me I was worried about.

eckett

IT WAS like I was ten again. Except a sleepover with a woman who'd be naked in my bed was so much better than Willis Jepson, who used to chew on my toy cows.

The workday was ticking down. A few days ago, I'd had Rick pick up cat supplies. He'd dropped a few armloads off at the house: litter boxes, a kennel for acclimation, cat food, treats, and a list of veterinarians in the area. He'd put the carrier in my car and sent me a few links about the best way to capture strays.

On the flight to Lincoln, while Eva answered emails and sent queries my way, I read up on how best to care for stray cats and their kittens. I knew some things. The stories about Dawson hadn't been a joke. Cats loved him. They didn't mind me and I didn't mind them, but Kitty would bring me closer to Eva.

When it came to Eva's home life, I was shut out like I was

standing outside Fort Knox with nothing but a lock pick. She had said her brother's name was Adam, but none of my searches on Adam Chase turned up anything. I was worried about him. She clearly loved him and if anything happened, it'd destroy her.

My phone pinged. Someone had entered. I glanced up and did a double take. What the hell was she doing here?

One of my exes, Terra Scalia, marched up to the desk and requested to see me, a congenial, but predatory, smile on her face. Instead of making Eva dance for Terra, I went out.

Terra awarded me her TV-ready smile, the one that could be seen each night on the six o'clock news. "Beck, how nice to see you again."

I smiled only as much as necessary. I didn't trust her as far as she could run in her pin-thin stilettos. "Terra, what brings you by? I thought you'd be getting ready for your segment."

She feathered her light hair out of her eyes and preened. "Didn't you know? I'm on the morning show."

"Congratulations." That was as much small talk as I could take. Since discovering that she'd tried to log in to my computer, I had told her I didn't want to see her again and let her figure the rest out.

Her smile faltered and she looked between me and Eva. "Did I read the announcement correctly?"

Eva's pleasant work smile dimmed and her eyes said that she'd rather melt into the flooring than face Terra. Eva had been born and raised in Denver and had worked at a sports bar. I could guarantee that the evening news had been on often enough that she knew who Terra was.

"Yes, we're engaged. Eva, meet Terra Scalia." Terra would want me to introduce her as an anchor on the local news, but I didn't have to make her happy anymore.

Terra stuck her hand out and smiled demurely. "So nice

to meet you, Eva. I can't believe Beck here actually thinks he can settle down." Her laugh grated on my nerves.

I was done with her games. "What brings you to my office?"

"Could we talk in private? Business." She winked at Eva.

That didn't relieve me like it should. People might claim I was a workaholic, but Terra was her job. Her job came first, and she would trash anything in her way up the news and entertainment ladder. "We're about to close, but sure, I can spare a few moments."

I exchanged a glance with Eva before I disappeared behind the partition. She looked more curious than upset, so that was promising.

When I returned to my desk, Terra sat across from me, her lacquered lips twisted in a smile that suggested we were sharing a secret. "Your assistant? I would think that would be bad for your image."

"It just worked out that way. How can I help you?"

Terra pursed her lips, but recovered with a wide smile. If I hadn't dated her and been on the receiving end of her displeasure, I might've missed it.

"I wanted to ask how your dad was doing."

A cold wave splashed through my veins. What the hell was she doing here asking about Dad? I set up shop in Colorado because my family's business stayed out of the state. We had oil wells in Montana and North Dakota, and Aiden was trying to break into Texas. But Colorado was my state and blissfully free of those nosy about King Oil. I should've known that of all people, Terra would be the one who showed up on my doorstep wanting to know more. "He's well. Why do you ask? You never even met him while we were dating."

There was that brief flash of annoyance again. "Not for

lack of trying, but you guarded your family almost as tightly as you guarded your business."

I hadn't needed to guard my family when I was with her. Up until a month ago, I'd been avoiding Montana and everything it involved.

"I heard that he'd been in the hospital, and so soon after he married that young girl. What does that mean for King Oil?"

I leveled Terra with a stare. "No comment."

She drew back like she was offended, but I knew her better. "Beck, I heard and I was worried about you. I know your dad is the only parent you have left."

"That's a low blow even for you, Terra."

She narrowed her eyes. "I wasn't using you to get a story on your company or your family."

"The ten failed login attempts say differently."

She blanched, and not even she could recover quickly enough. Busted. "You thought I was trying to hack your computer?"

Did she think I was stupid? That I hadn't covered all the angles? "I can pull up the security footage if you like."

Her mouth dropped open and a gasp squeaked out. She took a moment to gather her thoughts and I was okay letting her. This didn't need to end ugly. "You act all holier than thou, Beck, but you're fucking your assistant. Bad look for a CEO, isn't it?"

And it was going to be ugly. "Her name is Eva Chase and she's my fiancée." Sticking up for Eva didn't win me any favors.

Terra rose like a vengeful swan. "You think you're sitting at the top and the rest of us are so beneath you. You think your history is so spotless when your family rapes the earth for a buck. And then her." She whipped her arm toward Eva's desk. "You're just as fallible as the rest of us and I'm going to prove it."

I studied her. We'd dated for the typical six months before she'd started expecting more and I'd started suspecting her of more. But when I cut things off between us, she'd barely flinched. Where was this vitriol coming from? "Why me? Why now? I'm sure there are plenty of men in the world that did you wrong. Why are you here?"

She pressed her fingertips into the desktop until they turned white and leaned forward. "Because none of them can get me back into the anchor seat," she hissed.

Getting a straight answer from Terra was like squeezing a drop of water from a rock. It just didn't happen. But for once I believed her. "You're not going to find anything. Perhaps you should get a promotion the old-fashioned way." I rose and straightened my suit jacket. "By working hard and being good at your job."

Her glare could've curdled milk. She stormed out, but not before shouting at Eva. "You'd better hope you never make a mistake. That sanctimonious asshole will drop you like last year's iPhone."

She banged out of the door. For a second I was worried she'd leave a Terra-sized crack in the glass.

Eva was staring out into the hallway, her face white like Terra was her own personal nightmare. The tormented look was perplexing.

I crossed to her. "Are you all right?"

She blinked and cleared her throat. "That was eventful."

"That's Terra." I swept my gaze over Eva once more. One hand was closed tightly around her phone and the other was clenched against her thigh. "Are you sure you're okay?"

"Admittedly shaken up. I don't look forward to my name being splashed about like I'm tabloid fodder. What about you? What was she here for?"

"I'm surprised you didn't hear her shouting." I took a deep breath and cut my gaze toward the door. Terra wouldn't come storming back...would she? "She'd heard Dad was in the hospital."

"But not why?"

I nodded. "It's nothing more than a rumor. He might be charming, but when it comes to confidentiality, he's a pit bull. No one at the hospital would've talked." I shrugged because what else could I do? "But we can't stop the rest of the town from speculating."

"Does she have a grudge against you? Did things end badly?" She shook her head and waved off her question. "Never mind, it's none of my business. It's not like I'm gonna bring up Irving and how I found another girl's underwear in his glove box."

"One, I want to hear the story. Two, of course it's your business. She marched in here and yelled at you as much as she did at me." It was after closing time and we had to get her cat, but I perched on the edge of the desk like I had on her first day. We'd come so far since then. "It didn't, and as bad as it could've. She tried to get into my work computer, and after I found out, I broke things off. Told her I wasn't interested in seeing her anymore. She was hurt but she didn't pursue me."

"You didn't tell her why?"

"I thought she'd figure it out, but apparently she didn't. When I told her today that I knew what she'd done, she still tried to backpedal out of it. But since my last name is in the title of two successful companies, she sees me as an easy path to getting her anchor spot back."

"I guess that morning show wasn't quite the promotion she made it sound." Eva didn't sound spiteful. She wasn't championing Terra like she did Bristol, but she didn't look sympathetic toward her either.

I stroked my finger down her soft cheek. "You're not like anyone I've ever met."

Her expression flickered and her brows drew together. "What do you mean?"

"My ex came in here insulting you and berating me and you're not pissed at her."

I couldn't quite name her next expression, but she almost looked guilty. "I don't condone what she did at all. I guess I just know what it's like when you have a crazy moment and you don't feel like there are any other options. At least she didn't find anything."

"There's nothing to find." There was so much about Eva that I still didn't know. It was times like these that reminded me how new this relationship still was.

I held my hand out for her. "Shall we get Kitty and her five littles settled?"

She rewarded me with a smile. We locked up and went to the car, but the drive to her place was quiet. I didn't bother trying to make conversation. My mind was preoccupied with what Terra knew, how hard she was gonna try to find out more, and whether or not Eva would get dragged into it.

At her place, she took the lead with the cats. I was just fine holding the crate and watching her lure out the mama cat with a fresh packet of tuna. She didn't seem to care that the branches on the bush might snag her black leggings, or that her long cream coat could get smudged with dirt or worse. She gathered Kitty in her arms. The cat was not happy, but she was more interested in the tuna. We got her in the crate with fairly little drama and the rest of the packet of tuna.

I told her to stay with Kitty while I collected the five squirming kittens. "They're all here."

Relief crossed her face. "I've been so worried. We're

supposed to get snow soon and without leaves that bush isn't much protection."

"I'm sure she would've moved them somewhere else. You would've still seen her."

"She knows I have the food."

I tried not to be jealous of the cat as we drove to my house. Eva sat in the back with her and cooed and handled the kittens. When we entered the house, she carried the crate like it was a fragile vase. This part of Eva was fun to see. It was clear she hadn't wanted to get close to the cats only to lose them to traffic and weather.

"Go ahead and leave your coat and shoes wherever. I can put them away after we get the cats settled."

I showed her where my housekeeper Lois had set up a kennel. Eventually, they could have the room, then the whole house. I hadn't broached the subject of how many she planned to keep.

The cats got moved and she was on her knees in front of the kennel.

"Hungry?" I asked.

"Did I smell beer cheese soup and breadsticks when we walked in?"

"With extra breadsticks."

We ate just like the last time she'd been here. I had wanted her so much then. I always wanted her. This time we weren't going to be interrupted.

She was mine for the night. But I couldn't escape the feeling that even though she wore my ring on her finger, our engagement was more fake than ever.

va

I DIDN'T TELL HIM.

After the incident with Terra, I couldn't bring myself to tell him who Adam was, and more importantly, how innocent Adam was.

Montana certainly wasn't the place to spill my secrets. King's Creek probably didn't even have a taxi, much less an Uber, or a timely flight out of town when Beckett booted me on my ass.

Besides, I didn't want to ruin the holiday. Thanksgiving had been yesterday, but we were still at Dawson's with his dad and Kendall.

The guys were out looking at the renovations Dawson had made in one of the shops. I was in front of a crackling fire with Kendall. Talking to her was a weird cross between a nosy stepmother and a giggling best friend.

"So do you ride horses and stuff?" I asked.

"I had some friends in high school that had horses. They'd have me over for rides."

"I'd never touched a real horse until I was here last time."

Kendall's laugh was unreal. Light and delicate and it put me completely at ease. "A lot of people have never touched a horse. They need a lot of space and aren't like keeping a cat or dog."

I couldn't suppress my wistful sigh. "My parents planned to take us to a trail-riding place one year, but that year never came."

"I'm so sorry about your mom and dad."

"It's been ten years. I'm glad I can talk about them without getting swept under from the grief." An occasional tidal wave still toppled me, just not every day.

"I'm so glad you came into Beck's life. Things are going better between him and Gent."

That should help my guilt, but it didn't. What would happen to them if Beckett decided he was done with me? I guess it wouldn't be my problem.

But I'd worry. Gentry was a nice guy. Charming to the point of pushy, but he meant well. He pushed because he cared and I saw the difference even if it chafed Beckett and his brothers. I saw the difference because he reminded me of my dad, always encouraging me and Adam to do the best we could despite our limited funds.

Dad had been Adam's biggest champion. I couldn't imagine them not speaking to each other. But Gentry couldn't rule his boys like a boardroom.

"I hope that's all it takes for Xander." My heart practically stopped. Had I said that out loud?

"Right? And no worries. You're allowed to have an opinion about Gent and his boys. You can even speak it."

"It's rude and intrusive."

She leaned over the arm of the chair and whispered, "So are they."

We dissolved into giggles. The humor died quickly. Family dynamics. Like Adam and I. Our last conversation hung heavy between us. *Then two of us can feel worthless.*

She put her hand on my arm. "Oh, no. Did I say something wrong?"

"No, no. Just, since we're talking about family, I'm worried about my brother. We didn't leave things the best between us."

"Beckett mentioned a brother but that was it."

I nodded, allowing my floodgate to open an inch. "He's depressed. Severely depressed. He needs to get help. And I haven't had the tough talk with him."

"Why not?" Her tone was so warm, so concerned, that had to be why I said what I did next.

"Because part of it's my fault. Most of it, in fact. He gave up a lot for me and I took more in return. I was an ungrateful shit." I let out a long breath. There. I'd said it.

"I think it's natural to feel guilty. I don't know the story, but you're not the type to let someone suffer because of what you did."

She was right. She didn't know the story. "It's something I have to live with for the rest of my life, and it's something that Adam's living with every day."

Kendall's brows were drawn. She looks so earnest on my behalf, it was clear what a good person she was. I hadn't had the chance to get to know many Kendalls. "As the oldest, I can say that whatever happened, I doubt he blames you. You're here, healthy, and happy. That's the most important thing."

I wanted to believe her, but I concentrated on the flickers of flames to keep from crying.

"Have you been able to talk to anyone about it?"

The question wasn't humorous but it made me chuckle. "I know this is going to surprise you, but I don't have many friends."

"That does surprise me. Kate asked how you were doing. Did she ever get your number?"

That news surprised me. But then if I was going to marry into the family, Kate and I would be sisters-in-law. "I didn't have a chance to talk to her much. She seemed really nice."

Kendall's enthusiastic nod confirmed how nice Kate actually was. If she got that type of reaction from someone like Kendall, then she must walk around with a halo. "If you want to talk about gripes with brothers, mine is with Aiden. She's a gem and he doesn't know her value."

I didn't know Aiden or Kate very well, but I had been watching people my whole life. Others might feel that way about Aiden's behavior toward Kate, but I saw more. "Maybe with you helping out at the office, he can spare some attention for his private life. He seems like a guy driven by expectations."

"He does work really hard. He's always working." She wrinkled her nose. "I feel like shit now."

"I didn't mean to make you feel bad. Catering was one of my jobs. Waiting on people was my main priority, but anticipating their needs was another. We catered to a lot of affluent clients. I've seen people treat their spouses like they don't mean more than used toilet paper. At first glance, that's what I thought of Aiden, but I think there's more."

She sighed and rested her head in her hand, propping her elbow on the arm of the chair. "I'm glad we had this talk. Gentry is worried sick about all his boys and I try not to stress him out even more with my own concerns, but maybe I'm worrying too much." She chugged the rest of her wine until she'd drained the glass. "Anyway, I don't want to put my stressors on you."

"Friends talk. Or so I've heard."

She still had her glass in hand, but she scooted to the edge of her chair. "Well since you and Beckett are going to get married soon, you can call me Mumsie." Her smile was pure mischief. "I can't wait for the next family reunion, when I get to introduce Gentry's sons as my boys."

The image of a beaming Kendall showing off pictures of four grown men was hilarious. I could see her committing to the part and gushing about how well behaved the boys were and how good they were in school. "I want to hear all about it."

The guys came pouring in, a cold draft following in their wake.

My pulse fluttered when my gaze landed on Beckett. He had his cowboy hat on, his cheeks were pink from the bite in the air, and he was back in his boots. The beige coat he wore was similar to Dawson's. It must be some sort of Western workwear brand.

Dawson and Gentry took off their coats and gloves, but Beckett stayed dressed. "Want to go for a drive?"

I sucked in a breath. That was code for going out and fucking in his truck, which we'd done often, but that was after everyone was asleep.

Dawson snickered. "Is that what the kids are calling it nowadays?"

Beckett scowled at his brother. "To look at the stars. They're gorgeous this time of year. They look like they're so close you can touch them."

"He has a point." Gentry hung his hat on a peg by the front door. No matter how much I looked at him, I couldn't believe he'd just turned fifty. He could make millions off his skin regimen alone. "January and February are more spectacular. It's your reward for tolerating the cold in order to see them."

"You talked me into it." I left the warmth of the chair and the fire to get bundled in my coat and boots. A chill cascaded over my body, but Beckett would be warming me up soon enough.

I scurried into the big pickup that was becoming my favorite ride and not just because of the sex we'd had in it. I felt like I could relax inside of it and be me.

Beckett took his usual route out to the pasture, plowing through snowdrifts. I peered at the snow, worried we'd get stuck, but there wasn't enough to bog down the ride. Another ride, yes, but not this one.

He looked at me and my gut clenched at his hard profile in the dashboard lights. "You seem more relaxed than earlier this week."

"I needed to get away."

"Anytime, just say the word." He stopped at the top of the hill, but he didn't kill the engine. Heat continued to fill the cab, but he killed the lights.

This routine was comfortable. And so familiar. Doing anything with him was. I knew the flight crew and when their kids or grandkids had dance recitals. Rick's son was in hockey and he sent me videos his ex had taken of the boy playing. Then there was sleeping at Beckett's. With him and the cats in the house, and the fireplace going, it felt comfortable. And homey. To a level that exceeded my drab apartment.

Adam and I existed in that place. It wasn't our home. It's where we survived.

"What are you thinking about?" His tone was soft, concerned.

I had to be honest. "This engagement isn't so fake anymore, is it."

His expression didn't change, but he gave his head a little shake. "No."

"I told you it'd get confusing for us."

"Does it have to be?"

The next words spilled out of me. "My brother has done time."

"Like jail?"

I nodded and I couldn't look at Beckett. "He was found guilty of petty theft and breaking and entering."

He worked over my confession. "And he was in jail?"

"For a year. I had to drop out of school to keep our place, and then when we thought we were going to get back on our feet... Well, he was self-employed and it didn't work out." I was a fucking coward. Did I think that if I told Beckett sections of the story over the next few months that it'd be better? Obviously, I did because I didn't tell him the rest. "Then depression took him out like a wrecking ball and I kept working." And then I met Beckett.

"What'd he do?"

"He didn't do anything." *Just say it!* But it was all I could admit to.

"And you believe him."

"I know it," I whispered.

He considered me for a moment. "So he did time for a crime he didn't commit and then couldn't get his business off the ground?"

I nodded, a lump stuck in my throat, afraid I'd tell him everything and be flying home within the hour.

He took my hand and pulled it across the seat to him. "No wonder he's having a hard time. And no wonder you've kept your private life so private. You were afraid I'd treat you like a contract and walk away as soon as I found out about your brother."

Tears that I hadn't realized were gathered in my eyes streamed down my cheeks and I started shaking. How hard was it to be honest?

Impossible. Because I didn't want to lose Beckett. The guy who had been the villain in my story for so long was my Prince Charming now. Just like when I'd stolen that jewelry, I was greedy, looking out for myself. Only this time I cared who I hurt.

But we'd made it over this hurdle. Surely we could overcome the next one. The one where I told Beckett everything.

I'D BEEN AWAY for a solid week. Coming back into the apartment was a jolt back to reality.

Despite the late-afternoon sun and crisp, fresh air outside, the air inside was stale. Adam wore the same clothing I'd left him in and had built up a good scruff. So he wasn't shaving now. I slipped out of my boots.

He glanced over at me, my sudden entrance leaving him unfazed. "And she returns. How was the private jet and the ranch?"

"Good." Really good. I hadn't wanted to leave. The thought of sleeping on my thin twin mattress all alone was as unappealing as the rotting sandwich someone had thrown on the sidewalk outside of our complex. "Have you been eating?"

He rolled his eyes. "Yes, *Mother*."

The continuous clicking of the console was annoying. "When did you bathe last?"

"That would be none of your business." He kept his gaze on the TV, the glow giving him a nice cadaverous pallor. How much more weight had he lost this last month? Six weeks ago, when I'd met Beckett, I'd thought the extra money would help Adam.

I was a fool. It wasn't money he needed. And I had to quit coddling him. "You need help." Taking out my phone, I plopped on the couch next to him and started scrolling. "We're making an appointment."

He jerked his head at me, his stare incredulous. "What the hell are you talking about? I said I'd do it."

I gave him a steady look in return. "Have you?"

His jaw muscles flexed. I could see them way too clearly since his body fat was dropping.

"I think you should consider in-patient therapy."

"In-patient—" he sputtered. "You go away for a week with your boyfriend and you want to commit me? Are you trying to get me out of the picture so you can run off with him and not feel guilty?"

His words hit too close to home, but I'd replayed this conversation in my head on the flight back. Beckett had sensed I needed space and I took it. "I love you, Adam. You're everything to me. If I lose you too, I'll have no one."

"Except your rich boyfriend." He glared at the TV screen.

"Beckett isn't my brother. Only you are and you're killing yourself."

"Because of your boyfriend," he hissed.

"Because of me!" I shouted, then drew back. We never talked about what he'd done for me.

His jaw worked but he didn't say anything at first. "I should've been around for you more."

"You gave up everything to raise me. You dropped out of college and then kept working so I could go."

He shook his head. "I was so wrapped up in designing my own programs that I ignored who you were hanging out with, and what you were doing." The hand clutching the controller went limp, his precious device tumbling to the ground. "I was being selfish."

I scooted closer. When was the last time we'd hugged? "I was the selfish one. I was old enough to know better."

"You were only nineteen."

"You weren't much older when you had to finish raising me."

He released a long exhale and dropped his head on the back of the couch. "I don't want to be like this."

"I know you're capable of so much. I know you're not worthless."

He stared at the ceiling, his gaze fixated on a water spot. "Find whoever has the earliest opening and get me in." He squeezed his eyes shut. "I swear to God, Eva, I would've done it but I'm tired. I'm always so tired."

I squeezed his hand. "We'll find out what's going on. I'm not going anywhere."

While I was looking through listings, he watched me. "Did you tell him?"

My search stalled. "Not all of it. I said that you'd been in jail, but that you were innocent."

The corner of his mouth lifted, but there was no humor in the move. "You're missing some important details there."

"I know. I don't want to lose him, Adam." I couldn't look for another number through the fucking tears. Were all my repressed emotions coming back to haunt me this week?

"You won't. If he's foolish enough to let something like that scare him off, then he's the worthless one. Not you."

I appreciated his confidence, but sex only went so far and he could find an assistant that'd do just as well or better than me. What could I offer Beckett that'd be enough to put his mother's ghost to rest?

CHAPTER 20

eckett

THE ENTIRE WEEK was going to be spent in the office. The way Eva had been so quiet on the flight home convinced me she needed time at home. I had asked her to keep business trips off the schedule through Christmas. Holidays were harder when parents had been taken away. I didn't want to be the reason she left her brother at this time of year.

But we did have a date tonight. She didn't know where we were going, but I was pretty proud of myself for this one. And then she was coming over to see the cats. Since she'd shared her feelings the night we were in the pasture, I wanted to share my own.

I logged out of everything and rose. Had she been watching the clock as much as I had? When I got out to the main area, she had shut down everything.

"Ready?"

"For the surprise date? Of course." Her hair was styled

with a peak off to the side. One of my favorite looks, but they all were. Along with her outfits. Today, she was in maroon skinny pants and a fitted but fluffy white sweater. And those boots. Damn. Maybe it was the cowboy in me, but when she wore boots up to her knees, I was a goner.

Rick had the night off. I'd take her home when she was ready. No pressure to sleep over. Her brother needed her.

After we got settled in my car, she cut the silence. "Adam has an appointment. He's on board with getting help."

"Tough love?" I pulled out of the parking garage and into traffic. I'd never been to where our date was taking place, but I'd memorized the route. Couldn't have the GPS spoiling the surprise.

"A long talk." She peered out her window, her head tucked into the collar of her coat like the cutest turtle ever. "Where are we going?"

"Did I mention that it's a surprise?"

She chuckled. "I'm okay with a surprise."

"Hey, I was thinking…after Christmas, do you want to go on a getaway that doesn't revolve around my family?"

"I love your family, but what are you thinking?"

I hadn't realized how important it was to me that she got along with my dad and brothers. More than that, she liked them and they liked her. This woman was quickly becoming my world and it was about time I told her. "My cabin."

Her eyes went wide and she faced me. "The one in the mountains?"

I went there about once a year and had been thinking about selling it. Until meeting Eva. I couldn't wait to get her alone there. "That's the only cabin I have. Believe it or not."

"Wow." She reclined back. "That would be amazing. What do you even do out there?"

"Have sex."

She laughed. "Okay, I should've guessed."

"In the outdoor hot tub."

Her delighted gasp was worth it. "I've only seen those on TV."

"We can ski too. The lodge isn't far."

"I don't know how to ski."

I grinned. "You'll be the cutest newbie on the bunny hill."

"I bet you do, like, black diamonds and shit."

"When you grow up with three brothers, there's always competition. Xander broke his leg when he was fifteen. I goaded him into snowboarding a blue diamond before he was ready."

"You don't sound guilty."

I laughed. It'd been so long since I'd remembered the stupid crap we'd pulled as kids. "The previous year, I'd gotten a concussion from one of his bets. Dad almost didn't let us go skiing again."

She giggled. "Your poor dad." Delight brightened her features. "Look, there's the observatory. Have you ever been there?"

"Not until tonight."

The city shone in her eyes as she gaped at me. "That's our date?"

"Open house. I didn't want it to be so last minute, but I had to wait to see how cloudy it'd be. We get to see the stars up close." I pulled into the lot. "But I doubt we can have sex there."

For the next few hours, I was happy to let her take the lead, but I was just as interested. Never in my life had I thought I would be thrilled to spend an evening with a woman just looking at giant telescopes and a close-up of the moon. We pored through the history of the observatory, and when we left, Eva's smile made me think we had to do this a few times a year.

I was thinking long-term with her. This engagement was

no longer fake. I wanted to do everything to ensure that when she said "I do," she meant it. And that when the year was up, she wouldn't want to pocket her fifty million and bail. She was who I wanted my life to revolve around.

Who was I kidding? It already did.

≈

"I CAN'T BELIEVE how much they've grown in just a week." Eva was planted on the floor with two kittens in her lap.

Kitty had started our visit out by shifting around me, never quite touching, but I'd gotten a few pets in. She was a sucker for treats. Now, she was on my lap, purring up a storm.

"I think Lois spoils them." My housekeeper was on board with socializing them and it appeared she was doing a stellar job.

"She should add cat socializing to her resume. This is crazy." Eva nuzzled one cat and set it down, picking up another. Her stomach rumbled and she giggled. "I guess I'm ready for those breadsticks."

We said our goodnights to the cats and then washed up.

"I hope you don't mind beer cheese and breadsticks again." The moan she made when biting into a breadstick always went straight to my dick, and I wanted more of it. We'd have it every night if it were up to me.

"Mr. King, I think it's what comes after the breadsticks that you're after."

It was. But not quite in the way she thought.

We ate like we always did. At the island, turned into each other. I was rewarded with a moan, only she did it all the way through both breadsticks.

"God, Eva. You're killing me."

"Then I get what you didn't eat."

When had a relationship ever been this effortless? I'd been reluctant to date before and always kept my exes at a distance. I didn't blame them for wanting more. It was what healthy relationships progressed to.

This was the only relationship I wanted for the rest of my life and I couldn't hold it in anymore. "I love you, Eva."

She stopped midchew and swallowed. "Beckett?"

"I love you and I want this. I want you. And we don't have to change anything, and hell, if you're not ready to marry in two and a half months, we won't marry. But I want what we have forever."

"Are you…proposing…again?"

I gave her a small smile. "I guess I am."

She brushed her hands off and gave me her full attention. "I love you too, Beckett. And for now, I don't want to change anything. I want to take care of Adam and I don't want to let your dad down." She snuck her hands into mine. "I think we can keep our arrangement and keep on going. We can work it all out."

I lifted her off the chair into my lap. It wasn't easy on the stool, but I wasn't staying here long. I wanted to make slow, sweet love to her in my bed.

"You're everything I ever wanted." I nuzzled her neck.

"You're everything I never thought I could have," she murmured.

I carried her upstairs, leaving our soup half eaten.

I removed her sweater and she took off my shirt. I rolled down my pants and she rolled off her leggings. We worked in sync, anticipating the other's next move. I wanted to take my time with her bra and underwear. Unwrapping my fiancée was the greatest gift I could get.

When she was bare before me, I took my time putting the condom on, watching her chest rise and fall and her legs fall open, waiting for me. Climbing onto the bed, we didn't bother pushing the covers back or turning the lights on. She was bathed in shadow, her silky skin ready for my attention.

I dropped kisses all over her until I was settled between her legs, making her scream my name. Her knees were up to her chest and her back was arched and like my mind was a camera, I took a snapshot. She was so beautiful. Passionate. Because of me.

"Beckett." She laid her hands on my shoulders as I crawled back up her body. "That was intense."

I pressed a kiss to her neck, then to her lips. "I wanted to show you how I feel."

Her face filled with everything I felt about her. She felt the same.

I entered her, so slow it was painful. There was no rush. The way her body wrapped around mine, we were a perfect fit. "You're mine, Eva. You were made for me."

She put a hand on each side of my face. "Don't forget it. No matter what, please don't forget it."

Whatever she was getting at, it was important to her. So I set about showing her again. My muscles were tight and my body rigid, but I wasn't going to come without her.

I kept my pace relentless, stoking her passion until she was breathless and wiggling under me for more. I drew out the pleasure and watched her come. Ecstasy exploded across her face and her eyelids dropped shut and her mouth fell open. Her breasts strained against me and I kept pumping in and out of her heat, coated with her release.

Only when she was coming down did I let myself go. A hard thrust and I was spilling inside of her. We were closer than we'd ever been.

I wanted nothing more than to curl her in my arms and pass out with her at my side all night, but we'd each wish to clean up. Rolling to my side, I cradled her in my arms, my chin in her hair, our fingers entwined.

"Let me know when you need to go home."

She stroked a foot along my leg. "I can sleep over, but I'll need to run home before work in the morning for fresh clothes."

"Or you could just do laundry and walk around the house naked."

Her laugh made her shake in my embrace. "I guess. No one would see me. I assume you have a spare toothbrush."

"A King is always prepared."

"Then I'll steal one of your shirts and put my clothes in the wash. No one will notice I'm wearing the same thing."

"Only me, and I won't complain. But you should put those boots on. Just the boots."

She rolled away from me, but she was smiling. "I'll go grab them."

I enjoyed watching her select a T-shirt from the dresser. She grabbed her clothing and rushed out.

I lay on my back, staring at the ceiling, wondering how in the world I'd gotten to be such a lucky guy. A faint buzzing caught my attention. My phone was in my pants.

I slid down from the bed, grabbed my phone, and without looking at the screen shut it off. No one else needed to intrude on this night with Eva.

CHAPTER 21

va

"Fuck. Eva." His hips bucked off the bed.

I was bent over him, giving him morning head as my own way to show him how I felt.

His knees were spread, his ball sack tight, and he was propped on his elbows to watch everything I was doing to him. Then his head dropped back and he groaned.

I swallowed his hot release as it came, glad I could make him come apart like he did to me. When he was done, I snuggled into his side. He was splayed across the bed like I'd sucked all the energy from him.

"I need to—" He had to catch his breath. "I need to take care of you."

"You did last night. Several times." I hated to leave the cocoon of his body, but we both had to get to work and he was my ride. "Did you tell Rick that he didn't need to pick me up?"

"I'll do that while you're in the shower."

My clean clothes were already in the bathroom waiting for me. Even the boots were in his bedroom from last night. I couldn't quit smiling through the shower. No matter what happened, I was confident that we were good. We were tight. We were a couple.

Engaged. Holding up my hand, I admired how the ring twinkled under the shower lights. When was the last time I'd taken it off? Not since that disagreement with Adam.

Letting the six showerheads pummel any residual soreness out of me, I pushed my hair off my forehead. It was time to go back to work. Officially engaged.

I toweled off, and—damn, no hair dryer. After getting dressed, I found a spare toothbrush, then I was done.

In the bedroom, Beckett was perched on the edge of the bed, his slacks on but his pale blue shirt hanging open. He was hunched over his phone and the frown on his face cut straight to my gut.

It's about me.

No, that was just me being paranoid. We'd made love last night. He'd made *promises*.

"What's up?" I sat on the spare chair he kept in his room and slipped my boots on.

His gaze lifted and I stopped what I was doing, my breath stuck in my throat.

He knew.

This wasn't me being paranoid. He. Knew.

Without a word, he turned his phone so I could see the screen.

The sight of Terra Scalia on her insipid morning show made me sick. I fought the urge to vomit and forced myself to watch the video clip that began to replay.

Terra's grating voice carried across the otherwise stone-silent room. "And in other wedded-bliss news, big congratulations to tech giant Becket King, CEO of King Tech. He is engaged! We've learned his future bride is Eva Chase. She's the sister of Adam Dickerson, who developed the home organization app Organize You. Mr. Dickerson was charged for petty theft and breaking and entering and served a year in jail." She pasted a sickly sweet smile on her face and turned to her cohost. "Allegedly, when King Tech discovered Mr. Dickerson's criminal record, Mr. King withdrew his bid and Organize You floundered."

"Interesting." The cohost wrinkled her pert little nose and crossed her legs. "I guess all's well that ends well, huh?"

Terra nodded, her smile unwavering, but her expression was so smug I wanted to rub her face in the rug. "We wish them the best. You know, I had a chance to meet Ms. Chase. She's also Mr. King's executive assistant. Talk about a *working* relationship."

The two hosts let out throaty laughs. Terra lifted a shoulder and threw the camera a coy glance. "But I guess a guy can break the rules, even his own, when he's the boss."

Beckett threw the phone on the bed. "I can tell by your face that Terra's not lying. What the *fuck*, Eva?" He rose and paced the room, his hands on his hips, a storm raging on his face. "Is this what you haven't been telling me?"

"Yes." I could barely get the word out. I hugged my arms around myself. "Adam was devastated when you retracted your bid and the others pulled out."

"Why didn't you tell me?" He stopped and pinned me with a glare. "Why?"

Resentment snuck into my tone. "It's your business acumen. And the way you dropped Dr. Herrera. I was scared of how you'd drop me."

"So you lied? Like that was going to fix it." He swept his arm toward his phone. "I didn't know what to fucking say when I listened to all those messages. Your brother broke into *people's houses*?" The torment was clear on his face. It was like I was the sister of the man who'd beaten his mother.

"I told you he was innocent."

"And how do you know?" He *tsked* and spun away. "Why am I even asking? You won't tell me."

This was the moment I'd feared for six weeks. But he loved me. We'd work through it. "Because I did it."

He pivoted around, his astonished expression full of horror. "What?"

"I fell in with a bad crowd. We liked to think of ourselves as a lower class Bling Ring."

Comprehension worked through his tight features. "A bling ring. *You* broke into people's homes. Did you do drugs too?"

I lifted a shoulder. Might as well be honest about that too. "A lot of people have tried weed."

He reared back. "I told you everything and you kept this from me."

"I was going to tell you." My words were empty. Would I ever have told him?

He seethed. "You knew what this would do to my business."

"Your business is going to be fine."

"Is it? This is what the other companies have been waiting for. The crack in King Tech that makes me less desirable than them. My company is built on integrity. I was prepared to deal with any blowback about you being my assistant because I lov—" He cut his gaze away, the muscles in his jaw flexing. Too soon, the hostile glare turned in my direction. "What would it have looked like if I had married a criminal?"

"I'm not a criminal." My words rang empty. I *was* a criminal.

"Is your last name really Chase?"

"*Yes*." I rose, my volume creeping up to match his. "Adam

has a different dad. He was six when our parents got married."

He stared at me, his hands digging into his hips. "It wasn't a coincidence that we met. Were you casing the place?"

"No." He thought I'd rob him? "*No.*"

"Then what, Eva? How did you end up outside my building at the moment I pulled up?"

And I thought telling him Adam had taken the fall for me was the worst. But I was going with the truth. "I wanted to learn more about you. To find a mistake you made that would cost you everything like it cost Adam. But once we met—"

"God, save it. Get out, Eva. You got what you wanted. It'll take years for me to regain the brand trust I'd built."

He was exaggerating. He was still the one with the most money and the least to lose in the room. "Beckett—"

"I don't want to hear it. I don't trust a single word out of that deceitful mouth." He grabbed his phone and dialed a number. I could only stand and watch and hope he didn't mean what he said. "Rick, come get Eva as soon as possible. She's to go straight home." When he clicked off, he said. "I don't ever want to see you around here again. I don't want you around my family or talking to anyone in my circle."

His circle. Which didn't include me. "Beckett—" He was shaking his head and my patience snapped. "This is exactly why I didn't tell you. You're uncompromising. People make mistakes."

"Then take responsibility for your own this time." His voice was cold, no hint of the love we'd shared just an hour ago. "Consider yourself fired."

He was serious. He wanted me gone. I thought he'd grown past my fear, but he was the same Beckett King that I'd met months ago. He didn't want to know why I hung out with people who'd want to break into rich people's houses and steal valuables. He didn't want to know why I'd join in. My desperation and the gaping hole my parents' death had left behind were nothing to him. While he'd built a successful company off the back of his grief, I'd hung out in the gutter. Terra had been accurate. He thought he was so much higher than the rest of us.

"All right then," I said rigidly. "Goodbye."

"And leave the damn ring."

That last request stabbed through my heart worse than when he'd told me to leave. I slid the ring off and placed it on his dresser. Part of me had thought that maybe he'd seek me out after his temper died down. But the ring that he loved seeing on my finger, the ring he couldn't ignore while he was fucking me, was no longer mine.

I went down the stairs. I couldn't look toward the next level down. I'd break down in sobs at not being able to say goodbye to the kittens. Would he be so angry with me that he'd kick them out too?

Grabbing my coat, I slipped outside to wait for Rick on the front step. The bitter air permeated every stitch of clothing. I hoped Rick showed up quickly.

And he did. A few minutes later, he sped into the drive, stopping at the front instead of going around back to where I usually waited. His normally congenial expression was grim.

I should've called a different ride. But I wanted to say goodbye to Rick, and to know that maybe there was one person in Beckett's circle who wouldn't hate me.

The car was warm, but Rick was cold. "Ms. Chase."

I sighed. He usually called me Eva like everyone else. "I guess you heard."

He pulled away before I was buckled in. Beckett must've ordered an expedited ride. "It's all over the news. You know how this town likes its local celebrities."

"If Beckett hadn't dated a local celebrity, nobody would care about his business."

"*He* would have."

There was my answer. Rick didn't like me either. "Yeah. I guess it was coming either way, whether I told him when we met or now."

"Hurts you a lot more now."

"Yep." I laid my head back and watched the city go by.

He turned the corner that would take him to my complex. "Aw, hell, Eva. Prepare yourself."

Frowning, I peered out of the window. How many morning shows were there in Denver? It wasn't the press mob that swarmed a movie star, but the three TV station vans parked on my street felt just as overwhelming. It was too cold for them to linger outside. They just lay in wait inside their vehicles.

Glad that I had clean clothing on and had at least finger combed my hair, I steeled myself for the rush to the door. I didn't have to stop and check on cats. All I had to do was limit the amount of time they had to come at me with their questions.

"Goodbye, Rick. It was nice knowing you."

Hurrying down the sidewalk, the sound of a car door opening and closing quickened my pace.

"Ms. Chase. Can I have a word with you?" A guy. I'd probably watched him a million times on the news during bar shifts. That channel was now on my will-not-watch list.

"Ms. Chase, can you comment on your relationship with Mr. King? Did you meet through your brother?"

My boots clicked on the pavement. I was almost to the walk that'd take me to my door.

"Eva." That voice stopped me in my tracks. Terra Scalia. *That bitch.* "How did Mr. King react to the news?"

Don't do it. Don't do it.

I did it. Spinning on a heel, my gaze landed directly on Terra and that smug twist to her lips. "Ms. Scalia, care to share why Mr. King has it on his security footage that you tried to hack into his computer while you two were in a relationship? Care to elaborate why you broke this story about an ex-boyfriend? The public wants to know if it's a personal vendetta. He's the one that broke things off with you, after all. Seems like a conflict of interest."

Three large cameras swung toward Terra, her face losing color, then flushing. "You're just full of lies, Ms. Chase."

"Be careful, *Ms. Scalia*. You wouldn't want to lose a chance at that spot on your morning show. I hear slander isn't a good look in your field." I gestured to the news crews. "Or do you forget when you're being recorded?"

With that, I flounced inside, slammed the door, and slid down it until my butt hit the floor.

Adam was peeking under the curtain. "I didn't look outside until now or I would've warned you."

"It doesn't matter." I went to push my hair off my forehead but my hand was shaking.

"I take it he saw the news."

I looked at Adam. Really looked. Our talk had been only a few days ago, but his eyes were brighter and he'd shaved. His appointment wasn't until tomorrow, but his attempts to care for himself bolstered me. "He saw it all." I hitched my knees up and draped my hands over them. "He knows everything."

"And it's over." He gestured at my ringless hand. "I thought there was no way he could avoid it, but I'd hoped you two would work it out."

"He hates me."

"Then he's an idiot."

I didn't want to talk about Beckett. But at the same time, he was all I wanted to talk about. I focused on Adam instead.

"You look good." He gave me a dubious stare. "Better. You look better."

"I feel better. And I'm guessing it's time to pass the baton." What'd he mean?

He jerked his thumb toward the window. "I'll be the one getting groceries and you'll be the one stuck inside."

"Yeah," I choked out. Sinking into the couch and losing myself in a game sounded ideal about now. "Um, we should set a budget. I'm currently unemployed."

His brows lifted. "I guess that shouldn't come as a shock, but it seems a bit like salt on the wound."

"I doubt I'll get my next paycheck."

"Now that would be illegal, and you know how Mr. King likes to obey the law."

I didn't know if it was illegal. Adam probably didn't either, but I was grateful that my brother had come around in time to help me through this. But then, it's what he did.

"Speaking of illegal, remember that guy you were seeing whose bright idea it was to break into people's houses and steal jewelry?"

It'd been a long time since I let myself think about him. "Yep."

"Well, he texted me and said he'd leak to the news that you were the one who helped him and not me if we didn't pay him a hundred thousand dollars." I was about to shout a string of swear words when Adam looked at his phone. "So I took a screen shot. Then I sent it to him with a bunch of links on blackmailing and the legal ramifications. And then I sent him a picture of my middle finger."

It was enough to get a chuckle out of me. "I've missed you."

"You know what? I missed me too. The blackmail attempt was invigorating. I might use the spike of adrenaline to go outside." He shrugged. "Then I'll probably need a nap."

He came over and helped me off the floor. I was afraid I'd topple him over, but his grip was strong.

I threw my arms around him. "I love you. You won't have to carry me forever, but I need to nurse my wounds."

"We'll help each other through this. It's what we do."

eckett

IT'D BEEN three weeks and my chest ached each time I thought about Eva, which only happened every few seconds. Which was an improvement.

"You didn't." Xander eyed me over his tall draft beer. His head was shaking as he snagged another seasoned pretzel. "I mean I heard but I thought, no, man, I have to hear the whole story. There's no way he lost his shit and broke it off."

"Why wouldn't I?"

"Don't go on about that fake-marriage BS. You were crazy about her."

"She's a liar." My venom was all-consuming, like it'd been the last few weeks.

His eyes narrowed like he didn't believe me. "What about Grams?"

"I told her that I didn't want to hear about trusts or

MARIE JOHNSTON

marriage and I didn't want Dad and Kendall to pay for my lack of nuptials."

Xander whistled. "I think the last person to stand up to Grams was Mama."

"I think it was Dad, actually. She tried to toss Kendall my way, hoping I'd fall for her and get married. I can't imagine how the news broke that Dad had fallen for her instead. That he even went for it convinced me he was serious about her."

Xander's brows popped. "That almost makes me regret my stop in Indonesia. I'd give my left nut to see Dad light into Grams. She might've given you a reprieve, but she's starting on me now." He pulled out his phone and showed me the messages.

Anyone special in your life?

Do you know what next year brings? Wedding bells.

Not unexpected. "Did you hear the rest of the news?"

"Dawson forwarded the links. I was in Iceland or I would've flown back for like, moral support."

"I didn't need moral support." But I could've used him around.

After the blowout at my house and kicking Eva out, it leaked that she'd been the one her brother had done time for. Allegedly. My only consolation was that it hadn't been Terra reporting. In fact, I didn't see Terra's name on that news station anymore. Eva's low blows had done some hull damage. I tried not to be proud of her.

Just like I'd tried not to watch those segments a thousand times.

The three apps I'd been in the process of buying chose other backers. It was a hit financially. A small one that my company would feel in the next year or two.

To salvage at least a good-guy reputation, I made sure to add more money to my holiday charity donations. And for my efforts I'd been invited to a charity supper tonight and caught with no excuse for getting out of it. That, and my new assistant could talk me into gigs that I'd never go to otherwise. Since Taylor was also excellent at damage control and had promised to go with me, I listened.

Xander finished a long swig of his beer. "Did Dad get ahold of you?"

"I called and talked to him. Told him everything." After saying those words, I had to take a long pull of my own beer.

I wasn't usually an alcohol-before-five-p.m. kind of guy, but the gravity of Dad's voice over the phone... He'd been ashamed of me. But I couldn't tell if it was because I'd lied to him or because I'd dumped Eva over the scandal. The charity supper tonight also loomed over my head. I hated those things. I loved donating, and wished I could do more anonymously. But King Tech's brand had to be linked to it.

"You're just too used to being Gooder. Dad will get over it. Besides, it's been over a year and Aiden's still married. He could've gotten rid of her. That'll make Dad happy."

True. Maybe my brother really loved Kate in his cold, robotic way. And Dad hadn't seemed as worn as he was before the heart attack. His voice had been strong and he'd been astonishingly supportive.

"But I gotta ask." Xander leveled me with a no-nonsense stare that rivaled Aiden's. "What's the big deal over all this Eva drama anyway?"

"She lied."

"I lie all the time."

"Your lies won't take down my company, and we all expect it of you." I was joking, but he flinched. "Hey, man. I didn't mean it."

"No, it's just— You sound like Dad."

"You take that back." His comment gave me a little more insight into his relationship with Dad. "By the way, those pictures you sent were stunning. You should try to get published."

"Right. I'll think about it." I recognized the noncommittal tone as a fresh way to tell me to stay out of it.

"So, I've got a function to go to."

"And here I thought you dressed like that every day. Oh wait. You do."

"Jackass." I rose and straightened my vest under my suit jacket. "There are expectations."

Xander sobered. "Just don't let them rob you of everything you care about. You can't wake up to expectations in the morning."

"Actually, I can." I woke up to cats every morning. Purring, cuddly cats expecting to be fed. They'd been the only thing I'd been waking up to for the last three weeks.

RICK DROPPED me off at the splashy downtown Denver hotel. The entrance was off a side street, and there were ushers waiting out there to direct esteemed guests like me into the charity supper.

"Mr. King, sir. Right this way."

I wandered in, taking my time. Taylor was supposed to meet me here. My priority was looking for my assistant, the best hire I'd ever made. Even Wilma was put to shame under Taylor's watch.

"Beck, I was getting scared you'd ditch me here." The deep voice made me smile.

"Taylor, I'd never do that to you."

He ran a hand over his dark shaved head, then straightened his tie. He wore a vest with a suit like I did, but his vest was a trendy shade of pink and his suit a sharp gray. He was my dad's age but easier for me to be around than Dad. The guy could kill a spreadsheet and make any scheduling app cry. "I don't know. You didn't look too happy when I talked you into this."

I wasn't. I wanted to go home and play with the damn cats. All six of them. I hadn't found homes for them yet and my housekeeper had suggested naming them. "To make things easier," she had said, but I really think she thought names would make me want to keep them.

Kitty had been fixed and her litter—Orion, Dipper, Leo, Aries, and Ursa—had gotten their vaccinations. I'd taken them all to the vet. Alone.

"Where am I supposed to sit?"

"We're at the reserved tables up front. We get the food first and everything." He spoke out of the corner of his mouth as we took our seats. "I hope you never realize that I make you go to these things so I can get the VIP treatment by proxy."

"You deserve the VIP treatment."

Taylor led me to the table with our placards. On our way, local government officials stopped to chat, but mostly I could feel eyes on me, people who thought I looked familiar or maybe knew me from TV. Savory smells wafted across the room. My stomach growled, but I wished I'd eaten a burger and fries at the bar with Xander.

Awareness prickled along the back of my neck, though I didn't see anything amiss. Just a bunch of people with money celebrating that they were able to give it away and then throw themselves a party. I never understood these things. Logically, I knew that they brought awareness to their charity and make the donors feel special enough to fork over more next year, but I'd rather just cut a check and spend the night at home.

With my cats.

God, I was fucking pathetic.

What had I done when I was single? It seemed so long ago.

The urge to scan the room again hounded me. Taylor was chatting up the others at the table and I missed the whole conversation. I let my gaze wander, wondering what was nudging my intuition.

Then I saw her. Eva. I should've seen her before, but like the rich asshole I was, my gaze had automatically skipped over the help.

Her back was to me, but I'd know that hair anywhere, the way she stood, her mannerisms. She was talking to one of her coworkers, pointing out tables. Would she serve mine?

Then she turned and our gazes clashed. For the first time in weeks, the lonely pit in my gut wasn't so painful.

Her eyes went wide, then she turned and disappeared behind a dark curtain. And I was back to being empty.

"Excuse me." I got up and went in the same direction.

"Beck," Taylor whisper yelled. "The speaker is going to start soon."

I waved him off and kept walking. In my periphery, people approached like they were going to strike up conversation, but the look on my face must've told them to back off. No one stopped me.

I reached the place in the curtain where she'd disappeared. In the shadows was a cleverly concealed gap between the curtains. Without thinking, I charged through the opening.

Darkness surrounded me, but I followed the light. It'd lead me to Eva. The bustle of activity got louder. As I was rounding the corner, I rammed into a cart full of plates.

"Shit." Eva's voice was a caress to the senses. She was catching plates of chicken parmesan and risotto from tipping off her end. "Watch where you're going— Beckett."

"Eva."

Her gaze darted around, no doubt looking for another escape. A few of her fellow servers shot us curious glances.

"What are you doing here?" I asked.

She didn't answer, just looked down at her ruffled white shirt, black bow tie, and black slacks. "I need to get back to work."

"Wait."

She stopped rearranging the plates. A guy in the same outfit took the cart. "Move it or Carla's going to lose it."

He spun the cart around me and rushed out. Another server followed him. Eva scowled at a third cart and crossed her arms. "What?"

"What are you doing working? You made a lot of money in six weeks."

"A month. I didn't get paid for the last two weeks."

What? Ah, shit. She had been in charge of approving payroll and Taylor wouldn't have known that she needed to be paid. "I'll take care of it."

"Keep it. Donate it to the charity. I don't care."

"I pay my debts."

She sighed and brushed her hair behind her ear. It was getting longer. I could run my fingers through it now. An ache beat a slow rhythm in my chest. "Don't bother. I don't want your money."

"Why are you working here?"

"Because us degenerates need to make a living if we're not going to thieve and rob people every weekend. The catering company was generous enough to give me my job back in spite of my face being splashed all over the news. Looks like you're doing fine though."

The hostility in her tone pricked my nostalgic bubble. What had happened between us was not my fault. "What's that supposed to mean?"

"It means that people like you get second chances. No

one is going to remember Terra or her breaking story. Nobody's going to care that the King Tech CEO slept with his assistant or that he compromised his rigid morals for her."

"My company lost three bids."

"And next month you'll get three more. Meanwhile, I won't get a raise until my six-month probation is up. I would've gotten one last month, but I quit to work for you." She went to the cart. "Not every person who fucks up would beat someone to death if given the chance to misbehave again. You're so proud of sticking to this unrealistic no-second-chances ideal that you don't stop and actually *see* the people you throw away."

"You want me to feel sorry for the guy that killed my mom?" Did she even hear what she was saying?

"Maybe your mother would have."

She might as well have slapped me. "Don't you dare bring her into this."

"Why not? You bring her into all these decisions."

A woman dressed like Eva but wearing wire-rimmed glasses and a jacket over her shirt spun around the curtain. "Eva, what's taking so long—" She blinked at me, recognition flashing in her eyes. "Oh, Mr. King. They were just calling your name."

This must be the Carla the other guy mentioned. "I missed it." I didn't care.

"Is everything all right here?" She looked over her glasses at my torso. "Oh, dear. You have sauce on your jacket."

"It's fine." If the dry cleaners couldn't get it out, I'd buy a new one. I wasn't here to impress anyone. I was here because they were trying to impress me.

"Eva." The woman's voice rang like a bullet. "Those plates are cooling. We can't serve guests cold meals."

"Sorry, Carla." Eva's cheeks flushed, but she wheeled the

cart between us. I didn't want her to go, but it wasn't like our talk was going well.

"My apologies, Mr. King. Please send the dry cleaning bill to us. Can I help you with anything else?" Carla's tone was the opposite of how she spoke to her workers.

"No. And don't worry about the jacket. I won't."

Weaving my way back to my table, I managed to keep Eva in my line of vision. She disappeared with her empty cart behind the curtain and I took my seat. The guest speaker had started, her voice carrying over the tinkling of forks on plates.

Taylor spoke out of the corner of his mouth. "You missed their recognition of your donation."

His reprimand was clear and almost made me smile. He wasn't worried about kissing my ass as much as protecting it. Disappearing during the moment I'd been invited for wasn't a good look. And I didn't care.

Eva's words replayed in my mind. How dare she? She knew exactly why I ran my company the way I did.

I didn't hear any of what the speaker said. My attention was ready to catch a glimpse of Eva, but I hadn't seen her again since sitting down. I clapped when everyone else did and laughed at all the right moments, and when the speaker was done, I turned to Taylor.

"Eva didn't get paid for her last two weeks of work."

He cocked a brow. "And you'd like it paid out or absorbed into the company?"

"She did the work. She needs to get paid."

"I'll take care of it in the office tomorrow. Are you going to run off again, or can I take you around to work the room? The mayor's here, along with the folks you already spoke to, and I heard a state senator might drop by."

"I don't want to work the room."

Taylor turned in his seat so the woman next to him

couldn't hear. "And may I ask why? This night could go a long way to getting the local news to lay off you. You risk upsetting some influential friends of yours."

He had a point, but I still didn't care. That seemed to be my motto for the night. "Eva's working with the catering company."

Taylor covered his sharp inhale with a drink of his water. "So that's why you ran off. Do I need to do damage control?"

"For what?"

"You tell me."

"It's fine." I hadn't made a scene. Maybe some of her coworkers were wondering what was going on, but if they'd watched the news the last few weeks, they knew. Or maybe she'd told them. How close was she to the others? She'd never mentioned any friends.

What was she doing with herself? How was her brother? Was she back to working two jobs?

I rose again. Where was she?

"Dear Lord, Beck, don't tell me you're going to find her." The exasperation in his voice should be enough to get me to stop, but I had to find her.

"Work the room and have my dessert."

Taylor reclined back, kicking one knee over the other. "Don't make that offer lightly. It's cheesecake and I'll eat everyone's slices if they're not looking."

With Taylor mollified, I went searching for Eva. She wasn't working the floor. I checked out each server while I made my way to the same curtained exit I'd ducked behind before, but none of them were her.

Going through the curtains, I made it to the staging area. The guy that had taken the cart from Eva was walking by.

"Hey, where's Eva?"

He looked me up and down, his expression less than impressed. "She's not here, man."

"Why not?" Dessert still hadn't been served. Didn't they work the whole event?

"Got fired."

My face went cold. Fired? Why? "Where's Carla?"

The corner of the guy's mouth ticked. "In the kitchen."

He trailed behind me with an empty cart. I followed the sound of a ruthless voice commanding how many dessert plates per cart to load and which tables to serve first.

Amidst stainless steel shelves stacked with white plates, Carla was barking orders.

"Why'd you fire Eva?"

Carla cut off midsentence, her head whipping toward me. Her lips pursed. "Mr. King." She hustled toward me. "How can I help you?"

"By answering my question."

Carla sighed and propped a hand on her hip. I was in her territory and she wasn't going to go easy on me. "I can't have my staff be a distraction at events."

"So you fired her?"

"I can't very well ask if you'll be in attendance at each event."

"But I was the one who followed her back here. I was the one bothering her." It didn't make sense. Eva had gotten canned because I talked to her?

She stared at me from over her glasses. "You're not the one who'll lose business because of it. I employ a hundred people. I can't let one server cost me gigs."

"No one saw us."

"Plenty of people noticed where you went and who you talked to, Mr. King." She sighed. "I shouldn't have even hired her back after giving me no notice when she quit, but she was always so dependable otherwise."

"She quit because I paid her a thousand times more than you. What would you have done?"

I got the look over the glasses again. "Honestly? After my years of working these events, I would've known it was temporary and stayed where I was. And if she would've told me why, I would've informed her that if things went south, she'd be the one packing her bags. Not you."

Eva had said something similar. Now Carla. What kind of reputation did I really have? "Why does your experience catering events make you think you know this?"

Her mouth tightened, lines flaring all around like she was a coffee diehard—out of a mug, not a coffee shop cup. "Your lot protects yourselves."

"Wouldn't you?"

She sucked in a deep breath and took her glasses off. "A server sleeps in once, do I fire him? No. The third time, maybe, depends how short-staffed I am. But if my chicken parmesan is too salty tonight, do you think I'll get booked for next year's event? That's a hard no. I can have a stellar reputation, but one mediocre meal costs me the rest of that customer's business. They spread the word and I'm out thousands upon thousands of dollars and I have to start laying off people while they cry about the new baby they can't afford diapers for. Do I feel like doing that because so-and-so told so-and-so that King Tech's ex-fiancée works for the company and if you're coming, they'd better not hire me? No."

She put her glasses back on and craned her head around to inspect the cheesecake prep. "Make sure every slice is identical. For God's sake, if it's too small, set it aside. There's always someone on a diet who'll complain about how big the slices are. We can save it for them."

She marched off. I was forgotten.

Eva had lost her job because of me. She'd lost *another* job because of me.

The discussions with her and Carla mixed in my mind. I

took out my phone and called Rick for a ride and told him to pick me up at the service entrance. Then I sent Taylor a message that I was leaving. He'd cover for me and have a blast doing so.

Asking a few people for directions, I made my way out the back entrance. Leaning against the loading dock, I tipped my head back. The stars were hard to see over the light pollution, but it wasn't the stars I was looking at. I had a lot to think about.

va

When I entered the apartment, Adam looked up from his game. He still played a lot, but he did other things with his days too. And he ate without being reminded.

"What are you doing home so early?" he asked. He was sitting forward on the couch and not slumped back. I sniffed. Was he cooking? He'd been doing so well, going to therapy three times a week and really committing to treatment.

I hated to shove a rain cloud over his night. "I got fired."

He stopped the game, not even caring that he was in the middle of an epic battle. "What happened?" He even shut the TV off.

I could come home to that. As long as Adam was improving, it'd make the shit turn of events the last few weeks worth it.

"Yeah, we were catering this big charity supper, so take one guess who was in attendance."

"Oh, damn, Eva. I'm sorry. Did he demand it?"

I shook my head and trudged to the couch. Sinking down, I didn't care that I wrinkled the uniform. I wasn't sure I'd actually return it to Carla. "No, but he followed me to the back and we argued and Carla saw and canned me. Bad for business."

The other thing that was bad for business was to be publicly outed as the real criminal in the breaking and entering cases from years ago. I couldn't get my old job back as a bartender because the owner didn't know if he could trust me.

I'd worked there for three years.

"I'm so tired, Adam." That catering job had been my last chance. We were using the money I'd made working for Beckett to put Adam through treatment. Then there was insurance on the car and some TLC to get it running again. If we started tapping into it for regular living expenses, it'd drain dry quickly.

"What about that one place you put in for? The executive assistant opening? He called you back for another interview."

"His wife forbade him to hire me. I guess I'm a home-wrecker now too." After breaking up with Beckett, I'd started to believe Adam. How many applications could I put in without hearing back from anyone?

"It's not fair that you were vilified."

It was fair. I'd gone looking for something in Beckett's past to destroy him with, but it'd been my own shady past that had caused my ruin. He was a good guy with a stick up his ass for a noble reason. I was the petty thief.

"I put some pot pies in the oven. Want one?"

"No, thanks." I wasn't hungry. After serving a hundred people their meal and getting my walking papers, I didn't want to see anything edible right now.

I curled into the corner and pulled up a book on my

phone. Thank God for libraries. I was staying far away from the TV and any social media. With the library app, I didn't have to leave home. I could lose myself in a good book and not think about Beckett. Or wonder how Gentry's health was and if this breakup would cost him or Kendall a job.

Adam hadn't turned the TV back on. "I was thinking that I could dig out the Christmas tree. Want to help decorate?"

I'd put up the tree since I was strong enough to drag it out of the closet, but I had no cheer this year. "No. I think I'll just read in my bed tonight. Tomorrow I have to start the job search"—and the humiliation—"over again."

"I get that." The oven beeped and he disappeared into the kitchen.

How our roles had changed. I didn't think I was clinically depressed. Anyone who'd been through the publicity circus like I had would want to hide for a few weeks. Maybe years.

Seeing Beckett tonight had hurt. I was glad Adam was in the kitchen. I had to screw my face up ten different ways to keep from crying.

Beckett had been in a suit like the one he'd worn when I'd first met him. When he was talking to me, it had been all I could do not to lean in and smell him. That soap he used to lather me with. The shampoo he joked cost more than some appliances. The sauce stains on his tux I wanted to dab at.

He hadn't batted an eye.

I missed him. For weeks I'd tried to keep from having foolish fantasies, the ones where the hero comes back begging for forgiveness. But I'd been in the wrong, and even more, I wasn't worth his reconsideration.

NO MESSAGES. No emails. No job. A whole week had gone by and I was as unemployed as the day I was born. There had to be something I was qualified to do with a boss who didn't watch the news. My drama was dying down. Terra kept trying to reignite it on social media but it'd been a month. It was no longer juicy and there was always holiday drama. I guess if there was a time to go viral, the holidays worked.

Tossing my phone on my bed, I collapsed back. What the hell was I going to do? Logging into our bank account, I was going to run the numbers again. With what I'd made the month I'd gotten paid working for Beckett, Adam and I could make it—

I frowned. That was more money than when I'd checked yesterday.

Locating the deposit, my stomach fluttered, then a wave of grief swamped me. I'd been paid for those two weeks.

He'd paid me. What did that mean? Did it mean anything?

A choked cry left me. Then a sob. Then more until I was a puddle in the middle of my bed.

There was a knock on the door, but I was too lost in my heartache to answer. I was too ashamed that I'd lost it over a guy who couldn't be bothered twice by me.

The bed dipped and Adam's hand lay on my shoulder. "What's going on?" he asked softly.

"I'm being stupid."

"You hardly ever cry, so I know it's not stupid."

I hardly ever cried until Beckett gave me reason to. "It's about a boy, which is always stupid."

Adam's sigh was audible, but it wasn't because he was frustrated with me. It was his *I don't know what to do* sigh. "These are the times I miss Mom the most."

"I never cried over guys."

"No, but there were a few times you needed to. And if Mom had been around, you would've." My tears came harder because he was right. "Like Glove Box Underwear Irving."

A laugh interrupted my sobs. "Mom would've hated Irving."

"Dad could've talked you out of dating him."

"I don't know. I was eighteen and knew everything." I sat up, feeling better with Adam here. It had been me and him for so long. "Beckett paid me for those last two weeks."

He peeked at the computer and whistled. "That'll help."

"I don't like spending his money."

"Eva, you worked for it. That job was separate from your relationship with him."

"Not really."

He rolled his eyes. "Yes, really." His expression turned introspective and he glanced at the bank account again.

"Spill it."

"Hmm?"

It'd been so long since we'd done this back and forth, I almost didn't recognize it. His mind was churning over something. "You have an idea."

"I didn't want to mention it until the hoopla died down, which is taking longer than expected."

"You can thank a woman scorned."

His smile was brief. "With all the extra media attention being given to Organize You, I got a call."

My eyes flew wide. "Seriously?" All my problems washed away. That app had been his pride and joy, his baby. And people were interested again?

"Yes, but I told the rep that it's years old, that there are others out there that are up-to-date." He gave me a slight smile. "And he said he knew that but I should update it and get back to him, and to let him know about anything else I've been working on."

"But you'd need a new computer, and new—" My mind whirred over everything. It wasn't that expensive. Well, it was, but it had been like that four years ago when Adam was setting up the app too. "With the new deposit, we could easily upgrade what we needed. Though it'd take a month off our projected budget."

"They also…offered me a job. This company doesn't just acquire apps. They recruit the talent behind them."

My brows shot up. "That's…awesome. Where?"

"I could work from home, but I'd have to travel to Atlanta to the home offices a few times a year. Orientation would start right after the New Year."

Acid ate a hole through my body. I was so happy for him, so hopeful, but I'd be alone during the longest stretch of the year, trying to forget Beckett and applying for jobs I hated.

"I said no."

He what? "What? Why?"

"I'm doing well, and I don't want to mess it up by leaving my routine before I get it cemented. Or by leaving you."

Were we ever going to get out of this cycle? He'd give up opportunities for me when I was down, then I'd do the same for him. "Adam…"

"And I have an idea."

The sly look on his face was one I'd feared never seeing again. "For a new app?"

"Yes, for a game. I got the idea about a brother and sister." As he continued to describe his intricately versatile multi-player game, I was astounded by the detail. All those months on the couch, he hadn't been dead to the whole world. He'd been lost in his head, plotting and designing a game. Yes, he'd been depressed, but it hadn't stopped him from creating. Depression had just made him think there was no reason to try to go anywhere with his creation.

"So anyway," he concluded. "The relationship between the players can be anything, and you can play with more than two and it wouldn't change the functionality."

"That's fucking brilliant."

The flash of his grin was as welcome a sight today as it had been weeks ago. "Work with me on it."

Stunned, I stared at him. What did I know about games? I watched him play.

"And on updating Organize You. We can be Chase and Dickerson Enterprises, only with a more exciting name."

He'd done it all before, getting so wrapped up in the process that I had felt forgotten and found someone who'd pay attention to me, someone who wanted to break into houses. Graduating high school didn't mean I was exempt from the same insecurities that had plagued me once before.

But this time, I'd help him update his app. Go into business with him. Two kids who couldn't find a decent job to keep the roof over their heads doing it themselves.

"I happen to have some time on my hands." I smiled for the first time since Terra's news segment. "And I learned a few things in my last job."

CHAPTER 24

eckett

THE PLANE TOUCHED down in Idaho. The last time I'd landed at this airport ran through my head. Eva's first flight. Her anxiety, her curiosity, and her head for this business all came flooding back.

The flight attendant smiled at me. Shirley. I racked my brain to remember if she was the one who had a grandkid due next month, or if her daughter had graduated from college this past fall semester. I couldn't come up with it. The entire flight I hadn't spoken to her more than to let her know I didn't need anything and that I'd be working the rest of the trip.

Eva would've known what to say. Taylor too. He had stayed back in Denver. I wanted to talk to Dr. Herrera alone, and I didn't want to inspect my reasons too closely.

A driver picked me up and took me to a familiar office building. Everywhere I looked I was reminded of my time here with Eva. Our walk down this path. Her delight looking in the koi pond. And how I didn't mind that we appeared to be a couple in the waiting room.

I checked in at the desk and ignored how the receptionist looked behind me for my significant other. Sitting by myself, I clicked through my morning emails. There was one from Taylor asking if I was going to stop in at the office when I returned. I replied and said I would. I hadn't planned to, but his upbeat conversation would be a welcome distraction from all the emotions this trip was going to dredge up.

Dr. Herrera poked her head out the door. "Beck, come on back."

She was smiling, so that was a good sign. I'd expected her to reject my request for a meeting when I'd called in the first place. She didn't need to speak to me again. She had no reason to give me a second chance.

In her office, I sank into her cozy couch. The spot next to me was glaringly empty. When Eva had been here with me, I'd been so attuned to her. Her reactions to Dr. Herrera, Idaho, and the app itself. Nothing about Eva had escaped my notice.

Dr. Herrera tucked a dark lock of hair behind her ear. "So, needless to say, I was surprised that you're still interested."

"And I was just as surprised you were willing to meet again."

She laughed and a load lifted off my shoulders that I hadn't realized I'd been carrying around. I was so used to having the power. At home. At work. In my personal life. But this was Dr. Herrera's territory as much as it was new ground for me.

"I'm not in the business of giving up on people. But I have to ask you, why the renewed interest? You made it clear my son's past was a deal breaker."

"Life lately has been…enlightening."

A divot formed between her brows as her pleasant expression changed to professional concern. "I hate to say it, but I've followed the news on you the last couple of months."

It had been almost two months since Eva and I had broken up. The end of January was a few days away, and then beyond that was my birthday. Dad had been strangely silent on the home front, but I still got occasional texts and messages from him, asking me to call. My brothers had probably told him to lay off, maybe even explained that what was fake had turned way too real, and that these last couple of months had been the worst of my adult life. Nothing had changed, just that Eva was no longer in it.

"Eva was a strong supporter of your app. She believed in it, she believed in you, and she believed in your son. She told me over and over not to hold his history against him." I sighed, staring at my hands, feeling way too much like one of her patients. "I've been shown there are some flaws in my thinking. Like how rigidly I stuck to the idea that I shouldn't take a chance on some people who've made mistakes."

"You lost her, didn't you?"

I nodded, my body numb. I had lost her. She'd been mine and she'd stuck beside me and I'd driven her so far away that she was as good as lost. We lived in the same town, but I didn't have the guts to approach her again. Talking to me had gotten her *fired*. Why would she ever be willing to interact with me again? This was a foreign situation for me, and I didn't even know where to start to fix it. "We broke up, yes."

Dr. Herrera crossed one leg over the other and leaned forward, her tone quiet, comforting. "Were you two a couple when you first came here?"

I shook my head.

She nodded, like that had answered some of her questions. "There was a lot of information about you in the media. I don't need to ask questions, and you didn't come here for therapy. I'll just get right to it. My son is an addict. How do you feel about that?"

"Not the same as I did a few months ago. But I think that instead of focusing on keeping my reputation spotless, I should change my focus to highlighting the technical talents and abilities of others. If your son uses again, King Tech won't drop his program. If your son uses again, honestly, it's none of my business. I'm buying his program, I'm not employing him. You two will still be independent designers who can query and sell your apps to any company you want. But if something were to happen and your son relapsed, it doesn't mean that he wouldn't have King Tech's support. I would rather highlight his successes than concentrate on his problems."

Dr. Herrera considered my words, studying me the entire time. "That's quite a change of heart to have in such a short time. I want to be thrilled. Attracting the interest of your company was the biggest compliment for us. To go from zero to the top in such a short time, it was quite liberating. But your rejection didn't stop us. We pushed forward, and everything you said was true. I didn't have the capital to launch the app and make it become the next big thing, but we're trudging along, and we're learning a lot. So you'll need to tell me what you can do for me."

I smiled. She was proving to be as competent in this business as she was in her own, and I had no reason to think that she wouldn't hit her goals with the app just like she had with this big beautiful building and the waiting room outside.

"I can't imagine it's easy for a guy like you to admit that you were wrong," she said quietly, circling back to my change of heart.

"What do you mean?" Was I a masochist? I knew what she

meant. A rich bastard like me that thought everyone else was beneath him.

"It was part of your identity, stemming from childhood trauma. Those changes, through gradual realizations, or…" She lifted a shoulder, her lips curving up, softening her claim. "A sudden and hard lesson. Like losing someone you love because of what you've done to protect yourself from that happening."

She'd exposed me with her last sentence. Left me raw and aching. I had claimed I wasn't at fault, but I hadn't had to lose Eva. We could've talked and smiled at the cameras and moved on. Then, like it wasn't enough to sever the connection between us, I'd cost her a job.

I could prove I wasn't a complete bastard. "Let me take over your app. I'll triple the money you put into it within weeks."

"And updates? My son and I would like to control any and all updates to include a payout with each delivery."

She was going to be a delight to deal with. I often bought apps from people like… Adam Dickerson. Designers who didn't realize the profit potential of a well-marketed app, but with a fire in their belly that told them it could be great, if only…

I was the "if only." Dr. Herrera had done her research and thanks to my withdrawal she had experience. She wasn't going to turn control over to my people and take her one payout. She also knew that it'd keep her son in the game. If I'd truly had a change of heart, then that wouldn't bother me. And it didn't.

"What sort of updates do you have in mind?"

The corner of her mouth ticked up. We were in business. "The first is multiple languages. Then we have an outline to keep expanding it for all cultures, gender identities, and sexual preferences."

"Let's talk numbers."

∼

THE FLIGHT HOME was quick enough. I spent the time sending Taylor information on my deal with Dr. Herrera. He'd get all the paperwork ready and send it to her. I was confident that her app would make its money back and then some, just like I was confident that her son would come up with another. Whether he wanted to pitch that one to me or not didn't matter. This deal hadn't been just about business. It was the beginning of my amends.

Rick picked me up. After dropping Eva off at home for the last time, he'd been quiet. The last couple of weeks he'd gotten chattier again, helping me feel less like a loser that had given away his dog when he was at school.

Not a dog. I had six cats. Lois had tentatively mentioned that they were old enough to find homes for, but I hadn't given her the go-ahead. Eva hadn't seen how big they'd grown and if I gave them away, she never would.

And I'd spent some time figuring out what that meant.

Since Rick was concentrating on traffic, I pulled up the couples app. Switching the answers from my demo ones to what it was like between me and Eva, my finger hovered over a selection.

Relationship status. I chose *terminated*.

Relationship wish. I chose *to reconcile*.

Waiting for the summary of advice, I gazed out the window.

Hearts exploded across my screen. The advice was to have an honest talk but that doing something that'd show her that I understood what was important to her would go a long way toward repairing the relationship. All this followed by a disclaimer. I shook my head. Dr. Herrera thought of everything.

Taylor was waiting for me. He owned the space so well that it made it easier to enter without seeing Eva behind the desk, her head bent, concentration etched into her face.

"Hey, boss." Taylor swirled in his chair, tablet in hand. "Can I hit you right away?"

I'd stuck to the typical workday and had backed off on traveling for the winter.

"Lay it on me."

He followed me back to my office, waiting until I took my jacket off before he started in. That gave me a clue to how pertinent his information was. Full attention only.

I sat and held my arms out. "Ready."

"There's been talk." His pinched features told me I wouldn't like the subject.

"There's always talk."

"This is coming fast. It's a gaming app that could be adapted to most platforms. There's excitement and there's even a bidding war. And get this, it's not even complete. The designers laid tread getting the concept nailed and haven't wasted time building buzz."

"Sounds good. Send me the info and I'll take a look." I wasn't as confident as I usually was when it came to coming out on top, but that was okay. It forced me to default to the skills I'd built up to get to this position. No one could claim I was relying on family money.

Speaking of which, I needed to call Dad.

"The thing is, the designers…"

Taylor watched me, his body tense like he was setting a bomb, not defusing it. "The name of their company is Chase Dickerson Against the World."

The only sound I heard was my heartbeat slamming between my ears. My brain struggled to catch up to what my body understood. Chase Dickerson Against the World. Chase and Dickerson.

Eva Chase. Adam Dickerson.

She was working with her brother.

They'd built buzz. She'd used what she'd learned from my own marketing people and was gunning hard with her brother. A game? I didn't realize she played games, much less designed them.

She didn't. She worked hard for people she cared about. For people she loved.

Taylor continued, his tone cautious. "They've managed to recruit top-rated fans to beta test and leave reviews. Hell, they're alpha testing and leaving reviews. One of them said, 'A gaming app that combines the imagination of *Minecraft* and the universal appeal of *Fortnite* in its own unique and inclusive world.'"

"That's high praise," I mumbled.

He rattled off more reviews that would ordinarily stoke my interest until I approached the company with a bid. It was high praise for the designers when a company sought them out, but in this case...

Taylor crossed his arms. "She hit up your pool of reviewers and knew exactly what to say."

I barked out a laugh. "Yeah she did."

Taylor leaned back in his chair as if he needed to get a better view of me. "You do realize this is the next game they're going to make tournaments out of, the kind where some kid wins three million dollars. It's going to slip through our fingers." He made a choking sound. "We won't get close. I hated to even bring it up, but it's not my job to decide what you bid on. But Chase Dickerson Against the World are going to show you their backs if you approach with an offer."

A smile played over my lips. "Depends on the offer."

CHAPTER 25

va

ADAM WAS SLEEPING in and I could run into his room and bounce on his bed.

Three offers. He hadn't even finished the game, much less worked the bugs out of it, and we had three offers.

These last few weeks had been long and grueling, but we'd splurged and ordered in groceries and designed our little hearts out until well into the night. During the day I made calls and inquiries. Those first few had left me nauseous and swearing that I had an ulcer. But not all my attempts had been rebuffed and I hadn't been laughed off the phone.

Three offers. And we were in negotiations for the Organize You app. It had taken less than twenty-four hours for Adam to catch up with the market, current apps, and what changes he had to make, and another twenty-four to get Organize You upgraded.

I'd have to let him sleep.

Wandering away from his door and into the kitchen, I opened the fridge and marveled at the sight. The fridge hadn't been this full since Mom and Dad's accident. Grabbing a yogurt, I returned to the kitchen table, our new workplace. Adam was adamant that we work somewhere other than the couch and bed. It was our makeshift office with notes neatly arranged over the surface and our computers sitting side by side.

Refreshing my email, I took a bite. My gaze landed on a new message. I read the sender's name and inhaled some of my mouthful. Coughing and covering my mouth to keep from destroying our new equipment, I went to the sink. I cupped water in my hand to drink and swallowed, then wiped my chin off.

Had I read that correctly?

It had to be a mistake.

He wasn't... He knew... The CEO of King Tech had to know that Chase Dickerson Against the World was me and Adam. He had to.

So why was a message sitting in my inbox that read, *Let's talk about an offer*?

Going back to the table, I didn't sit down. I stared at the computer like it was a cobra ready to strike.

What the hell, Beckett?

I slid into my chair and opened the message. It provided no more detail. The same email template that Wilma had designed popped onto my screen. No more than two lines took up the body of the message, followed by Beckett's signature block. Beckett King, King Tech CEO.

When I sent emails to prospective clients, I used my own signature block. Surely he had a new assistant.

If he didn't, my nightmares that he'd found true love with

his next executive assistant were unfounded and a waste of nights spent tossing and turning.

I closed my laptop lid.

It had to be a mistake. He was fuming in his office because he had figured it out and couldn't go back in time to rectify his mistake.

Whatever. I was going to ignore it.

Minutes went by as I stared at the screen.

Okay, think about this logically. Professionally.

Beckett had heard the buzz. He knew a good thing when he saw it. Or he wanted to get back at me and offer a big-ass deal that we couldn't refuse.

Worst-case scenario: he was serious.

Oh God, what if he was? He'd offer more than the other three and we'd be kicking ourselves if we didn't accept.

Or…he could offer more than everyone else and then pull it like he had before. I didn't take him for a vengeful prick, but then I was single because I'd misread him, so…

I should tell Adam.

No, dammit. His head would be whirring with all the same thoughts, only he'd have flashbacks. I wasn't going to let Beckett sabotage Adam's recovery. My brother was back. That was the only good thing that had come out of my time with Beckett King.

That and the money I'd made.

But he wielded the power. He knew it. What I had predicted was right. He was back in the game something fierce, outbidding competitors and still the apple of the independent designers' eyes.

I wouldn't know that if I hadn't been following all things King Tech.

I went back to the computer and opened it. My email flashed back. I hit reply.

What should I write? *Kindly fuck off. Guess who? Do you regret it yet? Are you fucking serious because if you're not you're the cruelest human being alive? How are the cats?* Had he given them away?

Every time I went outside, I looked for Kitty as if she'd be there like before. No new strays had popped up.

I closed my reply.

Staring at the computer as if it'd tell me what to do, I sat there. I don't know how many minutes ticked by before I grabbed my phone. *Be back soon, had to run an errand.* I sent it to Adam.

I shouldn't shut Adam out of a business decision, but this one I might keep from him. Beckett wanted to make an offer? I'd tell him exactly what he could do with it.

THE AFTER-LUNCH CROWD rushed around me. I stared up at the building I didn't have the guts to enter. It had seemed a righteous decision to charge over here and get answers. But I was here.

What now?

The place looked the same. Colder. Was that just me or the winter weather? I stuffed my hands into my old thrift-store parka, but new snow boots were on my feet. Well, new in the discount bin, which was much more fun to go through when it wasn't my only option. Like the first time, I was wearing faded skinny jeans and a fitted hoodie underneath my coat.

How could he? He had to have an idea what his email would do to us. Was it eating away at him, my and Adam's success? He had to interfere. I didn't think that was like him, but again, I had misread him before.

"Well, don't just stand there. Come inside and get to work."

A jolt tumbled through my body. That voice. He'd said the same thing all those months ago.

Spinning on my heel, I tried to prepare myself, but it was useless. Nothing could prepare me for seeing him again. He had on a long black jacket that was belted around the middle. His hair was slicked to the side like it always was when he was working. Air puffed out of his mouth as he watched me.

"I didn't think I was welcome."

"I wouldn't have proposed an offer if you weren't."

That answered one question. He knew exactly who was behind the company. My patience snapped. I'd read his email less than an hour ago but I hadn't taken a full breath since. "What the fuck was that about?"

"Shall we talk inside?"

I didn't want to go in that building. Walking down that hallway to his suite was too akin to a walk of shame. Everyone would recognize me. Then once I got inside, I'd remember how he perched on the edge of my desk. And how we'd had sex on his.

But his offer was serious, though I had my doubts. He didn't look upset to see me. The humor in his eyes was forced, hiding a stark sadness that matched my own.

I needed to get this over with.

"Fine." Unlike the day we'd met, I took the lead, charging through the doors and down the wide hallway. I didn't turn my head, didn't see anyone, didn't care to. When I reached his door, I whipped it open and almost stopped. A man sat at my desk. A sharply dressed older guy who would've given me back several nights of sleep if I'd known about him.

It had been a stupid worry anyway. Beckett could sleep with eighteen assistants and marry in two days and it was none of my damn business. I shouldn't care.

But I did.

The man glanced up at me. His brows rose as his gaze slid

to Beckett. Then his mouth formed an O and he made a few clicks on his keyboard. Rising, he said, "Look at that. It's time for lunch."

Beckett walked up next to me. "Taylor, this is Eva Chase with Chase Dickerson Against the World."

Taylor power walked to us, his suit as sharp as Beckett's but more colorful. His shirt was pink, his tie had baby-blue polka dots, and the suit itself was pewter. He stuck his hand out. "Nice to meet you."

I gave him a perfunctory handshake while he assessed me, but I couldn't tell what conclusion he came to.

He released my hand and turned to Beckett. "Send me the details when you're done."

Code for "Tell me when it's safe to come back."

I liked Taylor. He seemed protective of Beckett.

Taylor left and it hit me that I was alone with Beckett. "Well, at least I can't get fired talking to you today," I muttered.

"You shouldn't have gotten fired last time." His vehement response gave me pause. He knew about that? He saw my expression and said, "I tried to find you after the speaker was done."

"Why?"

"Because I had to."

"So we could argue again?"

"I don't want to argue with you, Eva." His voice was quiet. Soft. It was how he used to talk at night. In bed.

"Okay, so the offer." My rapid subject change was pure cowardice but I didn't care. "Why the hell would you be interested?"

He lifted his chin toward his office. "Let's go somewhere where we're not on display."

I peered into the hallway. It seemed a few more people than normal were roaming the halls. I stormed into his office. His scent wrapped around me as soon as I stepped through the door. I kept my eyes off his desk and sat in the chair across from it.

He perched on the edge in front of me.

I stood and moved away. "The offer? Why?"

"It'd be a stupid business decision if I didn't." He was frustratingly chill.

"But I'm a thief and Adam was in jail."

"Petty thief. It's a misdemeanor. I looked it up."

He'd been reading up on me? It was Adam mentioned in the old reports, and even then, it wasn't much. It was nothing but a blip on Denver's crime radar. "Okay, so?"

"I'm sorry."

Two words that were loaded with emotion I couldn't identify.

"I miss you." He drifted closer.

Hold strong. I couldn't get my stupid hopes up again. But he'd read up on me. And he missed me. No, I'd trusted him once before. "Your birthday's in a week and you don't want to lose the money. Decided I'm better than a Cartwright?"

"Of course you're better, but I don't care about the money. I just want you."

My aching heart wanted to believe him. "The offer was fake then." A part of me withered.

"Absolutely not. With both Adam and you behind the project, I'd be a fool to sit this one out because of some prejudice that formed when I was twelve."

His offer was real and he wanted me back. I'd come so far since we broke up. I was making my own way and I was doing better than before. Maybe not in the pocketbook, but I was in a good place.

A good place that was missing him.

"I don't want to believe you," I whispered.

"Eva." He closed in, his hands on my shoulders as if he

was waiting for permission to do more. Permission I wasn't ready to give. "Guess who I signed last week?"

He was so close. I could lay my head on his chest. "Who?" Why was he asking?

"Dr. Herrera with Couples SOS."

"But it was already released." I'd been rooting for her, but the number of reviews had been underwhelming, and a couple of weeks later, it'd gotten buried by more popular apps.

"And I purchased it, along with a polite request that she and her son consider us for future designs."

This couldn't be real. Beckett couldn't turn that big a leaf over this quickly. "The GamesGamesGames rep said that they like to acquire the talent behind the programs. They offered Adam a job."

The corner of his mouth tipped up. "And you know that I prefer to let developers develop while running the front-end business. No shackling required."

"Why the change? You were so against people like me."

"Two things. I experienced firsthand that I can weather a bad publicity storm. And then you lost your job just for talking to me. My business rebounded before I could blink again, but I bet you had a hard time finding another job."

My nod was jerky. "If you hadn't paid me for those two weeks, Adam and I couldn't have afforded to go into business together."

"I saw how selfish and self-righteous I was. Before you, I worked. That was it. I have three brothers and I barely saw them. I hardly spoke to my dad. I almost never went home. I'd pushed them all away. Just like I ditched you the first chance I got." He ran a thumb down my cheek. I turned into the touch. "I couldn't stop what happened to Mama, but the little boy that found her wanted to stop it from happening to anyone else. He thought if he could keep all the bad guys away, nothing bad would ever happen to him again. Only he grew up into a guy who pushed *everyone* away."

"He grew up into a really good guy that a girl hell-bent on revenge couldn't help but fall for."

His smile was slow and sexy, one I never thought I'd see again. "I'd like to hear about your business. And to meet your brother again—to apologize."

"He's doing so well." My voice was ragged. "I'm so proud of him."

"Eva." His lips were at my temple. Then at my cheek. "I'm sorry. Can we try again?"

Try again. Try again. It echoed in my head, but the only reason why we shouldn't was because I was afraid to get hurt again. "Are you sure it's not about the money?"

"If it was about the money, I would be married by now. It's about us. Wait until I tell you about how my conversation with Grams went down."

I couldn't wait, but I'd been more worried about another person. "How's your dad?"

"He's good. I told him everything. If anything good came of the breakup, I hope it was that I left the name Gooder behind forever."

"Not with your brothers."

"And full disclosure—I have the ring in my pocket but only because when I touch it I can still feel it on your hand." He shifted so his mouth was at my ear. "I can see how it looked when you touched yourself."

A wave of heat threatened to make me swoon. I wanted to tell him to stop and I was terrified he would.

"I won't propose until after my birthday." His hands were going around my waist. "But if you let me, I will make you mine again. Over." His lips brushed my jaw. "And over again."

"Beckett." I fisted the lapels of his coat. Our lips brushed.

255

Once. Twice. And then we were lost. His tongue was against my tongue. Our coats were off and hitting the floor.

He backed me up until my ass hit the edge of the desk and I hooked a leg around his waist. The hard ridge of him pressed into the neediest place on my body. I could've ripped his shirt apart and sent buttons ricocheting around the room. He released my mouth to kiss his way down my neck. When he groaned and pulled away, a cold draft blew across me.

"I don't want to stop." He put his forehead to mine. "But the blinds are open and while I don't mind everyone knowing you're mine, I don't want you on full display."

"No, I don't want to be either." I pushed my hair off my face and took a steadying breath. "I came here to tell you off."

"Then my plan worked. Seriously, talk to Adam and bring me some numbers." He grinned and picked my coat up off the floor. "But you know how it works."

"I'll make sure we evaluate all the offers and make our decision based on what company suits us best and not who's the flashiest and offers the most money, though that's usually you."

His grin widened. "I told Taylor you'd be hard to beat. He took it as a personal challenge."

"Is he good?"

"I think he's made my tablets cry a few times. But I haven't taken him to see the stars."

I hadn't stopped to look at the stars since the observatory. "The cats?"

"Waiting for you to see them again."

If I'd had any concerns before, they were gone now. He'd kept the kittens. "Does Lois spoil them?"

"Yes. My Friday nights have turned into hanging out with them on my couch while we watch a movie. Now I get more pussy than Dawson ever did."

My heart melted and dripped down to my toes. "I want to see them."

He held up my coat for me. "How about this afternoon? I could call Rick. When he sees you he might start talking to me again."

Rick didn't hate me? Today really was a dream. I turned and let him help me into my coat. "I...have to tell my brother."

"Want me along?"

I did, but I had to think about what was best for Adam. "Maybe not today. He was there with me through it all. I should talk to him first."

"Then let me—and Rick—give you a ride."

He put his own jacket on and twined his hand through mine. We waited for Rick. After we were in the car, I told him about how the plan for our business had come together. Hearing how hard it had been for me wasn't easy for him, but I didn't hold back. He talked about Xander's visit and hiring Taylor. My apartment appeared much too quickly.

When I got out, Rick called, "Nice to see you again, Eva."

I waved at him and looked at Beckett as he was crawling back in and bit back a grin. It sounded like a foolish idea, but it might go a long way toward getting a vengeful news anchor off our backs. "Think we should give Terra the scoop that we're back together?"

CHAPTER 26

eckett

THE LAST FIVE days had been the best ever. I rolled to my side, careful to keep from pushing Eva off the bed. I'd stayed at her place last night. Adam had taken a couple of days, but he'd warmed up to the idea of me and his sister. But only after he and Eva had turned down my proposal without giving me a chance to pitch numbers.

There was an up-and-coming player in the market and while they weren't big enough to be on my radar, Adam wanted to pay his good fortune forward and help them out. As long as they brought the money, Eva brought the knowledge—and I'd be on hand for some advice.

"Mmm," Eva groaned and snuggled into my side. "It's weird waking up to you with clothes on."

Thin walls. I wasn't about to make her come with her brother working in the kitchen. "It's a novelty." I rubbed my hand up and down her arm, but that was making me harder than seeing her naked. Spending a night with her and going without sex was confusing my mind *and* body. "I gotta quit touching you or I'm going to do something extremely inappropriate."

She chuckled and rolled to her back. "I like it when you're inappropriate."

"Me too. But I'm not going to risk your brother's wrath."

She swatted at me. "He knows I'm an adult. But thanks. It'd still be embarrassing if he heard us."

I gave her a quick kiss and crawled over her to get off the narrow twin bed.

"Are you regretting sleeping over now?"

"Nope." She hadn't wanted me to. I had done it to prove a point. A tiny apartment with water stains on the ceiling wasn't going to scare me away. Neither was a creaky bed and grungy carpet. "I will sleep anywhere as long as I have you, Eva Chase."

I was pulling up my pants, giving her what I thought was a charming, romantic smile, but she was staring at the floor at my feet.

"Your birthday is tomorrow," she said.

"Yep. What should we do? Oh, you and Adam have to work, right? Maybe supper?" I quit with the twenty questions until she looked up. "Hey, I was thinking that if you're able to take some time off around Valentine's Day, we should go up to the cabin. I haven't been there this year."

She didn't answer. Her brows twitched and a myriad of expressions passed over her face. "I think… I think we should get married."

I was in the middle of zipping my slacks and jerked. The zipper pinched the skin of my finger. "Ouch. What?" I finished zipping myself and sat on the edge of the bed.

"We need to save that money. Your trust."

"I don't need the money, Eva."

"Your grams—"

"Will have to live with seeing Old Man Cartwright drive a vehicle from this century." I stretched out in front of her, lying on my side and propping myself on my elbow. "Don't get me wrong. You're the one I want to spend my life with, every single day of it. You're the one I want to talk to about my day and go back to Montana with. And we have a lot more stars to see. But I'll make sure my next proposal is done right. Exotic location, romantic dinner, down on one knee."

"I liked the horseback proposal."

I feathered her hair behind her ear. "That wasn't a proposal. That was a deal."

"Are you saying that because you think it's what I want to hear?"

"What do you mean?"

Her gaze swept over my face and she put her hand on my arm. "I was ready to marry you for real two months ago. Were you?"

"Yes." And I ruined it. We would've been united right now.

"Then do you think I want you to wait for a right time and right place?" She frowned and rubbed her thumb across my lower lip. "Are you afraid I'll take the fifty million next year and leave?"

"No. If you do, then it means I failed somewhere." My true fear came pouring out. "I don't want you to think that I'm only marrying you to secure my trust."

"What if I didn't see it that way?"

"Then I'd abscond with you to Vegas today." Was I getting married today? To *Eva*? I'd been sick without her for so long, this had to be a delusion.

Her sexy smile told me that no, this wasn't a delusion. "I'll tell Adam."

I leapt off the bed and helped her up. She might be

wearing clothes, but it was just underwear and a white T-shirt that was thin enough I could see her little pink nipples. The only thing that was keeping me from tonguing them was that we weren't alone.

She rummaged through the storage bin that subbed for a dresser. She and Adam worked well together. How would their schedule be when she lived with me? Would she live with me?

"You think Adam might want to move in?" I asked.

She had dropped to her knees and her ass was swaying in the air. It was enough to keep the logistics of our nuptials from interfering with my sex drive. "Move in where?"

What were we talking about again? I had to drag my gaze away from her round cheeks. Oh, yes. Moving. "My house. You, me, Adam, and the cats. I hardly use the office, but we could convert one of the bedrooms so you have a larger work space."

She peered over her shoulder. "I'll talk to him. How many of your family can meet us in Vegas?"

I sat on the bed and dug out my phone, keeping my eye on her butt and the sloping curve it made up to her waist, how her thigh muscles flexed as she moved. My dick wanted to take over, but I'd wait. The next time I was inside of her, we'd be married.

The first person I called was Dad. He'd be the only one I needed to call. For this, he'd rally all three brothers while Kendall planned travel arrangements. When he answered, I didn't bother with chitchat. "Eva wants to get married in Vegas. How soon can you and the others get there?"

"I'll have to play Where in the World Is Xander, but Dawson, Aiden, and I will be there. You know Grams won't miss it. We'll land in Denver and pick you up."

"That'll be three extra passengers." The jet would be full. I wished Xander could make it, but he wouldn't want me holding up the ceremony for him—or being anywhere Grams could reach him for the next year.

"Good deal." Before I hung up, he said, "And Beckett. Congratulations. I'm happy for you. I really am."

Eva shimmied into jeans. When I groaned, she shot me a promising smile. "Soon."

"Not soon enough. Time to break the news to Adam."

"I DO." Eva's smile was almost shy. Her cheeks were flushed and her heart was probably racing as fast as mine.

I slipped her ring on her finger, a part of me breathing a sigh of relief to see it on her hand again. The official ran through the vows, but I was focused on Eva.

On the flight, we'd found a hotel with a chapel and a clothing store. While Eva bought her wedding dress, a sexy, white, off-the-shoulder cocktail dress with a pair of short heels, I'd reserved our room and one for Adam. Xander had buzzed in an hour later, delighting us all and good-naturedly griping about missing some epic northern lights photos. He'd been in the Seattle airport when Dad had called, ready to catch his flight to Russia.

Dawson and Aiden were standing next to me with Xander while Dad used Xander's camera for pictures. Kendall and Kate stood with Adam next to Eva. The ink was still drying on our marriage license and Grams was getting copies of it for our lawyer.

It was finally my turn. "I do."

Our family cheered and I yanked Eva in for a kiss.

"Save it for upstairs." Xander poked me in the ribs.

I lifted my head. "Better take notes. You're next. Ticktock."

He shuddered. "Now Beck, this is your day. Don't go

worrying about me." He leaned close and whispered, "And if you mention it around Grams again, I'm going to tell Eva about the time you said girls should be the ones who have to do dishes."

"I was ten and Mama made me do dishes for a month." I curled Eva under my arm. "You want to make sure Adam has more fun than Aiden, but not Dawson's type of fun?"

"One Xander Tatum King Vegas special, coming right up." He grinned. "Only I won't be Xander tonight. I'm testing out my pseudonym and Vegas is the perfect place to do it. Tate Boyd." He nodded at Eva. "Speaking of using other names, welcome to the family. Mrs. King or Mrs. Chase?"

She tapped her chin. "I was thinking of doing the same as you. Eva Chase professionally. Eva King personally."

Dad broke in, his arms going around my shoulders and Xander's, but he was beaming at Eva. "Time to go celebrate. I made a reservation at the restaurant on the top floor. My treat. Come on."

He left to collect everyone and I stole another kiss with my wife. Today was perfect. There was no other venue or locale that would've made this better. I had married the woman of my dreams, surrounded by our family.

My big empty house was full of cats and a new brother-in-law would be moving in, armed with allergy medicine and daily housekeeping, while I honeymooned with my wife anywhere she wanted—and she wanted the cabin with the stars. We'd be together because she'd given me a second chance.

EPILOGUE

 ander

Beckett raised his champagne flute. "And a toast to my lovely wife. One full year and she wasn't waiting with divorce papers when we woke up."

Glasses clicked around the table. I joined in, finishing my drink off in one gulp, the bubbles fizzing down my chest.

A year had gone by since the last time I'd been in Vegas—for Beck and Eva's wedding. Today was their one-year anniversary. I sat at the far end of the table with Aiden and Kate, and as far away from Dad as possible. The steakhouse in The Venetian was one of my personal favorites. Maybe that's why Beck had chosen it—to lure me here.

It hadn't been enough, not until he'd messaged and said that no one was telling Grams what the plan was and that he and Eva were covering the trip for everyone.

That had been enough.

I had planned to be far out of the country on my twenty-ninth birthday. The things we do for family. The things we don't tell our family.

"She's going to be richer than you soon," Dawson drawled.

Eva grinned. Her hair was even shorter than when I'd met her, making her eyes wide and expressive. "We're having a friendly competition: who can give away more."

Beckett leaned back in his chair and slung his arm across the back of his wife's seat. They couldn't go long without touching each other. "So far, we've got donations planned for recovery centers, scholarships for low-income kids, and programs to help tech designers do their thing and not go in the hole financially."

Envy curled at the base of my spine. Their giving wouldn't be arbitrary. All that money. I'd grown up with it, but I wouldn't get to keep any of it, much less have enough to help others. My birthday was two days away and I was still as single as a priest on Valentine's Day. And look at that. It was Valentine's Day.

Aiden swirled his wine glass like the arrogant prick he was. He glanced at me out of the corner of his eyes. "So... Tate Boyd. Is that what I should call you?"

"In public? Yes. Especially since Dad was spotted outside the hotel and some environmentalists decided to protest big oil." The demonstration made me antsy to leave. Grams might be lured here if she learned I'd shown up. Months of missed calls and increasingly harsh messages might catch up to me.

Aiden's jaw hardened. He'd probably sic his people on the media coverage the protest would attract. So much for a vacation for him. He looked like he needed one.

"I'm going to go take photos of them after dinner. If they're still outside."

Kate's face lit up. There was a bit of a rebel in her. Did

Aiden even see it? "Aren't you afraid you'll get recognized?"

"Nope. I'll change clothes, and I have a hat I wear backward while shooting and a backpack. With the different name, no one will know it's me."

Kate smiled. "You'll have to send me some of your pictures." She leaned closer. "I show them all to my boss. They're just stunning. Do you think maybe you'd allow her to do an exhibit in the library?"

She sparked a proud glow deep inside me. My sister-in-law was the only one who built me up instead of tearing me down. I hoped she never tired of Aiden's inattention and left the family. But knowing Kate, even if she did, she'd still support me and show my photos everywhere.

Beck cleared his throat and looked at all of us. "I want to take a moment before the food comes and thank you all for coming. Eva said I could make the announcement: she's not divorcing me."

Laughter rippled up and down the table. As Beckett continued his speech, I stared at the empty spot in front of me. I didn't need to see Dad shoot disappointed looks my way, or witness the tension in Dawson's shoulders as he prepared to deal with the obstacle that would be the Cartwrights getting a shit ton of money.

Beck said my name, snapping my attention back. He grinned. "And best of luck to Xander. You still have time. Anything can happen. It's Vegas, baby."

————

BECKETT AND EVA have a special epilogue, just for you. Find it here.

. . .

I'D LOVE to know what you thought! Please consider leaving a review for King's Ransom.

WANT to read more rugged heroes while waiting for King's Treasure to release? Check out Conflict of Interest.

ABOUT THE AUTHOR

Marie Johnston writes paranormal and contemporary romance and has collected several awards in both genres. Before she was a writer, she was a microbiologist. Depending on the situation, she can be oddly unconcerned about germs or weirdly phobic. She's also a licensed medical technician and has worked as a public health microbiologist and as a lab tech in hospital and clinic labs. Marie's been a volunteer EMT, a college instructor, a security guard, a phlebotomist, a hotel clerk, and a coffee pourer in a bingo hall. All fodder for a writer!! She has four kids, an old cat, and a puppy that's bigger than half her kids.

mariejohnstonwriter.com

Follow me:

Printed in Great Britain
by Amazon